Keep Me Safe

Sazerac Series, Volume 1

Bellamy Gayle

Published by Bellamy Gayle, 2022.

KEEP ME SAFE

First edition. August 31, 2022.

ISBN: 978-1736528211

Written by Bellamy Gayle.

Table of Contents

Chapter One....1
Chapter Two....5
Chapter Three....10
Chapter Four....17
Chapter Five....21
Chapter Six....28
Chapter Seven....38
Chapter Eight....42
Chapter Nine....44
Chapter Ten....48
Chapter Eleven....54
Chapter Twelve....57
Chapter Thirteen....60
Chapter Fourteen....69
Chapter Fifteen....74
Chapter Sixteen....78
Chapter Seventeen....81
Chapter Eighteen....89
Chapter Nineteen....96
Chapter Twenty....103
Chapter Twenty-One....107
RIO FRIO....113
Chapter One....114
Chapter Two....118
Chapter Three....125
Chapter Four....128
Chapter Five....133
Chapter Six....135
Chapter Seven....138
Chapter Eight....142
Chapter Nine....146

Chapter Ten 153
Chapter Eleven 161
Chapter Twelve 165
Chapter Thirteen 168
Chapter Fourteen 175
Chapter Fifteen 181
Chapter Sixteen 185
Chapter Seventeen 187
Chapter Eighteen 191
Chapter Nineteen 195
Chapter Twenty 197
Chapter Twenty One 200
Chapter Twenty Two 209
Chapter Twenty Three 211
OAK ALLEY 213
Chapter One 214
Chapter Two 218
Chapter Three 222
Chapter Four 229
Chapter Five 237
Chapter Six 242
Chapter Seven 245
Chapter Eight 253
Chapter Nine 257
Chapter Ten 263
Chapter Ten 267
Chapter Eleven 269
Chapter Twelve 274
Chapter Thirteen 278
Chapter Fourteen 281
Chapter Fifteen 282
Epilogue 285

Dedicated to my husband, who gives me his unwavering support, and dedicated also, to those we love and who love us in return.

Chapter One

Cecile Forest collapsed into a wicker chair at the desk, a flash drive gripped in her trembling fingers. The licorice-colored gadget was causing her nothing but angst. She stared up at the slim laptop, its green pinpoint pulsing its readiness.

She felt as captive to reluctance as Tess had to the ropes binding her to the rails with a train bearing down. Like Tess, Cecile had to free herself, to view the flash drive's contents. Would she suffer more emotional damage? ...As though she had a choice. *They* required it; they guessed that just by viewing it she might be able to identify her husband's killer.

The shiny black flash drive slipped smoothly into the USB port. Cecile's index finger double-clicked the computer mouse, and she shivered with unexpected emotion.

People who looked familiar appeared on the screen, snaking in a sinuous procession through the headstones and mausoleums grounded beside a graceful, ivy-covered old church—it was her funeral, their funeral, hers and Barley's. Somber people blotted hot, damp necks and fanned their faces as they trudged behind two coffins.

Cecile nibbled at the skin next to her thumbnail as she watched, imagining wisps of miasmic steam rising above the whitewashed tombs of the New Orleans cemetery. The heat and damp of that September day seemed to come right through the clear computer screen.

The presence of so many mourners weighed her down. She suspected more than a few were there only for the gossip. Not typically a cynic, Cecile didn't feel her usual sanguine self—though it wasn't grief making her struggle, it was the guilt of vast relief.

She was hidden now, and safe, far from New Orleans. Cecile didn't want to watch her funeral, but she had a job to do.

A movement on the screen caught her eye. It was a *Times Picayune* reporter she recognized, with a small video camera dangling at her hip. She couldn't fault the woman for doing her job. What could be more newsworthy in New Orleans than a double homicide in a fancy Uptown neighborhood?

Cecile had caught the dryness in Tammy Avenetti's comment, "An invitation to the funeral is the hottest ticket in town." DEA agents, in her limited experience, were not known for irony.

Cecile pressed a hand to her bandaged head to ease the ache, and leaned closer to the screen. She spied someone most familiar, and blinked away moisture as the woman walked sobbing across the churchyard. It was her best friend, Mary Ann Fitch. She had her black hair pulled back into a tight bun and wore the kind of clothes an earlier generation called widow's weeds. Not everyone knew, though, that Mary Ann always, always wore black from her skin out. Or that she'd been doing so from her early teenage years.

Cecile felt a tear trickle down her cheek. She hadn't thought her subterfuge might hurt someone she cared for. At the time, she had been too stunned to think.

One of the DEA men she'd met appeared on-screen. His head was on a swivel, scanning the crowd. He was keeping pace with Mary Ann, but a few steps behind. Was he tailing her friend? Was Mary Ann a suspect?

She'd thought there wouldn't be many flowers at the funeral. Neither Cecile nor her husband had any family to mourn them, unless she counted Karl Schmitzer. She had known her Aunt Hattie's venerable lawyer friend *forever*.

And her next-door neighbor, Odette Freyou, was there, practically family. Cecile and her husband, though in their thirties, had had few close friends.

She watched the funeral as she sat isolated in Puebla, Texas, hundreds of miles and many days removed from the scene. Cecile wondered how appalled her friends had been when they'd heard the news. Murder was always obscene, but the *double* homicide of a married couple? Beyond awful—outrageous. In their place, she'd be wondering if she'd missed something terribly wrong about the marriage.

There was nothing wrong with her, Cecile knew, unless it was the way she shuttered herself off from reality to protect her emotional self. Strangely enough, she was an excellent lawyer who argued ferociously on her clients' behalf. Yet she herself had grown up in a stilted home, then married a man who'd wrapped chains around those stilts. She didn't know the "why" of this horrid thing that had happened, but she did know she was determined to find out.

Barley. Cecile couldn't believe he was dead. She hadn't believed it that awful night the DEA chief told her, just minutes after she regained consciousness. It had taken some convincing. She hadn't said it out loud, but in her resistance she'd thought her husband was trying to confuse her sense of reality again, typical of his usual torments.

The DEA officers, however, had been on the scene and heard the shot; they'd quickly discovered her lying unconscious next to her husband's body. It was the DEA who'd delivered Barley to the morgue, and taken her, bleeding and unconscious, to a doctor's office rather than a hospital.

In the Uptown neighborhood where they lived, Cecile was the better known of the couple, though her husband, Barley Forest, had once been a well-known Tulane University football star. Cecile had grown up in the comfortable Uptown neighborhood, and had attended and graduated from Dominican Academy and Tulane

University. Both high school and college campuses were just short streetcar rides from her home. Before she married, Cecile and her great-aunt Hattie DuMond attended Sunday Mass together at the very church she was now viewing on the humming laptop.

The electronic images on the screen included her neighbors, and Cecile winced at the distress her deception had caused. Her wound's stitches were pulling, and the infernal itching was driving her crazy. She decided she deserved it all.

The DEA had manipulated her, but she had allowed it. Now she had to live with the agreement until she figured a way out.

Cecile shut down the computer, having seen more than enough to make her nauseous. Stuck in this new place, in a different state, she debated ways to get home to New Orleans. Leaving would break two contracts, really: one with the Drug Enforcement Authority and the second with the US Marshals Service, who were hiding her from whoever had tried to kill her.

Without thinking, Cecile plopped onto the sofa, which made her head wound throb more. She closed her eyes against the pain. Despite everything, she was optimistic because of a paragraph she'd insisted be added before she would sign the DEA agreement, stating that she would have an integral role in the investigation.

Who had tried to kill her, and why? What did she recall about that day? Had she seen something or done something before leaving the office that day that led to the shooting? The DEA people seemed sure that something she'd seen or done had put her in danger. She massaged her temples and thought back to that terrible day.

Chapter Two

Cecile's watch chirped. She checked the time, dropping her pen onto paper-clipped pages. It rolled to a stop as she massaged the kinks in her back and looked around.

This spacious law office was her safe and comfortable place. She had decorated it using green and khaki toile-patterned drapery and cushioned, Chippendale-style chairs that pleased the eye. Sturdy bookcases faced her on either side of a door, rising to the ceiling and full of useful law tomes and fascinating legal extracts. She liked her surroundings and loved her career.

Even better, she liked her right-hand woman, glancing in her direction.

Jan Yokum, her paralegal, frowned over notations on her electronic tablet.

"Let's stop here." Cecile stretched and rubbed her neck. "I have to get going. I'm meeting Mary Ann."

She snapped the file closed and handed it to her efficient assistant. "The deadline on this is a week away, so it can wait until tomorrow morning. I have to hurry. I'm already almost late. And Jan, you need a break, so please leave soon."

Jan had an admirable work ethic. First to arrive in the morning, she was last to leave at the end of the day, a diligence that sometimes troubled her boss. Too much work and no time for play could mean Jan would suffer an early burnout, and Cecile relied on her paralegal far too much to allow that.

"Thank you, I will," Jan answered over her shoulder, already on her way to her desk, file and tablet cradled in her arms. "I'll leave as soon as I finish up a few more things."

Cecile breezed past Jan's desk, her purse over her shoulder, and a suit jacket, superfluous in the hot weather, over her arm. As she crossed the threshold to the corridor, she said, "See you tomorrow."

Barley insisted Cecile tell him where she was headed whenever she left the building. He, however, didn't extend her the same courtesy. Her husband's tight rein chafed. They'd been married for ten years, but he still insisted on knowing where she went, and when, and what she did. She headed to his office to say goodbye. Better that, than having to listen to his rant later.

She swerved into the short corridor that lead to his office suite. Cecile disliked the over-decorated yet sterile appearance of the firm, with the exception of her own two rooms. There was monotonous gray carpeting, and tall, fake plants set next to walls covered with cold metallic paper. It was depressing. Overly high ceilings gave the hallways a counter-intuitive, claustrophobic feel.

Barley had insisted they join the same law firm, though she'd said she wasn't interested in practicing law at the same place he did. He had finally worn her down. The couple was hired by the Authement and Gaudet Law Firm before they passed their bar exams. Cecile passed on her first try. Their boss had had to pay the exam fee twice for Barley. He called the fees he'd paid their bonus for joining his firm.

The couple's paths seldom crossed during the day; none of their cases overlapped and they'd agreed there would be no law talk at home. Cecile was pleased to know nothing of Barley's cases, nor he of hers. That had suited her just fine then, and even more now.

The door to Barley's private office was closed, with his ornate nameplate positioned at eye level clearly visible. His secretary was not there; her desk was so clean it looked sterile, her computer invisible beneath its plastic cover. She appeared to have left early.

Cecile hesitated, but thought he wouldn't mind her intrusion. Rapping briskly, she opened the door and walked in the room, already speaking.

"I may be a little late..." She stopped mid-sentence, disconcerted to see René Gaudet, the firm's swarthy, middle-aged boss, standing with her husband. The heavyset man's face, disfigured by broken blood vessels, showed visible discomfiture at her abrupt entry. The two men each had a hand on a rectangular package. In his other hand, Gaudet held a thick, rubber-banded stack of money. He snarled at her, and jabbed his chin at the door.

"What the hell? Get out of here, Cecile. Barley's door was closed, which means you need to knock and wait until you're invited to enter. This is private business."

Mortified, she flushed and looked at her husband, who stood silent, wearing a disgusted expression. *Is it* me *he's disgusted with? Why doesn't he say something?*

She stammered an apology, and hurriedly backed out. She swung the door nearly shut behind her, but not before she saw her husband's shrug in response to René's frown. The incident rattled Cecile, her heart painfully aware of her mate's failure to intercede on her behalf.

She had no idea why her entry had provoked such an extreme reaction. Her *faux pas* was the sort of thing Barley hated, and she was sure he'd make her suffer for it later. Worse, he'd looked ready to leave. He disliked walking into an empty house, so the visit with Mary Ann that she'd been looking forward to would have to be briefer than she had hoped.

⁂

Cecile's paralegal glimpsed her boss rounding a corner of the hall heading in a different direction as she approached Barley's office to return a file. As Jan placed the folder on his secretary's desk blotter, she heard two familiar voices from behind Barley's office door, which was cracked ajar. She crept closer. Mr. Gaudet's gravelly voice was unmistakable.

"She saw what we were doing, and you know it. I don't care how good a lawyer she is, I can't afford for her to have any kind of leverage." Jan heard Forest's strained voice reply after a pause.

"What are you saying, boss? We're talking about my wife."

"Yeah, I know how much you care about Cecile, how you treat her. You love your wife, Barley?"

"No, boss. She's a convenience," he said. "But I'm stuck with her for a couple of reasons."

"I hear gossip that you don't spend much time at home. You giving somebody else your pillow talk?"

"That's a funny way to say it, but yeah, I've been with someone for a long time."

"Then if you don't care, get yourself unstuck. It might solve this little predicament we seem to find ourselves in. Mick's the answer. Give him a call before you leave tonight and tell him to take care of it. Don't give her time to think about what she saw in here."

Mr. Gaudet's brazen demand left Jan paralyzed. The woman who'd taken a chance on her, given her a job she loved—she was in danger. Unlike Cecile, Jan was hardly naïve. She made it her business to see everything around her. She'd been suspicious of René Gaudet from her first day, and she was certain his legitimate law firm hid a shadow business.

The Mick he mentioned was Mick Shaughnessy, and she knew his reputation. He and his partner, Shawn Leary, were dockworkers when they weren't hired out to kill someone—something they called wet work.

Jan crept away from Barley's office, thankful for her crepe-soled shoes as she dodged around the fake plants in the hall. Back at her desk, she fired up her computer again, navigating to the employee list of phone numbers and copying what she needed onto a Post-It.

Checking the time, she turned off the computer, doused the lights, and left the firm to stroll around the streets outside for a while. She enjoyed looking at artfully arranged store windows. It was her favorite pastime, but tonight Jan couldn't concentrate. She had something else planned, something much more important.

Chapter Three

About the time Jan left the office, Cecile stepped from her car many blocks farther south on Decatur Street, looking forward to a pleasant interlude with Mary Ann.

She and Mary Ann had been best friends since elementary school and all the way through college, inseparable until Cecile met and married Barley Forest. They talked often and visited, though not as frequently these days. She and Barley got along well, which was a helpful bonus.

More infrequent visits had been Cecile's choice. She always had tried to give Mary Ann the impression she was perfect; she liked being thought of that way. She was reluctant to discuss her deteriorating ten-year marriage with her best friend, so she'd backed away. Cecile didn't have enough self-confidence to admit her problems.

By the time she arrived in the *Vieux Carré,* the French Quarter of New Orleans, the late afternoon sun had slipped lower in the sky. Heat waves still shimmered off the sidewalks, pedestrians materializing like voodoo dolls out of the haze. Cecile struggled free of her moody self-absorption, determined to act upbeat.

Slender into her late teens, Cecile had blossomed late into a classic beauty possessed of pleasing bodily proportions. Graceful and athletic, she weaved through the crowd to her destination, stepping at last into an open-sided restaurant, the Café du Monde, where outside noises contributed to the din of the patrons seated inside.

A street musician's off-key jazz grated like musical fingernails on the street's rough cobblestones, the acoustics moving beneath and through the many rumbling conversations. Fluttering awnings added a lulling undertone. Decrepit ceiling fans, hanging too high to be effective, struggled to circulate currents in the September humidity.

The anemic movement of air did little to cool the sultry afternoon—pigeon wings would have generated a better breeze.

Outside on the brick streets near the Cabildo and the Cathedral, mules flicked their tails at pesky flies and pulled carriages with gaily painted wooden wheels that creaked and rumbled. The clopping hooves offered a staccato counterpoint to the conversations in the café.

Servers who looked as ancient as the café scurried about beneath the high ceiling, dodging narrow metal supports to slide steaming mugs of café au lait and plates of powdered-sugar beignets to their customers.

Cecile, just into her thirties, had a blithe, open expression and amber eyes which invited people to smile with her. She dressed with a quirky flair, though she wore the necessary lawyer clothes—a crisp, collared white linen blouse tucked into a lightweight, pleated, dark skirt. The skirt's hem flirted with her bare, toned knees. A matching jacket stayed in the car, the weather making it far too warm to wear. Open-toed snakeskin high-heeled shoes added the quirky touch. They fit well and were comfortable. The overall impression was of an approachable and slightly sexy woman.

Mary Ann sat alone on the far side of the room. Cecile called to her across all the Tommy Bahama shirts and Lilly Pulitzer dresses seated at the tables.

"I'm here, Mary Ann." People within hearing glanced up at the sound of Cecile's cheerful, musical voice.

Her target whipped around, startled, a sour expression tempering her sultry beauty. Cecile noticed the strain, but ignored it as her friend's smile appeared. Instead, she grasped Mary Ann and pulled her up into a bear hug.

"I'm grinning like an idiot." Cecile said, "You're gorgeous, and I've missed you. Hard to *believe* it's been a month since our last visit. That's way too long for us."

Holding her friend at arm's length, she looked her up and down. Mary Ann's hair shone. Her skin glowed with health. She squirmed out of Cecile's grasp and returned to her chair.

Cecile dropped onto a flimsy metal chair, tucking strands of loose dark auburn hair into the low bun coiled at the nape of her neck. The setting sun behind her glinted off her gold wedding band into Mary Ann's eyes. Cecile leaned forward to touch Mary Ann's arm.

"You look sexy, girlfriend, but I'm not surprised. You called yourself *Hussy* in college, remember?" She made air quotes with her fingers. "You said you 'wanted to sleep with every man on campus, professors included.' You still got that tally sheet tacked next to your mirror?"

"Hell, Cissy," Mary Ann sputtered, "You have a memory like an elephant. I'm stupid to spend time with people I've known forever. I should've left town long ago."

"Aw, I promise I won't tease you anymore, baby." Cecile raised crossed fingers to show Mary Ann not to count on it, and just then, their server interrupted, arriving with an order Mary Ann had placed earlier.

The man's scrawny right hand thunked two heavy white ceramic mugs of steaming *café au lait* on the table, quickly followed by two small plates stacked high with delicious-looking pyramids of puffy golden beignets smothered in powdered sugar precariously balanced in his left hand.

Wiping his hands on a stained apron, the server spoke with an accent less French than straight out of the Bronx when he pronounced, "Fresh out da erl, ladies, dey hot. Be careful."

Cecile asked for a knife and fork, the same routine Mary Ann heard every time they were there. The man rolled his eyes, but produced utensils rolled in a napkin from deep in his apron pocket. Crazy as it seemed to drink hot coffee and eat steaming beignets this oppressive afternoon, the two women weren't alone; the place was bustling with activity.

Mary Ann's stomach gurgled. "Sorry about that, I'm ravenous." She pinched a hot beignet between long red-painted fingernails, bending to nibble at its hot, crusty edges. Powdered sugar drifted off like snowfall.

"What's new, Mary Ann?" Cecile gave her coffee a tentative sip, deciding to let it cool. She relaxed with a sigh as her best friend prattled about her day. Mary Ann worked sporadically at the convention center during special events. Her stories were interesting and amusing, often about her rejections of handsome men who focused on her striking appearance.

The Café du Monde had been part of their lives since their first school field trip when they'd held hands in a daisy chain of tittering little girls. The colorful sights and musical sounds swirling around them, endemic to the French Quarter, had entranced them then as now. Though now, as adults, the pleasures were more subconscious.

Mary Ann finished her recitation. Eyeing Cecile over the rim of her cup, she asked her friend probing questions.

"How's your hubby, Cissy? And your marriage? Any trouble in paradise? I mean, are you *really* happy? Ever wish you were single?"

Her inquisition was so unexpected, so personal, that Cecile inhaled the moist sugar of her beignet. She choked a cough and reached for a swallow of water. A gulp or two later, she had gained some time, and her voice.

"Trouble? That's a laugh. Barley's wonderful. We still enjoy each other. There're lots of hugs and kisses in our house." She couldn't tell Mary Ann the embarrassing truth—that she didn't like her husband very much, and that the man she'd once thought she loved now slept in the guest bedroom and seemed to barely tolerate her.

"Same old, same old," Cecile continued. "I suppose he's still at the office talking to the boss." An image of Gaudet's snarling face and the stack of money in his hand flashed through her mind, and her ears reddened. "Our cases don't overlap, even though we're working at the same firm. Neither of us knows what the other is doing."

Cecile looked down and picked at the mauve polish on her nails, peeling away bits of color, so she didn't see Mary Ann's frown or her confused expression. She had evaded all the questions about her marriage and happiness.

Am I making sense? She examined the destruction of her polish. *I'm such a bad liar.* She'd been traumatized more than once, and so treaded life on its surface. She'd had to hunt for joy these past ten years, tiptoeing in the few times she found it. It was a shock when she realized her husband disliked her, and she hid the hurt beneath an armor of denial, pretending to herself and the world that everything was fine. Her thoughts focused on herself, Cecile didn't sense anything amiss on the other side of the table.

She chewed a piece of beignet. They *were* delicious, fried in fat and coated with sugar. Working the bite to a manageable size, Cecile swallowed. She looked up at Mary Ann and her eyebrows shot up.

"Are you wearing a padded bra?"

"What? Of course not." Color suffused Mary Ann's cheeks. She covered her chest with her hands before going on the offensive. "I do *not* wear padded bras. You're the one who needs falsies." They'd had this conversation many times over the years, Cecile often ending up defensive. This time, she surprised Mary Ann by laughing.

"Look at yourself," said Cecile, as gleeful as a schoolgirl.

Mary Ann looked down at the stark white, powdered-sugar handprints on her black dress. Snorting helplessly, she brushed at the sugar. "For Pete's sake!" A ship's deep whistle on the river startled them into more laughter, reminiscent of their earlier carefree days.

Cecile worked on her last beignet after she regained control, then said, "Okay, your turn. Tell me you're finally in love."

Mary Ann abruptly stopped brushing the sugar from her dress and asked, her face ashen, "You know? You've been spying?"

Cecile choked again on the powdered sugar from her half-eaten beignet. "Spying?" Her mug clunked on the table while she covered her coughs. She wiped her sticky mouth with a handful of paper napkins.

"Know *what*? You *are* in love? Now I'm seriously confused." Cecile lowered her voice, looking around. The place teemed with people, several tables of them within range of their private conversation. "But I'm your best friend, and you're just now telling me? Who is he? Do I know him?"

Cecile reached over to touch Mary Ann's wrist, but she moved it away, a napkin over her eyes. "Are you crying?"

Between hiccups, Mary Ann confessed, "I'm in love, and... pregnant." And her expression told Cecile she was the last person in the world her friend wanted to tell.

Cecile couldn't assimilate this astounding news. *This is soap opera material. Am I missing an undercurrent? Is something else going on?* She lowered her voice more.

"Pregnant? Wow. Are you okay with that? You were always so careful."

"Yeah, mostly okay." Mary Ann took a deep breath. "He doesn't know. His... divorce isn't final."

Cecile struggled with unexpected jealousy, when she should be congratulating her friend. "Wait until Barley hears this news."

"No! I mean... I'm not ready to tell anyone." Mary Ann dabbed her upper lip, agitated. "Please don't tell anybody, Cissy. It's a secret." She drew her purse onto her lap. "I... I'm feeling a little nauseous. I'm sorry, I'd better leave."

"Don't go," said Cecile. She rested her hand on top of Mary Ann's, but her friend flinched away again. Outside the café, the late afternoon shadows flexed, stretching across the sidewalk toward the coming night in their regular evening exercise. Cecile looked at her watch and was surprised at the hour.

"You're right. We do have to go," she said. She walked around the table to hug her gorgeous friend goodbye, gently patting her cheek. "You're going to be okay. In fact, you'll be a wonderful mama.

"Let's do this again next week. Same time? It'll be cooler by then, and you can tell me about your mysterious lover boy." She walked away, but paused when Mary Ann didn't respond.

"Fine," answered Mary Ann. "And..." She sounded constricted. "I'm sorry. These pregnancy hormones make me act like a flaky idiot. See you next week, girl." Head down, her expression unreadable, she fumbled in her purse until Cecile's footsteps receded.

Cecile mounted the city's shady stairway to the top of the levee, an avian advance guard of pigeons flapping and scattering as she walked along. At the top, her slender figure was silhouetted by the setting sun. She looked back for a moment, then pivoted with a flair of her skirt and dropped from sight as she walked down the far side of the protective levee.

Mary Ann watched, then hit speed dial #1 on her cell phone. Cecile couldn't see that, of course, nor could she hear Mary Ann ask, "Did you do it?"

Nor, after a slight pause, could she see Mary Ann nod and say, "See you later, then. I love you, too."

Chapter Four

Cecile's placid Buick waited in a sea of parked cars. What little color remained on the old chariot was gray with swirls of rusty brown. The frayed cloth interior could have been a faded black. It was anybody's guess.

She slid under the steering wheel into the superhot car. *I could bake bread in this dang oven.* She cranked the ignition and turned up the blower, tilting into the slowly cooling air before she slammed the door shut. The hot September days in the South were brutal. She tented her blouse away from her body to let the blower hit her chest and threw up a prayer the erratic AC would work long enough to lower the sweltering heat inside the car. It was too much to ask that the AC would dissipate the odors of dust, old motor oil, and the lingering hint of Aunt Hattie's *Arpège*.

Shifting into drive, she knew the car had earned the right to make unseemly noises.

Cecile followed the queue headed out to Chartres Street. The line inched forward, giving Cecile time to watch a tiny red tugboat maneuver a string of enormous gray barges ten times its size down the wide, brown Mississippi only a stone's throw away. She loved the river, owning it as hers, and never tired of watching it carry all the industry from America's heartland to the rest of the world.

As the Buick idled forward, she frowned, thinking about her unsettling visit with Mary Ann. *That was a weird vibe going on the whole time. She doesn't seem very stable. What's next for her? Her parents—they're already old. What if that man, whoever he is, doesn't divorce his wife? Will she live with her folks? That pregnancy must be a shock. Poor Mary Ann. Who could the father be?*

Cecile had once yearned to have Barley's child, but he adamantly refused to even discuss having a baby. Period. They'd met at Tulane, both of them college seniors, just after Cecile's adoptive mother died, making her an orphan for the second time in her life.

She thought about that freak accident overseas that killed her parents and brother. She'd been cut adrift at the age of nine. Her great-aunt Hattie, her mother's aunt, had stepped in and welcomed her into the Octavia Street bungalow in New Orleans. Aunt Hattie had suggested the grieving child use the name on her birth certificate, Cecile Valois, instead of her nickname Sunny, hoping it would give her a fresh start. A year later, she adopted Cecile, changing Cecile's last name from Valois to her aunt's DuMond.

For a dozen years, Aunt Hattie had shared her life lovingly with her new daughter, teaching her everything she knew. When Hattie died, Cecile was advised she was her aunt's sole heir. She'd also just been admitted to Tulane's law school. Neither of these consoled her; she was once again alone and bereft.

She knew it was from the fear of being alone that she'd clutched Barley as a lifeline and accepted his offer of marriage. She hadn't recognized that there was no love in their union, only convenience. She'd known for some time that her dependency was in its third iteration: first, her parents; then, Aunt Hattie; and now, her husband. A husband, it seemed, with plans of his own.

Cecile was devastated that Barley hadn't defended her when she'd stumbled into his office and surprised him with their boss. It was the final humiliation—the last straw that would send their haystack marriage up in flames. It had taken everything she had not to tell Mary Ann about it, about how it had hurt her. In retrospect, Barley's refusal to have a child with her was the best gift he could've given her. And it was easier to take the next step now, than it would have been when he'd left their bedroom, saying he didn't get enough rest lying beside her.

She'd experienced vast relief when he abandoned their bed, but it hadn't stopped his verbal abuse or his vicious pinches. Cecile didn't care *where* her husband slept. She'd stopped caring years ago. The past ten years had been a painful waste of time, and it was time for a divorce, but the man was vengeful. She had to be careful, she thought, or he would hurt her badly.

For years she had tried to believe they were a couple, but he had never felt that way. It was as though she was a shipwreck survivor and Barley was driftwood in the sea that she grabbed to stay afloat, afraid to swim for shore. But she was stronger now, more independent. Now she knew how to be alone, and she was okay.

Escaping the downtown traffic congestion, Hattie's car chugged past the stately mansions along St. Charles Avenue, each structure seemingly lovelier than the last. The moss-hung branches of ancient live oaks shielded gracious examples of Victorian, Romanesque, and Grecian architecture. This part of New Orleans was more like the Old South and less like the flamboyant Vieux Carré section of the city.

Cecile relished the commute alongside the rattling streetcars, and on this afternoon she saw swirling dust motes above the cars turn a shimmering gold in the rays of the setting sun.

New Orleans was exotic even to her natives. Built on flat, subsiding terrain and perched uneasily on the alluvial floodplain of the Mississippi River, it was protected by levees and pumps. There was much to recommend the city, but not its streets. Porous soil and political graft combined to produce potholes that made the streets feel like a never-ending washboard. Mechanics loved them.

Cecile reached Octavia Street and turned left across the neutral ground of the Avenue. She was almost home, on a street where fathers grilled hamburgers and played ball with their kids. Her stomach muscles clenched thinking of the coming confrontation. When she was working out the intricate details of a legal case, she felt competent and assertive. At home, she felt hesitant and alone, but she knew she didn't want Barley in her house—not for another night. Cecile grimaced, admitting she was scared of him and what he might do.

He would be angry when she told him to leave, though he was already gone most of the time. His eyes would be murderous and his hands would curl into tight fists, ready to strike a blow. Barley had always had the upper hand in their marriage, and he would fight to keep it that way.

Gritting her teeth, Cecile shivered convulsively. A cat walked over my grave, she thought. She would end this farce of a marriage tonight.

Chapter Five

Three miles upriver from the Vieux Carré and the Café du Monde, the Mississippi River flowed around a horseshoe bend on the far side of a high levee two blocks from Cecile's bungalow on Octavia. The street, higher than most in the city, ran along a gentle rise. The pretty neighborhood was relatively unscathed by seasonal floods and hurricanes, as evidenced by old moss-draped oaks and the magenta blooms of Formosa azaleas grown taller than a man. One could imagine a time two centuries earlier, when gentlewomen rode in open carriages and common men strolled the verges of dusty roads, picking their way around tree roots.

Carriages had disappeared from Cecile's street more than a hundred years earlier, but as she approached her bungalow, she saw that cars were much in evidence and that her next-door neighbor, Odette Freyou, was watching every one of them. Every evening, the elderly widow swung on her front-porch swing, occasionally touching her toe to the floor. She missed little of the activity on Octavia Street, noting in particular the few unknown cars that were anomalies in the quiet neighborhood.

For the past week, Odette had noticed the dark sedan that maneuvered into a parking space directly across the street from her, arriving in late afternoon and remaining there for hours. At dusk today, there was a change in the routine. A different vehicle, a van, had pulled into that space before the sedan arrived, so the sedan had to circle the block and find a spot a half-block farther away. Odette hadn't heard any doors "thunk" shut, nor seen anyone get in or out of either vehicle, though with her fading eyesight she wasn't sure about that. Neither vehicle was breaking the law, but something about them was worrisome to her. She could hear their motors running, perhaps to cool whoever was inside.

Something was off about those vehicles, but she set those thoughts aside when Cecile's old car entered the driveway next door. Odette waved, automatically taking note of the hour on the timepiece pinned to her bosom. Odette missed the girl's great-aunt, who'd been her best friend, but at least her adopted daughter and the familiar old car remained. Hattie had always been so kind and wonderful, since she'd long ago befriended her timid new neighbor.

Cecile dodged the old Buick around the giant oak tree that had buckled the sidewalk next to her driveway. As always, she glanced to the lush white oleanders growing at the far end of her property. She and Aunt Hattie had planted them a dozen years ago. She intended to keep this beloved, comfortable property forever, so full of happy memories, but tonight she couldn't think about that. Tonight she was jittery, thinking about something much less pleasant.

Peering through her dusty windshield, she searched for the thin, stooped octogenarian on the porch next door, and there she sat—on a varnished swing, her wiry salt-and-pepper hair skewered on the top of her head in a topknot. That wrinkled dark skin contrasted with the starched white lace collar pinned to the neckline of her navy blue dress. Her feet, in sedate navy blue shoes, nudged the swing.

Unlike her neighbor, Cecile didn't notice the cars along the street. They were like street furniture, always there. She focused on the home she'd shared with her aunt. Her Buick crunched down the uneven oyster-shell drive toward the backyard. It, like everything else Cecile owned, had belonged to her aunt.

Giant ferns peeked from beneath the bungalow's raised foundation. Cecile inhaled a whiff of rich forest loam that passed through the AC. Ferns had always grown under the house, the sight of them pleasing her as much now as they had the day she arrived as a child. Families of endearing tiny frogs lived among the fronds, too, climbing up the wood siding during rainy weather and burbling the nights away.

She returned her neighbor's wave. Cecile had inherited her aunt's friends along with everything else—the car, the house, and its antique contents. And Odette Freyou was the closest and dearest of them all. The two of them missed Hattie terribly—her adopted daughter yearning for more of Hattie's love and her friend missing her neighbor's loyal companionship. With Hattie gone, Odette and Cecile had filled the void by forming a close bond themselves.

The younger woman paid the old woman a brief visit most nights, walking across their adjoining gardens to sit and recount the events of her day. She spoke sparingly of her home life, knowing Odette was no fan of her husband. Instead, they often reminisced about her aunt.

Hattie had been a spinster, but the word didn't describe the woman. "Spinster" conjured a prudish woman wearing a pinched expression and an old-fashioned black dress, but Hattie was nothing like that. She smiled—a lot—and laughed. She was a superb cook. She dressed beautifully in stylish white, blue, and red clothing and the spectator pumps favored by that generation of well-to-do New Orleanians. She blended into society, whether high or otherwise. There was hardly a hint that she was extraordinary, though somehow Hattie imbued everything with a French *je ne sais quoi*. Her hairdos and hems went up and down with current fashion, though settling to mid-range when she reached her seventies. Cecile's aunt had been lovely, smart, and fun. So much fun. And she'd loved her niece, her home, and her friends as much as was humanly possible.

⁂

The gracious, comfortable bungalow Hattie bequeathed Cecile sat beneath a canopy of moss-draped oaks, similar to other homes on the block. Seen from above, they looked like pastel toys lined along the two sides of shady Octavia Street in a tidy double row.

The house had expanded since its double-shotgun construction. The original Cajun French structure had two front doors, each with a direct view through a chain of rooms to a corresponding rear door.

Subsequent DuMonds had tacked on deep porches, more bedrooms, a dining room, and eventually an inside kitchen. Toilets moved from behind the gardens outdoors to plumbed bathrooms inside the house. Cecile's bedroom in the "new" wing had been built more than one hundred years earlier.

It was Aunt Hattie's grandfather who tore out walls, raised ceilings, and combined the two front rooms into a welcoming foyer that opened into a spacious living area with fireplaces at either end. Her own father enlarged the front windows, using multiple smaller panes separated by muntins. The house was extraordinarily graceful. It had an aura of permanence, as if it had always been there, and would be there forever.

While Aunt Hattie was alive, the bungalow's cypress siding received a fresh coat of pale aqua paint every three years, but that changed after Barley and Cecile married. The paint looked faded, overlaid with something that looked like a chalky frost that came off on one's skin and clothes. The paint had begun to peel in curling flakes, but Barley was the boss. He wanted to wait a few more years to repaint, so they waited.

Barley's car wasn't in the backyard. Relieved, Cecile bypassed the shady spot he preferred and parked where morning sun would heat her car's interior. Why argue over parking in the shade? She wanted him in a mellow mood. It might make for an easier confrontation. The dappled shade would be hers soon enough.

Cecile slammed the car door and a squirrel on a high branch barked in alarm. She took the time to say, "Stop your fussing. You have a good life and you know it."

When Aunt Hattie planted that oak, Cecile's arms could still wrap around its trunk. That wasn't possible today. *Where had the time gone? If I could erase the past ten of those years...*

She walked across the grassy backyard on her tiptoes in her high-heeled shoes. The redolent smell of the warm river mud wafted in on a soft breeze. Cecile tried to feel a hint of autumn in the air, though no one could anticipate a change of seasons this far south. In New Orleans, Mother Nature broke people's hearts—raining on weddings, blowing away ball games, sending stinging sleet down on Mardi Gras parades. Better to be happily surprised once the cool breezes began to blow.

The screened porch's warped door squealed its welcome at the top of the back steps. How many times had she heard that squeak? Its hinges were never well-oiled and silent. She had asked why that fix wasn't on her aunt's famous list of projects. Her answer was that it was their "poor man's advance warning system." Its sound had announced many visitors over the years.

Cecile crossed the porch to the heavy kitchen door. She pushed inside the dim, cool house, her fingers scorched by the hot doorknob. Dropping purse and keys on the scarred table, she blew on her fingers and kicked off her shoes. The cool ceramic tiles felt heavenly under her bare toes and she moaned with pleasure.

The updated kitchen offered more than cool shelter. It reminded her of her aunt. Her thoughtful renovations, in warm earth colors and polished granite, had all been done for her adopted daughter. Cecile kept a ceramic pitcher stuffed with yellow wildflowers on the windowsill to commemorate Aunt Hattie. It was like taking a trip to French Provence each time Cecile entered the room, invariably evoking a smile. *So characteristic of her. She thought of my comfort even as she grew sicker—not that she told me about her illness. If she had known Barley, she would have warned me that he was a big mistake.*

Cecile rummaged in the refrigerator, refreshed by the frigid air that poured out. She uncorked a chilled white wine and poured some into a stemmed glass, taking a sip.

She wanted Barley to see food the moment he entered the house, so she padded about the room barefoot to place skewered marinated shrimp from the refrigerator into a shallow, clear glass bowl, then arranged a softened wedge of buttered brie, thinly sliced French bread, and pickled okra on a white oval platter.

Marshaling her thoughts as she would before a judge or jury, Cecile rehearsed her words to ease her anxiety. She worked on his cocktail next, at least the beginnings of it. Taking absinthe liqueur, she swirled a little in a wide-lipped glass, running a wedge of lemon around the edge, before coating it with sugar. She completed the Sazerac except for ice cubes, using bitters and rye whiskey, stirring the drink to dissolve a single sugar cube. Ice cubes, added once Barley arrived, would dilute the booze. She'd performed similar chores nightly for the past ten years.

Breathing deeply to slow her heartbeat, she exhaled to calm herself. She realized she'd first been focused on law school, and then had transferred that focus to a new law practice. She'd pushed her personal life into a far corner of her brain. She and Barley had never developed a connection, and never would. He treated her like household help. And she'd reacted by becoming a creature of habit, her activity tonight in the kitchen just another example.

I want Barley out of my life. There was no question that ten years before, he'd pursued her with determination, but it couldn't have been for love. She was certain he'd manipulated her into marrying him.

Cecile blamed herself for lacking discernment when it came to Barley. He had entered her life only a few days after Aunt Hattie died and left her on her own. She'd wanted nothing more than to feel safe, and Barley popped up. *I brought him into this safe place my aunt created.* Her vision blurred for a second, then Cecile squared her shoulders, determined to free herself. *It's time for him to leave, but I'm afraid of what he might try to do.*

Chapter Six

Barley hated his life.

He cursed *sotto voce* as he strode down the dim hallway to his office, chafing that he'd been summoned to meet his boss there. His secretary had left for the day, dousing most of the lights. The murky gloom deepened his annoyance.

A handsome, fit man, Barley's personality could be off-putting. Certain women were attracted to his broad shoulders and sun-lightened brown hair. He wasn't stupid—not smart like his wife Cecile—but not stupid, either, though he felt an inadequacy that he tried to hide with aggression and expensive custom-made clothes. Most of his paycheck and some of his wife's trust dividends went to his wardrobe—and to maintain the mistress he thought of as his side-woman.

Barley controlled the household checkbook because he was "the man of the family," leaving Cecile to run their household on her income from the law firm.

To be fair, he didn't hate *everything* about his existence. There were parts of Barley's life he liked quite a bit. He smirked as he sauntered down the hall thinking of his paramour. Her perfume got a Pavlovian response every time it wafted his way. The affair made his marriage to Cecile an unhappy one. He'd only married her because he had a goal, and Cecile was his means to achieve it.

Barley flicked the lights back on in his office and settled into his desk chair. As he waited, he thought back to what first set him on this journey.

*

Barley grasped a sweating can of cold beer at a postgame beer blast and idly watched as a staggering, inebriated student speculated loudly that Cecile DuMond would be a great catch. He ticked off the callous reasons on his fingers: she had money, she owned a house and a car, and she was an orphan—how perfect was that? Barley paused with his can halfway to his open mouth. Could this girl be the answer to his problems? He clasped the tipsy student's shoulder.

"What girl you talking about, fella?"

Barley wrinkled his nose. To this day, he recalled that noxious beer breath. Overwhelmed to be directly addressed by a Tulane football star, the boy had staggered back a step.

"Cecile DuMond." He had to yell over the noise in the bar. "She's kinda cute. She's an Uptown society girl. You know what I mean. She's an orphan now. Her adoptive mother just died and left her everything."

The word "Uptown" revealed more than neighborhood location. It meant "old high society" to New Orleanians, but Barley *didn't* know about Uptown, and he emphatically wasn't familiar with high society.

He arrowed in on the only thing that mattered to him. "What does 'left her everything' mean?"

The boy talked, Barley listened, and the germ of an idea began to ferment. He decided to find this Cecile DuMond, who was somewhere on the Tulane campus.

Barley was broke and about to graduate. Soon, he'd have no athletic dorm room and no more meal ticket. He'd be homeless.

A law degree might give him a successful career, but he had no idea how to pay law school tuition. Things would get worse unless something good happened soon. It was a cinch that his parents wouldn't help him. Barley was spending most of his time worrying about his immediate future.

This girl, though... Cecile's inheritance presented him with tantalizing possibilities. If he handled things right, she could be the answer to all his problems.

❋

The next morning was Sunday. He crossed campus and opened the coffee shop door to a wall of noise in the crowded space—spoons clinking against heavy china and loud laughter from young voices—and mouthwatering smells of roasted coffee and fried bacon.

Like a predator searching for weak and vulnerable prey, he hunted, looking for Cecile, asking a server for help. He frowned when he saw the wan, colorless girl who slumped beside a coed whose exotic looks were more to his taste. He sauntered their way, unable to imagine his presence might not be welcome in a grieving young woman's life.

Barley spread both hands on the table when he reached their booth, speaking in his kindest voice.

"Cecile?"

Surprised, she glanced around, then looked up at him. A hand to her chest, she said, "Me?"

"You, yes." His smile was sympathetic. "I was sorry to hear about your aunt. Can I do anything to help?" His synthetic version of earnest friendship worked with the grieving girl; she teared up, and a flush mottled her pale skin. This is so easy, he thought, it's almost embarrassing.

Marriage was the only solution he could see. He manipulated their relationship, though Cecile refused to engage in sex. He had to concentrate on courtship, which was an alien concept to a man so much in demand. But, in his opinion, his performance was flawless, better than any Hollywood hero.

They necked in her car, which he drove beneath the low-hanging branches of a campus live oak tree. He nibbled her smooth, fragrant neck and cradled her in his arms. He prided himself on seduction as his strong suit, but his art didn't work on the reluctant Cecile.

When he broached the subject of money, she said, "I won't talk about finances, Barley. Aunt Hattie told me nice people don't talk about money, politics, or religion." She'd blushed and added "or bathroom habits." Cecile looked down and added, "She also said to watch out for some gold-digging man to come along and try to marry me for my money." He took that to mean she had inherited a large bank account, though she hadn't explicitly said so.

He choked out an urgent, "Marry me, honey. I want to spend my life making love to you." He let his warm breath tickle her ear.

He'd repeated that refrain all through the spring. Graduation was fast approaching.

"We're moving too fast," she'd reply, but would snuggle closer. Barley remembered having a powerful urge to strangle her, which wasn't easy to control. If I hear that objection even one more time, he thought, there's no telling what I might do. Instead, he'd said, "You're torturing me, honey. Men have needs, you know that." Cecile hadn't the faintest idea about men's needs, so he should've known that wouldn't work, and it didn't.

At that point, he was back to having regular sex, having seduced his girlfriend's best friend. Or maybe she'd seduced him. Either way, they both enjoyed it. After a few weeks, he told her about his dilemma and its possible solution, enlisting Mary Ann to help convince poor Cecile she might as well get married, now that she was alone.

With Mary Ann's encouragement, Cecile finally agreed to marry Barley just two days before their graduation. Less than an hour after collecting a marriage license, a justice of the peace pronounced them husband and wife. There were no flowers, no music, and very little ceremony, but Barley Forest's prayer had been answered. Their only witness was the amoral, cynical Mary Ann, who watched her lover wed her friend.

*

Barley figured he could tolerate marriage for the three years it took to finish law school. He could handle *anything* for three years, especially if it came with a fat bank account. And once he had a law degree, he could handle his own divorce.

He knew nothing about divorce law or how personal property was divided. He believed

half of Cecile's assets would be his when they divorced. He couldn't see past his vision of the big dollar signs or the possibility of fashionable new clothes and shoes, though he had no idea of Cecile's wealth. A drunk student had told him she was rich, and he believed it.

"Gold digger" described Barley well, though he kept it well hidden. He and Cecile weren't aware of the much larger second trust Aunt Hattie established in secret for Cecile, only of the smaller "maintenance" trust that issued a regular monthly stipend. Her great aunt intended her to learn of the larger trust only as her 35th birthday approached, which was the day she would receive her full inheritance. When Barley learned the terms of Cecile's maintenance trust, he was apoplectic. The trust provided only a pittance compared to the income he had expected, although it was more than enough to cover his needs, even allotting some for Cecile's modest expenses. It would take decades locked in loveless marriage for the maintenance trust to make him truly wealthy.

No way would Barley accept such a fate. He insisted his new wife arrange an appointment to meet the trustee. He was completely unaware of the history between his bride and the trustee, who happened to be her deceased great-aunt's beloved friend. He was the man who had helped Hattie raise Cecile.

The trustee, Karl Schmitzer, was a dapper gentleman much older than Barley expected. Cecile had known him since infancy, well before she'd become an orphan. He'd tickled her little round tummy until she chortled with glee and bounced her baby bottom on his knee. Cecile's unexpected wedding had taken him by surprise and the shock was apparent when he had offered Barley only a perfunctory handshake, his lips glued in a grim, disapproving line. He smelled of wintergreen mints and a hint of expensive cologne, his intimidating greeting stabbing Barley with its patrician chill.

Barley detected a trembling huskiness in his wife's voice when she said, "Remember the happy times we had with Aunt Hattie?"

Barley bristled as she held out her arms to the old man. Mr. Schmitzer gathered her into a hug, the two as comfortable with each other as a father and daughter.

"I miss you, too, sweet little Cecile." Barley thought the man's voice oozed an artificial, syrupy affection. "Sit. Sit. How can I help?"

He retreated to his orderly desk, arranging its papers while he waited for his visitors to sit. Immediately, Barley asked him to describe the structure of his wife's inheritance. The old lawyer gathered himself, looked down at the gleaming desk top. He ignored Barley, looking directly at Cecile.

"Your aunt loved you more than anything else in the world. You know that." His mouth and Cecile's drooped, mimicking each other. "What she wanted was to keep you as safe as possible and she accomplished that with this confidential trust. She didn't live a frivolous life, as you know, and she chose the same kind of moderation on your behalf."

Yeah, yeah. Get on with it. Barley rolled his eyes.

"She used the goals you had set for yourself when she chose your 35th birthday for full distribution. You gain your full inheritance on that day, in another, what, thirteen years? In the meantime, you'll continue to receive a generous monthly disbursement. Hattie's intention was to support you long enough to complete your education and become self-sufficient. She made me the trustee until that time."

Schmitzer now looked at Barley, still speaking to Cecile. "She could never have imagined you would marry the minute you graduated from college—before you entered law school. That, however, does nothing to change the terms of the trust."

Barley erupted, furious, his face an alarming magenta. He banged his fist on Mr. Schmitzer's desk, sending the row of pens skittering. Cecile flinched like a kicked puppy, her stomach dropping. She'd been married less than two weeks, and already saw her new husband's boorish behavior like an awful TV show.

Barley growled, "That's my money, Schmitzer. You can't keep it from us."

As if expecting inappropriate behavior, Karl Schmitzer remained unperturbed and courteously expressionless. He leaned back in his chair before he spoke, hands laced across his chest.

"This is an ironclad trust which cannot be overturned, Mr. Forest. Challenge it a hundred times, as often as you like. You will not break it. I can't change it, nor can you. I suggest you live with it."

Barley bounded up and pulled Cecile to her feet. He stormed from Schmitzer's office, yanking his wife along. She stumbled in her hurry, trying to keep up, unable to say goodbye. Karl frowned as they left, worried for the young woman's safety.

Barley couldn't rectify the situation right away, but he would do something soon. *Surely Cecile knew what her aunt was doing. She took advantage of me, and I'll make her pay for it.* He couldn't think more than a few months into the future, much less thirteen years. He couldn't possibly stay trapped in this marriage for that long.

Within weeks, Cecile cowered whenever he approached. He relished her fear, and it spurred him to ever more tormenting behavior, until she began studying for long hours in Tulane's law library, which her husband never entered.

*

After ten miserable years of marriage, the thought of Cecile's trust still made Barley livid. He glowered at his bare desk as he waited for Mr. Gaudet's arrival. It was unusual for the boss to lower himself to visit an employee's office. He clenched his teeth, pinching the fleshy inside of his cheeks. He still believed the trust was a dirty trick, abetted by Cecile. *I sure as hell have paid my dues and it's time to cash out. I want all the money, everything.*

What was taking Gaudet so long? He knew his boss thought of him like a younger brother, but he knew better than to test the man. Whatever Mr. Gaudet wanted, legal work wouldn't enter into it. Barley was getting impatient.

The leather of his chair crackled when he leaned forward, his elbows digging into his thigh muscles. Barley tried willing the door's intricately carved doorknob to turn. The sounds of business had evaporated, and the law office was now eerily silent. The whooshes of the ascending and descending elevators had become less frequent, and had now ceased. The quiet was unnerving. *For crap's sake, it's been a long day and I'm thirsty.*

He picked up his memories where he'd left off.

Not long after he joined the firm seven years ago, Mr. Gaudet had summoned Barley to his opulent corner office and weighed the young lawyer who stood before him in silence.

"I've been watching you, Forest. You're not much interested in the law, are you?"

Barley's heart sank. Within a week of starting work at the firm, he'd known he didn't want to practice law, but he'd thought he was doing a decent job of faking it. All that reading, stuck behind a desk, all that writing—that wasn't him.

When Mr. Gaudet said he had noticed, Barley shook his head, his shoulders slumped, and he focused on the tips of his shoes. He waited for the ax to fall. His career would end before it could take off.

"Don't worry," said Mr. Gaudet. "You're gonna like my new plan much better. You won't have to write another thing, I promise."

Barley was to replace Mr. Gaudet's current assistant, Jimmy Costanza, who would remain with the firm in a different capacity. One hand on Barley's shoulder, Gaudet outlined exactly what he envisioned, ticking off each item on hairy knuckles. They included allegiance, silence, and an unquestioning willingness to follow whatever orders he received. A fat raise would accompany the new position. He was forbidden to tell Cecile about his raise *or* his new job. Fine by me, he thought.

Barley hardly heard a word past the boss calling him "son." He liked the sound of that and he liked where the conversation headed. Mr. Gaudet rocked on his heels, hands thrust deep into his bespoke silk pockets. He waited for his new acolyte's decision.

"Deal. You're the boss, boss." They smiled at each other, complicit.

He was astounded, but titillated, when Mr. Gaudet offhandedly told him the law firm was only camouflage, and that its real business was distributing street drugs. The firm had started off small with marijuana, but over the years had added cocaine, crack, methamphetamines, heroin, and now fentanyl.

The work had a dangerous edge that smacked of risk, but drugs made perfect sense to Barley. The New Orleans port was located close to the Gulf of Mexico and it was a unique conduit for transporting illegal drugs. The major clout his boss must be wielding would rub off on Barley and satisfy his yen for power.

The new position meant he didn't have to practice law, though his wife wouldn't know that. Barley knew how to keep a secret from Cecile. He added it to the one he was already keeping from the wife he hated. She would never get a whiff of how he earned his money.

Mr. Gaudet had put him to work the same day he accepted his new job. The drug trade was perilous, but Barley would have agreed to anything to keep his job—and this was an *anything* he enjoyed. He had a romantic vision of life alongside a drug kingpin. A criminal career was more to his taste than was scratching out a living as a lawyer.

"This gives me another problem, Forest. With you working this side of the business, I'm short a lawyer. I need someone legit—someone bona fide to keep the firm legal and out of trouble. I'm a lawyer, yes—but I can't do everything. Anybody from your class worth a look?"

Barley immediately thought of his wife but hesitated, not sure he wanted her in the same firm. She was in demand, but hadn't settled on a firm to work for. There was the small matter of whether he could conceal the drug business from her, but she was so naïve he felt confident it wouldn't be a problem. It *was* one way to keep tabs on her *and* her paycheck, and in the end, both his greed and his need for control led him to recommend Cecile.

She would have done better with a top firm in the city, but this solution suited *him*.

Mr. Gaudet strode unannounced into Barley's untidy office, holding a rubber-banded stack of currency and a package he was holding tight to his left side with an elbow. Barley jumped to his feet, walking around the desk to shake hands.

Gaudet barked precise instructions instead, wasting no time on pleasantries, looking with distaste around the disorderly room. He took the package from under his arm and thrust it at the young lawyer.

In that unfortunate moment Cecile barged in.

Chapter Seven

The New Orleans twilight was a golden pink that enhanced Octavia Street and its surrounding neighborhood. Cicadas sawed their romantic yearning, ignoring the signals of coming autumn days.

Parked on the street most nights, a nondescript, dark-colored sedan sat across from the Forest and Freyou houses. Tonight it was half a block from its preferred location.

Two men sat in the car, their postures portraying superiority and their eyes hidden behind dark Oakley shades as darkness advanced. They sat as far apart as possible, wearing similar dark suits and narrow, inconspicuous ties, but the men's similarity stopped there.

Harry Smith was behind the wheel, the deep furrows and pale, sagging skin of his face a clue to his age. He was retiring the next day, and he was ready to take off for his one-room cabin in the Alleghenies. He would decompress from his so-called career in the Drug Enforcement Administration. It was a miracle he had tolerated his latest partner, Rick Bernard, as long as he had. The man was weird, but Harry put that aside and craned his neck for a better look at the van usurping their usual spot.

"Who d'ya think those guys are? They took our spot across from the Forest place." He could only see a sliver of the van because of the parked cars between them.

"How should I know?" Rick shrugged. "They would've told us if it's more people from our office." Rick had a useful memory for numbers, and he would automatically memorize the van's license plate once he saw it. He checked the time on his phone.

"End of the day. They're probably waiting for a maid to get off work," he speculated.

Harry rolled his eyes, already bored, thinking *duh*. He and Rick were field agents, both recently assigned to this region in moves coordinated by someone at a higher pay grade, which meant that agents rarely had time to become invested in their surveilled subjects. Harry shifted, seeking a more comfortable spot for his generous haunches. Rick was a squirrelly guy, and the only friend Harry had ever heard him mention was that Deputy US Marshal guy, Gene White.

Stuck on Harry's earlier dumb question, Rick squinted for a better view of the van. Harry scraped his five o'clock bristle, wishing he'd kept his mouth shut and thinking Rick should maybe develop X-ray vision to go with his eidetic memory. This would be a boring night.

"Tell you what, Rick, I might want to keep an eye on *her*." He jerked his chin toward an old car that was turning into the bungalow's narrow driveway.

In the preferred parking place, another two men sat on the sprung seats of a dirty white Dodge van with "Handy Man" scrawled on the side panels. Their fit physiques were difficult to see in the car, but in fact the two young men were as strong as the stevedores that worked the docks at the Port of New Orleans. They sat oddly, one behind the other on the driver's side, and not in the more usual grouping side by side on the front seat.

At ease behind the steering wheel, Mick Shaughnessy's eyes swiveled, looking for anything unusual or out of place. He adjusted his mirror-in-a-mirror, careful not to smudge it, and mugged at himself. He checked his smile, then his teeth and hair. This van was the first set of wheels he had ever owned. After the job today paid off, he'd paint it matte black with a thin red stripe. He flashed his gold-veneered teeth, liking how his scruffy beard squared his chin.

Mick and his buddy, Shawn Leary, had driven across the city to Octavia Street and found a perfect parking place for tonight's job. They'd been parked at least an hour, the van's air-conditioned breeze blowing in their faces, Mick's eyes roving the neighborhood. Out of the corner of his eye, he watched an old lady dressed in Sunday clothes, sitting on a porch swing like she had nothing better to do. She seemed to watch the activity on the street, but Mick suspected her eyesight was too poor to see much.

An older sedan had parked half a block behind them, but nobody left the car.

"M'man, you see that old car behind us?" Mick asked. "The dark one?"

He and Shawn had grown up in the New Orleans' Ninth Ward, displaced from a gentrified Irish Channel neighborhood.

Both men pronounced Ninth as *Nint,* with a long *i*. The letter *d* replaced *th* in several words—dis, dat, dese, dem, dose. The Ninth Ward was known to spawn sociopaths like Mick and Shawn, thugs for hire who did anything for a price.

"Huh?" Seated behind Mick, Shawn gave a loud sniff. He had the look of an Irish model with his freckles and ginger curls, but that pretty face hid a ruthless soul. He glanced up and cleared his throat.

Shawn stared at Mick's dark blue eyes reflected in the rearview mirror, thinking the street had too damn many trees and flowers. His eyes itched and his nose dripped like a leaky faucet, both interfering as he tried to load his favorite short stock rifle. Gun oil made the van smell bad, but the windows stayed shut to keep it cool inside, better than the oppressive outside air even with the odors.

"Who you think those guys are?" asked Mick. He tapped a finger on his mirror. "They not be watchin' *us*, are they?"

Shawn couldn't care less. Not in the mood to look over his shoulder, he gave a sullen shrug. "Hell, no. They prolly bill collectors waiting for peeps to get home. Gonna tell 'em 'pay up, or get beat up.'" After issuing his opinion, he wiped his dripping nose on his rag and threw in a loud sneeze for good measure.

An old Buick turned from the street onto a narrow driveway right in front of them.

"Hey, there's the missus. We finally got some action," said Mick. "She should be 'shamed to drive a car looks like that."

His hip vibrated with a heavy rock and roll sound, alerting him to a call. In a passing thought, he realized the vibration could be pleasurable. Multiple calls on the prepaid phone were unusual, but not unheard of. Cheap, bottom-of-the-barrel, throwaway phones were what he used for jobs like this.

He held the phone to his ear. "Yeah? What? Who is this? Oh." His voice bland, Mick said, "What do you think? Of course we're ready." He listened for a minute. "Okay, that'll work." Disconnecting, he relayed new instructions to Shawn, crammed the phone in his hip pocket, and settled back to wait.

Mick chucked his used-up phones in the Port's dumpster every morning, giving him a chance to flirt with the pretty secretary who sat inside a flimsy office door. She'd act all business-like, typing on her computer, but Mick believed he had a chance. One of the secretary's tasks was to keep track of how full the gigantic dumpster became. When the trash got close to the top, she called the supplier to replace it. Not often, maybe once or twice a year.

Chapter Eight

Jan Yokum replaced the receiver, a smile transforming her into an attractive woman. *That might do the trick.* She abandoned Alyssa's desk, returning to the elevator. She sagged against the wall as it descended, surprised her knees were unsteady. Her riotous dark curls bounced into tangles as she left the office for the second time that day. She knew her way around the place quite well, having worked there only one day less than her boss, Cecile Forest.

She had come to New Orleans years ago by bus, fresh from north Alabama, eager to improve her life. She relished her first breaths of the heavy, moisture-laden air, full of unfamiliar smells, and thumbed the two-hundred-dollar bankroll pushed deep in her puffy jacket. Born with bright intelligence into a dull, overfull household, she never dreamed she'd break away to a place where she could exercise her brain, but she'd made it this far!

There'd been a single suit carefully folded into her big backpack with tissue paper. It was a shiny, dark green polyester suit that she would have to wear every day until she'd earned her first paycheck. She would cycle her four blouses that first month, scrubbing them in her bathroom and hanging them on the shower rod to dry.

In those early days, the employees at Authement & Gaudet had tactfully avoided commenting on Jan's limited wardrobe, but she'd quickly bought new things. After seven years on the job, everything had changed—her wardrobe *and* her living conditions. She'd moved up from a dusty boarding house to a one-bedroom apartment carved from a former mansion in the Uptown area of St. Charles Avenue. Her closet now held tasteful clothes of mostly natural fabrics.

She gave Cecile Forest a complete dedication that bordered on the obsessive, arising from an extraordinary bond that dated back to the day she'd been hired. Jan had been rejected time after time during her job search. Although she'd achieved a fourth interview, she drooped that fateful day. Jan knew she could prove her worth if someone would just give her a chance, but it seemed a high school diploma and basic typing and shorthand skills were not in much demand. She'd never done legal research and didn't even know the vocabulary of the law.

But the empathetic Cecile sitting opposite Jan was herself new to the practice of law. She observed her interviewee's exhausted desperation and appreciated Jan's forthright candor about her weaknesses. She understood Jan's willingness to learn, having that same earnest feeling herself. Taking everything she saw and learned about Jan into account, she decided she had nothing to lose this early in her career, and offered her the job.

Together, Jan and Cecile, both bright women, learned how to run a law practice and developed into a well-meshed team. Jan adored Cecile—a naïve, kind-hearted, generous boss who had given her, once just a country girl, a career that fit like a second skin.

Her inquisitiveness led Jan to learn everything she could about her workplace. She made friends with the rest of the staff, including a strong, wiry man who made her heart stutter.

Jimmy Costanza had an attractive, brooding, dangerous edge to his personality that Jan did her best to avoid. He had been Mr. Gaudet's assistant until he was demoted in favor of Cecile's husband, Barley. It was Jimmy who'd warned her in his sexy growl to stop asking so many questions. Jan doubted *Cecile* knew Mr. Gaudet ran a criminal enterprise, but she wasn't positive. She kept her mouth shut, just in case.

Chapter Nine

"Where is that frigging Forest?" Rick shifted in his seat, speaking impatiently. "He's late tonight."

"Shut up with your whining, Rick." Harry visualized himself backhanding his partner's face. "We're gonna sit here anyway, so who cares?" Rick ignored him.

"This job sucks big time. Man, it's boring." He drew out the word, "bor-r-r-ring."

Harry's jaw muscles rippled, but he remained silent. His retirement cabin beckoned and the quieter he was tonight, the better off he'd be.

Occasional cars hissed by, disturbing the quiet street. Shadows grayed beneath the oaks. A soaring osprey screamed, flying home from the river to its isolated nest on a snag at the top of a swamp tree.

Nothing else moved until a red Jaguar materialized from the gloom of the Avenue. The Jag's snarling cat hood ornament stopped a half block further down, pointing in their direction on the other side of the street. Harry flicked a glance at the van sitting ahead of them. Its presence concerned him.

"About time he's home," said Rick. "Why the hell did Forest park way down there? Wanna bet he's not going to stay home for long?" The change in Forest's usual routine had their attention.

"Think he's trying to catch his wife fooling around?" asked Harry, before adding, "Nah, she's scared of him. She's too nice, anyways, but there's gotta be a reason he parked there. He's too lazy to walk half a block."

"You crazy? You think a few hours with that Fitch broad ain't a reason?"

Harry couldn't disagree. Both men fell silent, sinking into private reveries, recalling their sightings of Barley's girlfriend in the nude.

Their conversation was only bored speculation. Forest would enter his driveway at the end of the workday, but his stay was always brief and he'd leave again after an hour. By the time Harry and Rick followed the Jaguar back home, it was usually well past midnight.

That was their job—keeping track of Barley Forest. They speculated that drugs and money were cached under a false floor in the Jaguar's trunk. Whatever else he had to do each night, Barley always managed a few hours with the luscious Mary Ann Fitch, who was living in a luxury apartment at Barley's expense. Occasionally, she left her shades open when welcoming her lover in the nude, a distraction the bored DEA guys thoroughly enjoyed.

Sitting in his van, Mick watched the Jaguar approach. He jerked his chin toward the windshield.

"That must be Forest in his show-off wheels. That damn car's too cool for a bastard like him." The Jag backed into a parking place and purred to a stop.

Mick looked over his shoulder. "You 'bout ready?" There was nothing discreet about the two men, but then, New Orleans wasn't a subtle town.

Shawn grinned. "Yeah, bring it on."

In the kitchen, Cecile heard the thunk of a solid car door slamming shut outside. She trembled, a staccato pulse thudding in her ear as she peered through the window. The sound made by Barley's car door was unmistakable.

Hurriedly, she jammed her shoes on to give her more height and an added sense of assurance. The accomplished lawyer had turned into a quivering mass of insecurity, and nervousness was taking her nearly to the point of paralysis.

Quickly dispensing ice cubes, Cecile added them to the waiting Sazerac. Her hands shook, the ice clinking as she stirred. She fought off a growing edge of hysteria.

Barley jumped the back steps two at a time, his heavy feet thunderous. Screeching through the screen door, he slammed into the kitchen on a gust of hot air. With his bulk and his cocky attitude, he occupied more than his share of any room he entered. Cecile hurried to safely barricade herself by putting the kitchen table between them. It was Barley's routine to give her a vicious pinch whenever he closed in on her. He saw what she'd done and pulled to a stop with a grin, his head cocked. He was delighted to see he had scared the hell out of her.

"You some sexy, girl. Be ready when I come back tonight. I'm gonna get me some of that." He made exaggerated kissing sounds.

Her eyes widened, afraid he meant what he said. *Oh, God. This is not good.* Too intimidated to respond, she remained mute as Barley pushed through the swinging door into their living room.

"And bring my drink to the living room." He flung the words at her over his shoulder as he walked out.

He's even more rotten than usual. Has he figured out what I plan to do? Cecile was hyperventilating. She could scarcely swallow, but she had to act while she still had courage or she might never escape this nightmare she'd brought on herself.

A heavy bass rap began to reverberate through the walls, its screaming misogynistic stanzas full of murder and rape that soiled the air. The sound itself felt like a violation.

Cecile muttered "show time" under her breath and grabbed her wine glass for a gulp of liquid courage. Setting Barley's Sazerac on a tray with the hors d'oeuvres, she followed him through the swinging door and paused in surprise, the door hitting her back.

All the lamps were lit, as well as the ceiling light, and the curtains were pulled completely back. *What the heck's he doing?* She walked slowly, her eyes looking at the heavy tray to keep it level. Barley sprawled against the cushions under the big picture window at the far end of Aunt Hattie's old sofa in a self-conscious GQ pose.

It was all enough distraction that Cecile didn't notice Barley had pushed the coffee table further away from the sofa to give his long legs more room. The pounding, pulsing beat of rap music vibrated every cell in her body and she doubled her concentration on the tray so the whiskey wouldn't slosh out of its glass.

A sharp corner of the coffee table painfully gouged her bare leg, and Cecile stumbled. She yelped, and her hand stretched out for balance. Held by a single hand, the heavy tray overbalanced and the tumbler of Sazerac and ice tilted, its amber alcohol splashing out. Cecile twisted to catch the tumbler, but the coffee table was in the way. She fell, horrified to see everything—okra, shrimp cocktail, whiskey—cascading onto Barley's lap. Cecile thought *Barley will hurt me for this*.

"You bitch!" Too late to avoid being doused, he jumped up to strike her as she fell.

She felt a painful blow to her head and Cecile's world went black.

Chapter Ten

When Barley opened the curtains covering the big front window, Harry and Rick could see into the Forest house from an oblique angle. They saw an overhead light flash on, followed by several lamps. It was like watching a drive-in movie, but without a hot date or a tub of barely warm, greasy popcorn.

Harry hung over his forearms, draped over the steering wheel, as he watched. "That's a strange man. Who turns on all the lights at the same time?"

Rick grunted, "I *always* do," as he leaned forward for a better view.

Harry snorted, unsurprised at Rick's comment. He was eager to be free of the man. "Hell, it's so bright, it's like an interrogation room."

Voyeurs, they were transfixed, invading the unwitting Barley's privacy. They watched him slide to the end of the sofa, the back of his head to the window. On the opposite side of the room, a door swung open and Barley's wife entered, carrying a tray.

"Look at that," said Rick, envious. "The perfect wife serving her husband a drink the minute he gets home. Not many wives do that."

Suddenly, a piercing, reverberating *thwack* very close by splintered the humid air without warning. Instinctively recognizing gunfire, both DEA men ducked as shattered shards of glass fell from Barley's picture window into the house. Across the street, Mrs. Forest dropped from sight and a vermilion bloom spread across the room's far wall.

"What the hell? Where'd that come from?" Keeping low, they peeked over the dashboard, trying to understand what had just happened. Mr. and Mrs. Forest had disappeared. To take cover? Something worse?

Later, when they submitted their reports, neither of them recalled who spoke first after the gunshot. Each remembered ducking and recalled a brief flash of red tail lights when the dirty white van down the street pulled away, and the scrape of a car fender as it left.

"Shit," yelled Harry, thinking *and on my last night on the job.* "You check the Forests! And call the boss. I'll follow the van."

Already out, Rick tore across the street, his phone connecting to a speed dial number. His jacket flapped, holstered handgun banging against his ribs and clearly visible. If Harry could keep up, Rick thought, there was a chance he'd apprehend the shooter.

The skinny little old lady who lived next door to the Forests was struggling to her feet from her porch floor. Holding out his shield, Rick yelled as he ran.

"DEA, ma'am. Stay down." He hesitated a beat, concerned she might be injured, then shook his head, deciding she was okay. "Stay where you are, ma'am. Someone will come to talk to you."

He leapt up the wide brick steps of the faded bungalow two at a time, crunching across broken glass. He stared through the front window, wild-eyed and nauseated at the ghastly scene inside.

Two bodies sprawled across the floor. An obscene volume of blood obscured the details, except that three-quarters of Barley Forest's head had been obliterated with overwhelming finality.

Gray matter mixed with blood oozed down the back wall. A red snakeskin high-heeled shoe lay on the coffee table, an ice cube melting beside it. Rick forced himself to remain calm and not tremble. *Odd the details I notice at times like this.* Cool, vaguely coppery-smelling air poured out through the broken window, engulfing him, filling his nostrils, and making him gag. He imagined he tasted blood's powerful smell until he felt the sting of a bitten lower lip. No one gets used to the smell of human blood and brains.

The heavy front door wouldn't budge, but the killers had easily bypassed the useless lock by shooting through the glass. After one futile shove, Rick decided not to try the shattered window, but the back door instead. His awkward jump from the front porch sparked a sharp jarring pain in one ankle as he hit the ground. He limped around toward the back door while his phone dialed out. His boss, Steve Morley, was personally managing not just this surveillance, but the entire operation. His team's phones used encrypted transmissions to discourage eavesdropping on their sensitive activities.

They'd been warned to call only in an emergency, and one of the surveillance targets getting shot certainly qualified. Morley finally answered.

"Talk." Morley, the chief of the local DEA office, was a middle-aged, no-nonsense veteran agent with gray strands sprinkled in his dark hair. Deep lines radiated from the outside corners of his eyes, and his neck bulged over a tight shirt collar. Excellent New Orleans meals had thickened his torso.

"Shots fired, boss. At the Forest house. Both hit, they're on the floor. Lotsa blood." Rick's voice jerked as he ran to the rear of the house.

"What the hell?" Morley got loud, agitated. "You inside? Got your Kevlar on? Where's Harry?"

"Not yet. No. He followed the shooter."

Rick vaulted the painted back steps three at a time, out of breath. He yanked open the screeching screened door. The heavy kitchen door wasn't locked and he cautiously poked his head into the dim kitchen. Flicking off his gun safety, Rick checked the empty room, whispering in the phone to Morley. He was pretty sure everyone in the house was dead, but you never knew.

"The shot came from a van parked a few spaces in front of us. It peeled out in a hurry. I'm inside the house."

"Alone? Wait for backup, I'm calling dispatch."

Too late for backup, Rick thought. He tried to talk quietly while he crept through the kitchen. His hard leather heels thundered on the ceramic tile floor.

"Rick!" Mr. Morley sounded panicked. "You didn't call 911, did you?"

"I did, boss." Morley lost his temper, his anger radiating through the microwaves. Rick thought he heard something break.

"Crap! Why? Dammit to hell."

"For that van, boss—so Harry would have backup. Didn't say nothing else." Rick, too, should've waited for backup, too, but he'd followed his instinct to save a life.

"No more calls. I'm on my way." Rick heard Morley gasp like he was running. "The Forest house, right? Not Gaudet's place?"

"Right. The Forest house on Octavia Street." Rick crouched to make himself a smaller target, listening to Morley breathing in his ear. Slowly, he pushed the swinging door into the living room. The place was as soundless as vacuum, as though the explosive gunshot had blown all the air out of the house. He straightened to inspect the room.

"Got two bodies here." Nauseous, Rick swallowed spasmodically. The noxious smells of sudden death—blood, brains, and loose bowels—penetrated his sinuses. Too much saliva was filling his mouth. He fought the urge to vomit.

"Holy crap," Morley growled. "Don't touch anything and don't *do* anything," His voice jabbed Rick like an ice pick. On the phone, he heard a car door slam.

Rick moaned. "I'm gonna be sick. Hurry."

"On my way." Morley's words went unheard. Rick ran outside, leaning over tree roots to barf and spit. He forced himself to return, inspecting the rest of the house for unseen dangers before re-entering the murder scene.

*

During his race to the scene, Morley wondered what the hell happened and what it would mean to his investigation of René Gaudet's illegal drug empire. The operation was so sensitive that only the two top New Orleans officials, the police chief and the mayor, knew about it, and they'd been advised solely as a courtesy at the beginning of the investigation with no updates.

Experience had shown that when the DEA coordinated raids on local drug dealers with the NOPD, there often was nothing to find. Morley suspected there were corrupt cops protecting Gaudet's illicit operation, at least through alerts, which was why he had changed the way the DEA operated. They would never be successful otherwise. He had asked the police chief to involve no more than a few officers, which she did. She seemed relieved to have the DEA's help dealing with the city's overwhelming drug problem.

Illegal substances flooded the Port in a massive stream impossible to stem, and not all of them left the city, creating havoc. Users strained police resources with their crimes, and clogged hospital emergency rooms. If the feds could solve the problem, the city would gratefully keep hands off.

The lengthy pursuit of Gaudet was a chess match, each side making strategic moves, with one of the players—the DEA—hampered by legal constraints.

These particular murders of the Forests, who were secondary targets at best, were aberrations which confused Steve Morley. Had Gaudet ordered the hit to forestall exposure of his organization? This was a high-stakes, winner-take-all game, and the very next move could determine who came out on top.

The regular surveillance of Barley Forest was a small part of the DEA's plan. The overarching goal was to find enough evidence to arrest and prosecute René Gaudet and dismantle his far-ranging massive drug and money laundering operations. Until tonight's killings, the DEA couldn't prove Gaudet engaged in murder, at least not in New Orleans. There was a great deal of violence and intimidation, yes, but murder, no. This attack on a known associate of the mighty Mr. Gaudet could hand the DEA some much needed additional leverage.

Chapter Eleven

Rick stood unsteadily next to the bodies sprawled on the bloody living room floor. Still nauseous, he dutifully watched as a paramedic worked. Barley Forest's nearly decapitated body spoke of death. Mrs. Forest's body told a different story, one of life.

Her diaphragm rose and fell imperceptibly as she lay amid the debris. Rick compromised the crime scene, aware the forensic team would complain, when he'd found a towel and pressed it to Mrs. Forest's head to stop her bleeding. Long auburn hair, matted and saturated with blood had escaped its pins and was plastered to her skull. She was alive, but for how much longer? Rick gritted his teeth, maintaining steady pressure until a paramedic nudged him aside.

"She gonna die?" Morley had arrived, skirted the carnage, and was bending over the paramedic.

"No," the paramedic answered. "Her pulse is weak, but it's steady. Respirations are light and regular. Bleeding is good—it means her heart is beating. She's lost a lot of blood, not unusual with head injuries. The bullet didn't penetrate her skull, but it gouged a shallow furrow in her scalp. Looks pretty nasty." His tone sounded detached and impersonal, as though he were an objective instructor.

Rick found a dry corner of the towel and wiped off his hands as best he could. The knee of his right pants leg slowly dried and stiffened, drenched with Mrs. Forest's blood. The unconscious woman looked fragile, sprawled on the floor. She appeared to be a lovely woman, in her early thirties he guessed, and completely unaware of the medic or those around her.

Though they were impeding the forensic team, Steve Morley stood with Rick close to Mrs. Forest and listened in silence to Rick's detailed account of the attack, then cleared his throat.

"The bullet hit Forest first, but his wife was a target, too," Morley said. "Something put them on Gaudet's radar. I can't swear to it, but this is how he operates." Rick frowned, as though not sure he agreed.

Morley looked around for untainted space and made his way to the back yard. He walked in deep thought, his fingernails scratching a five o'clock stubble already a couple of hours older. The sun had disappeared, taking the heat of the day with it.

Rick sat on the porch steps and watched his boss, his stomach still queasy, and a dull headache blossoming behind his eyes. Finally, Morley slapped his thigh.

"We have to protect Mrs. Forest now. Something we don't understand yet makes her important to our investigation. If Gaudet wants her dead, let's make sure he *thinks* she's dead. He'll try to kill her if he finds out she's still alive. That can't happen, because we'll need her testimony when the bastard goes to court. Let's get the US Marshals involved so we can hide this little gal."

Rick stared at his boss, struggling to hide his irritation. *What the hell? That's a live woman—not some kind of "gal."*

"I know a local deputy marshal we can call. He could put the wheels in motion," Rick offered.

"Good. Take care of it." Morley snapped out some other rapid-fire orders, then called the head of the NOPD. The Chief cooperated and gave Morley the green light to manage the crime scene, unaware the work was in progress. The DEA forensic team had begun their search of every room for evidence and data, already hard at work.

When necessary, the DEA used a discreet private emergency service which Morley now called, asking for two gurneys and two body bags—one for Barley Forest, legitimately dead, and a second bag to disguise the removal of the living but still unconscious Cecile Forest. Everyone at the scene was sworn to absolute secrecy.

*

Odette Freyou trembled with shock. Her arthritis was making her sore and stiff, so she clambered back onto the porch swing, still trying to understand what happened. A pleasant woman, a DEA investigator, casually mounted Odette's steps to write down her eyewitness account, along with her name, address, and phone number.

At the interview's conclusion, the investigator smiled gently and cautioned, "Don't mention this 'incident' to anyone, Mrs. Freyou. It's serious. It's top secret and everyone has to keep it quiet."

Odette snapped out a feisty, "Just who do you think I'm going to tell? You worry about yourself. I have bigger things to worry about." The investigator, already quickstepping across the yard, may not have heard the elderly woman who hugged herself in the warm evening air. Odette was shocked at the attack and stunned by all the crackling radios, revving engines, and loud voices. The chains of her swing creaked, and Odette worried the thin chain around her neck, grasping its cross.

Vehicles and uniforms clogged the street in front of Cecile's bungalow. Odette moaned under her breath when she saw two gurneys crush Cecile's flowerbeds before being hauled up the steps and through the open front door.

She sobbed, her gnarled hand covering her mouth, when the men wheeled out a zipped body bag on a gurney. When a second gurney emerged holding another body bag, Odette covered her eyes and keened. Cecile, that precious girl, Hattie's child and Odette's darling young friend, was dead.

Chapter Twelve

Curtains of tropical rain drummed in the night as clouds released accumulations of steamy moisture. The soporific shower fell straight as an arrow, enveloping the city in a cocoon of white noise. The late September heat dissipated, gurgling with declining rainwater down the city drains to leave a moist nighttime coolness in the air.

A trio surrounded a gurney. Snugly sheltered and looking down, they could have been three figures frescoed high on a cathedral ceiling. An unconscious figure was the object of their attention.

Steve Morley, chief of the DEA office located in New Orleans, was the most well-known member of the group. Next to him was a new face, Gene White, his silver metal badge clipped to his belt, a Deputy US Marshal who was now assigned to assist Morley. He swayed slightly, exhausted, longing for a hot shower and a soft bed, and wishing he were home. He had a backache and had no idea why his presence was required.

A draped stethoscope established the third member of the group as the physician charged with caring for the patient. They stood in the building the physician owned.

Marshal White scrutinized his companions with oblique glances, though it was the woman who lay unconscious under the blanket who should have had his attention. His buddy Rick with the DEA had found her, and that was probably why Gene had been assigned to the case. He hadn't decided yet whether to thank Rick or punch him for pulling him into the situation.

The owner of the office, Merle Miller, MD, ME, was an invisible contractor with the regional federal agencies. Her ordinary appearance belied her profession, though she was dressed well except for her shoes. Those no-nonsense, crepe-soled, black wedges elevated her height to a fraction over five feet. Tonight she wore a long white coat over her clothing. Pulling her stethoscope from around her neck, she checked her patient's heartbeat. She had directed that the patient be delivered to her office, knowing they were less likely to be discovered by the media than at an emergency room.

Merle Miller had established her medical practice in an attractive building. Outside, the street was quiet at this hour. During the day, the sounds of midtown commerce penetrated the wavy, hand-blown glass of the antique windows. The meticulously restored Victorian structure nestled hidden among its surrounding high-rise neighbors, which included the DEA's regional headquarters. Dr. Miller believed her office location was why she had snagged the DEA contract.

Dr. Miller was generally right about most things, but she was wrong about the contract. She'd secured it because she was an assistant coroner with unlimited access to the morgue and, more importantly, its records. For example, the report on the Forests she would file the following day would show two bodies awaiting autopsy. Anyone who checked the official record would see this, until the DEA advised Dr. Miller to change the status. Only then would the official public record be corrected.

The shiny chrome gurney sat on its ridiculous small wheels in an examination room converted from a bedroom. Tubes and cords sprouted from the unconscious woman who was lying on its flat black padded surface. The gleaming equipment looked out of place in the warmth and comfort of the honey-colored walls, though framed and ribboned diplomas hanging there spoke to the room's use. Gene's mouth twisted, scornful. Comfort and warmth were incompatible with a doctor's office.

A plastic IV line snaked from the vulnerable bend of the patient's elbow to a hanging bag of saline solution. Dr. Miller had injected short-acting sedation into the IV line before she shaved and debrided the wound and sutured the long, shallow furrow. The sedation would soon dissipate and the patient would waken. She had good, stable vital signs. The bullet wound wasn't life-threatening, and Dr. Miller believed Mrs. Forest's concussion was temporary, though she might suffer headaches for a few days.

Cecile moaned small involuntary sounds as she surfaced to consciousness, having traumatic dreams in which she ran silently screaming as giant waves tried to drown her as they had done to her family.

Then her dream changed. Barley told her over and over she would never be perfect. He laughed at her until she wallowed in unhappiness. He fitted a vise on her head and began to squeeze it tighter and tighter. No! she gasped out loud.

Cecile thrashed about on the narrow gurney, an excruciating pain threatening to burst her brain like a pulpy grape. Starbursts of bright light flashed behind her closed eyelids, but a soft voice calmed her. Gentle hands on her arms brought her to consciousness.

Chapter Thirteen

Cecile startled awake, dazed and stunned by a ferocious headache, and frightened to find herself lying in some kind of strange room.

"Wha...what happened?" She was hurting—a lot. Not all over, just her head, but it was a nauseating ache that made her see double.

"Have to throw up," she mumbled, and tried to roll on her side. A spotless metal bowl appeared in front of her. A strong, competent arm steadied her while she purged what few contents her stomach was willing to release. Rolling back, she saw shadowy figures staring down at her.

A soothing voice crooned, "It's all right, Mrs. Forest, you're safe. I'm a doctor, and you're in my office."

Cecile turned her head and winced, the movement making her gasp. *Oh God, that hurts.* She sniffed, the air carrying a faint, disagreeable, antiseptic tang. She squinted, seeing high ceilings, long windows, and darkness outside. Was that rainwater she heard dripping from a roof? Half-hidden behind three blurred figures, her eye snagged on a graceful Hepplewhite desk like Aunt Hattie's. The desk was plopped in space where it didn't belong, an anomaly in a room of glittering metal and astringent smells.

"This isn't a doctor's office," she whispered, though she saw one person wearing a starched, white coat. Cecile's voice grated roughly and her sore, parched throat made swallowing difficult.

"But it is," the white-coated woman answered, half-laughing.

"It's...nice." Cecile saw the woman's pleased smile before her neutral expression returned.

"Did I faint?" She squeezed her eyes shut. She remembered tripping, but nothing else.

"You lost consciousness, Mrs. Forest—Cecile. I'm Dr. Miller.... Merle." Cecile blinked to focus on the woman speaking in a quiet professional voice, her kind blue eyes reflecting a genuine concern. "What's the last thing you recall?"

Through her painful headache, Cecile struggled to marshal cohesive thoughts. Her words, hesitant and separated by tears and long pauses, spoke of tripping over the low table and Barley's drink sloshing onto his lap. And that the next thing she knew she was waking up here in this unknown place, in the presence of people she'd never seen before.

"Your head is bandaged, Cecile, but let's find out if you can tolerate sitting up." The doctor slid careful, supporting hands behind Cecile's head and neck, helping her sit erect. The movement caused overwhelming vertigo, forcing her eyes shut. She swallowed convulsively, choking back the rising bile.

"I want to throw up," she groaned. "Not good." She swayed against Dr. Miller's steadying arms.

"What happened to me?" Lifting a hand to her head, Cecile's fingers encountered rough gauze, bulging well outside her head's normal size, bandages wrapped as fat as a football helmet. She saw she was moored by a needle taped to her elbow, and that there was plastic tubing attached to a bag of a clear solution dragging across her face. *Something must be very wrong.*

"Someone please tell me what happened." No querulous question this time. A demand, whispered and polite, but more assertive.

The older man stepped closer, speaking slowly as though to a small child.

"Mrs. Barley—uh, Mrs. Forest—I'm Steve Morley. I'm in charge of the regional DEA here." He placed a hand on his expansive chest. Except for dark stubble, Morley looked nothing like Columbo, the

TV hero he admired. Cecile saw a man graying at the temples, heavy though fit for a man losing the athletic edge of a younger man. His height helped disguise the effects of a desk job that had undone years of assiduous exercise.

"DEA?" That factoid forced Cecile's eyes open wide. She struggled to concentrate. "Why and how do you know *my* name?" And turning to Dr. Miller, she demanded, "Take this needle out of my arm."

Impassive, the doctor made no move toward the IV, but attempted to lower the shaking woman to a more prone position. Cecile's headache worsened, now centered near the top of her head. Her nausea made her angry, and she resisted, refusing to lie back.

Unaware of Cecile's reaction, Morley droned out the full story of their surveillance. *He likes to hear himself talk, but I've had enough.*

"Where *is* Barley?" Cecile broke in and Morley abruptly shut his mouth. Weighted silence saturated the air. Through her pounding headache, tasting bile at the back of her throat, she considered everyone's expressions and tried to interpret what she saw there.

Morley slapped his thigh, making a sharp sound. "This is ridiculous. Why are we beating around the bush?"

Brusquely insensitive, he announced, "Your husband is dead, Mrs. Forest." The air seemed to withdraw from the room, leaving only a cocooned vacuum of roaring silence.

"What? I don't understand," said Cecile, bewildered. She saw Dr. Miller's lips tighten as she reached for a syringe. Not even Morley spoke as comprehension seeped into Cecile's battered brain. Her lips formed a silent "O."

She whispered, "Oh my God," and blanched as white as the sheet that covered her. Her eyelids fluttered as blackness returned. The monitor's tone changed pitch.

Dr. Miller pierced Cecile's IV line with the syringe and depressed the plunger. Medication flowed into the clear liquid, dripping steadily into a vein. Color returned to Cecile's cheeks, and the monitor's beeps returned to normal. The doctor palpated Cecile's erratic pulse, counting the beats and frowning in Morley's direction.

Barley had bruised and torn Cecile's heart to pieces for the past ten years, but her shock was genuine. In the role she had played for all the years of their marriage, that of a loving wife, she automatically showed the face of bereavement. Perhaps she was fooling herself, too, she thought, mourning this man, but it wasn't for the Barley of today. It was for the Barley she'd once thought she loved.

The panicky, free-falling sensation wasn't something new. It was the same fear she remembered as a child when she had learned her family had died, leaving her alone in the world.

Cecile's composure evaporated in front of the strangers in this odd room. She wept, great gulping sobs not for Barley, but for what she truly missed—butterfly kisses, a mother's caress, the smell of her father's aftershave, her brother's laugh, playing with a puppy in the grass. Happy childhood memories that were bruised by a cruel husband. She grieved for her Aunt Hattie, for her dream of love and a happy marriage, and for her innocent youth. Lying in bloodstained clothes on a hard gurney, her head wrapped like a mummy, she sobbed out of fear for her future.

The men shrank back, finding something fascinating on their shoes, but Dr. Miller comforted her with a tissue before stepping back, removing herself emotionally. In this room, sympathy was hard to find.

After she shivered violently, Dr. Miller plunged a second syringe of fast-acting sedative into Cecile's IV. The doctor draped a heated blanket over the quaking woman, who gratefully hugged the warmth. Cecile wanted Odette, her friend and neighbor, beside her, but knew she was too old, then thought of Mary Ann, really her best friend. She was a better choice.

"Will someone please call Mary Ann Fitch for me?" She recited the phone number from memory. "She'll take me home." Cecile's eyelids drooped as the mild sedative dripped into her vein and relaxed her. Dr. Miller looked an inquiry at Steve Morley, who gave a negative headshake. Morley took advantage of Cecile's new passivity to resume speaking with new impatience. It was the middle of the night, past time to wrap this up.

"Madam, do you have your wits about you?"

The marshal and the doctor smothered chuckles with an exchanged glance. Who in this century called anyone "madam"?

Morley's question penetrated Cecile's sedation, her response given in such a strident tone, she horrified herself. Her voice grated sharp as shattered glass. She struggled up, pulling her hand's taped IV line painfully taut.

"My wits?" Cecile fought the sedation and faced Morley. What she wanted—what she expected—was honesty. Normally a gentle soul like Cecile wouldn't mimic the man, but nothing was normal tonight. She gingerly touched her bandaged head and winced, painfully aware of every stitch tightly suturing her torn scalp.

"I *have* my wits, thank you. Plus, I have a raging headache, I feel awful, I'm confused, I don't know where I am, *and* I have questions. How did I get here? I don't believe Barley is dead and I want to know where he is. Why hasn't anyone called my friend for me? And what have *I* done? Am I your *captive*?"

Cecile noticed Marshal White smile as she bombarded Morley with questions. Even traumatized as she was, Cecile thought the man's reaction seemed off kilter, not quite normal.

Morley made a tamping motion with both hands and apologized, unwilling to alienate the wounded woman. He needed her cooperation for his plan to work, a plan he thought would be pivotal for a successful conclusion to his investigation of Gaudet and his criminal enterprise. Pointing to each person, Morley introduced them and explained why each was in the room. Then he gave his theory about what happened to Cecile and her husband, without mentioning any names.

The horrific details made Cecile whimper as she listened, tears tracking down her cheeks. Morley paused, pleading, "Mrs. Forest—Cecile—we promise to protect you if you will help us catch... the killer. We need your help."

"Protect me?" Her head shake sparked a stab of pain. "I can't think about protection. I want to go home. We didn't do anything to deserve this... this nightmare."

"Don't be too sure about that, Mrs. Forest." It was a mistake for Morley to use Cecile's last name. They were taught to encourage others to view them as friendly authority figures. To do that, they used informal first names. "Maybe *you* didn't—the jury's still out on that—but Barley was definitely a bad guy, worse than you maybe know, and he has been for a very long time."

In response, Cecile fought the residual sedative effects and ripped off her Velcroed pressure cuff, then yanked away a handful of wires stuck to her chest. The monitor leads made popping sounds as they came off, leaving a few adhesive dots behind. The machine's lights flashed, beeping like an imaginary alien spaceship set for takeoff. Ignoring the monitor, Morley extended pudgy hands in a placating motion, speaking in his most reasonable voice while Dr. Miller tended to her equipment.

"Don't forget you were supposed to die, too, Mrs. Forest. You're only alive because you tripped and fell. You're about to hear things that are very confidential, things that you cannot repeat. Do you understand?"

After waiting for Cecile's nod, Morley described his investigation into René Gaudet's illegal activities. "Your husband is...was...his right-hand man. Whether it's true or not, Gaudet believes you know something that can put him behind bars. If he finds out you're alive, he won't stop. He'll keep trying to kill you."

Cecile's mouth fell open in disbelief.

"You think my boss did this? René Gaudet? I don't believe it for a minute. Why would he do that? My husband was like a son to the man." She could never have worked for a killer for seven years without suspecting something, but Cecile recalled how René had treated her in Barley's office. A niggling fear Morley was right hit her with a pain so visceral, she doubled over.

"I can't see it," she said, "but I'm only a busy lawyer who does nothing illegal, I swear." She groped for a dry corner of the sheet, wiping her face dry. Barley's bad behavior had cost him his life. All the while, a cool stream of relief ran beneath the surface of her thoughts.

Instinctively, Cecile hid her ambivalent state. She'd hidden most of her feelings for the past ten miserable years. This wasn't the time to show the relief in her eyes, so she stared down at her fingertips.

"René believes you know about his activities," said Morley. "That's why he wanted you dead. We"—he thumped his chest—"the DEA, want you alive as a witness. Our friends at the US Marshals Service, like Gene here, are willing to help."

"I still don't think it's René," said Cecile. "Maybe someone else in the office, but not René."

Morley ignored Cecile, pacing the floor as he continued. "Now, how do we make that happen? We keep you somewhere safe and hidden, that's how. You want us to get the bad guys, doncha? You wanna be safe, doncha? Well, that's what we want, too."

Stubborn, Cecile said, "I want to see Barley for myself. Otherwise, why should I believe you? I don't know you."

Morley grimaced, shaking his head. He made no attempt to soften the impact of his words.

"That's not gonna happen. The gunshot messed him up pretty bad. His body's still there, but most of his head is gone."

Shocked by those horrific words, Cecile cried out, her sobs increasing with the DEA man's next words.

"Besides, you're supposed to be dead, too, remember? We have a double funeral all planned. Going to bury your empty coffin next to his, but don't worry. We'll pay for a monument with the correct dates. We've got everything ordered, and you'll be far away by the time the funeral takes place. Get used to it, Mrs. Forest...Cecile. This is your new reality." He patted her on the shoulder.

"No. Just no. I won't do it, so leave me alone." Cecile's jaw was clenched, but she was wringing her hands, as though not quite certain.

"Look, Cecile. I'm telling you this is the right thing to do." Mr. Morley was persuasive, someone of authority forcefully telling her the proper course of action. Morley kept wheedling, and the exhausted young woman finally gave in.

Let him take charge, she thought, and agreed to his plan. More than anything else, she wanted someone else to make these important decisions—her parents and then Aunt Hattie always had. Barley had, too. Her parents had sheltered her until they died and then Hattie. When Hattie died and Cecile married Barley, he took over her life, telling her what she could and couldn't do, and where and when to do it. She'd never made her own decisions. It was the DEA's good luck that she wasn't ready to start now.

"Okay then, right," Morley said, and with a solitary loud clap of his hands he began speaking in clichés. "The wheels are in motion. Let's get this show on the road." He kept his eyes on Cecile as he laid out the rest of his plan. When he finished, he told Gene to check outside then turned away, drew out his phone, and began jabbing at the numbers.

Cecile had relinquished control of her life—again. She sank back on the thin pillow of the gurney. Her throat was parched. The salt in her tears had tightened the skin of her jaw, and the throbbing intensity of her pain drained away the last of her energy.

"Please take me home," she begged, yearning for the home of a dozen years before that had meant laughter and good food and conversations with Great-aunt Hattie and their friends, her home before Barley spoiled everything. Now home just meant a place to snuggle between soft sheets in her own bed and sleep away the pain. Cecile longed to be home.

Morley heard her and whirled, holding his phone to his chest. Speaking, he emphasized each gruff word. "No, Mrs. Forest. You may *not* go home. You are *dead* in the eyes of everyone except the Drug Enforcement Administration, the US Marshals Service, and Dr. Miller." His actions made Cecile redden. She wiped her nose, helpless against his boorishness, like a baby bird in a cruel world.

The midnight world outside the doctor's office entranced a tired Gene as he checked for the presence of media spies. The rain had ceased, but drops plopped wetly to the ground, providing a counterpoint to the burbles of tiny tree frogs and the sawing of cicadas. City lights provided enough illumination to see without the light from his phone, so he tucked it away and quickly scanned the small, shorn yard and the sidewalk in front of the doctor's old house. Except for the eerie moss and looped vines hanging from an enormous oak, he saw nothing of note. He went back inside to report an all clear, then helped a shaky Cecile up onto her bare feet.

Chapter Fourteen

René Gaudet's day didn't end the way he expected. Ten minutes more, and he would've made it out of his handsome office, heading home. Instead, the prepaid phone only a few people knew about vibrated in his pocket. He listened, sighing after he disconnected. His bribed police contact had paid off again, and this tip-off was a biggie. He sank back into his soft leather chair and put his feet up on his expensive burled honeywood desk. He considered what actions to take.

René hadn't always been a criminal. On the contrary, when he graduated from Loyola law, he'd considered himself an honest defender of souls. He hung out a shingle as a defense attorney and put himself on welfare and food stamps while he waited for clients to find him. From the beginning, René had called his practice the Authement and Gaudet Law Firm because he liked the way it sounded. Authement wasn't a real person; it was simply a placeholder name to add weight and authenticity to a new practice. He slept on a secondhand Salvation Army sofa in his one-room office. Success in those early days meant being able to afford groceries *and* pay his utility bill the same month.

His starvation phase ended when René lucked into his first regular client.

Clive LeBlanc was incarcerated in the state prison, located in a rural area more than an hour from New Orleans. The call came at a desperate time for René. He was hungry and penniless. His car was running on fumes, and that morning he decided to take on any client who could pay.

⁕

Getting past a surly guard at the prison check-in was an irritation for the unknown attorney. When René finally got past the gatekeeper, he found himself walking down a long, echoing corridor keeping pace with a guard. The corridor was puke-green and smelled of industrial chemicals overlaid with the sweaty odor of a men's locker room. René snorted out his first breath of the crappy smell out and tried to hold his breath. The guard chortled, amused.

Sound reverberated off every surface, his trepidation increasing as he went deeper into the prison with the burly guard. Their steps echoed with an unsettling tympanic effect making René realize he should've worn soft-soled shoes. He would never make that mistake again. They reached their destination and he entered a windowless concrete chamber, so small it felt claustrophobic. Left alone, he stretched out his arms, almost able to touch the opposing walls of the secure visitation room with his fingertips.

René set his briefcase onto the room's narrow metal table and settled in the chair farthest from the door and the remaining chairs. His heartbeat gradually slowed to normal as he looked around the bare, windowless room. The four pieces of furniture, a table and three chairs, were immovable, securely bolted to the cement floor. René pulled at his scratchy collar, looked around and waited, his heel making a staccato tapping sound against the floor. This lasted a full twenty minutes until a guard pulled the door open and Clive LeBlanc walked in, completely unrestrained. This, then, was his new client.

René hadn't known what to expect, why Mr. LeBlanc was in prison, or why he, René, had been summoned. In his imagination, he'd pictured the man heavyset and dangerous-looking, dark-skinned, with long hair pulled into a ponytail and a scraggly beard. René had worked up a real apprehension that caused him to flinch when the door clanged open.

When LeBlanc entered wearing a prison-issued orange jumpsuit, his appearance left Gaudet speechless. He was short, rather thin and pasty-white. Clean-shaven, he had a buzzed haircut that left him looking skinned. His jumpsuit flapped around his arms and legs. It swallowed his scrawny frame. He waited calmly without speaking, staring at René with penetrating eyes, until the guard left and locked the door behind him.

"Mr. LeBlanc, I'm René Gaudet." He'd talked with no idea what to say to this harmless, scrawny felon, anxious to fill the silence.

"Yeah, I know. It was me called *you*." LeBlanc snickered, his mouth lifting in a sneer. René disliked the man immediately and irrationally. He was uncomfortable in the ominous place, regretting being there despite how badly he needed money. He felt off-balance.

A question had been uppermost in René's mind since LeBlanc first called and he politely asked, "Who gave you my name?"

"Simple. It was nobody. The prison library keeps all the phone books. Your name ain't in the old book, but it's in the new one."

"Yes, so?"

"So I figure you're a brand-new lawyer and might be hungry."

René marveled at Mr. LeBlanc's simple ingenuity.

"Listen, you wanna be my lawyer, or not?"

"Don't you have a lawyer?" René imagined Clive could've had his lawyer bumped off somehow.

LeBlanc said, "Yeah, Alvin Boudreaux. You know Alvin?"

"No. Should I?" René hated this man to think he didn't know other lawyers in the city, and said, "There are a thousand lawyers in New Orleans."

LeBlanc grunted, picking at a torn fingernail. "It's good to know old Alvin stayed outta sight. He's been my lawyer a long time. He has all my stuff, but he says he's too sick to keep working. He's quit lawyering and told me to find somebody quick he could turn my files over to. Call him if you have to, but that's all I'm gonna say until you tell me yes or no."

René had some concern, but it wasn't like he was swamped with work. He agreed to represent LeBlanc, quoting half again more than his usual hourly fee. Clive LeBlanc didn't bat an eye, countersigning the representation contract in René's briefcase. Folding his copy of the contract, LeBlanc told René about the large-scale drug business he was running in New Orleans from behind bars. He needed René's help for the rest of his time in prison—another five years.

"What exactly are you asking?" A drop of sweat inched down from René's sideburn and his heartbeat ratcheted into overdrive.

"It's simple, René." Patient, LeBlanc slowly drew the young lawyer into his web. "Don't get your panties in a twist. I *can* call you René, can't I?" René nodded, his lips clenched. It was too late now to insist on formalities. Clive LeBlanc was probably a con man who wanted to get something for nothing and René thought he'd have to chalk this meeting up to experience.

When he called his bank to check the balance an hour after he reached his office, the outrageous fee he had quoted LeBlanc was already there, swelling the sum to many times larger than it had ever been. With the snap of his fingers, he could suddenly pay his bills *and* find a more comfortable place to sleep.

He retrieved Clive LeBlanc's files from the dying lawyer, Alvin Boudreaux. After that, he did three simple things for LeBlanc: he ferried messages to LeBlanc's street pushers, he picked up their drug proceeds and deposited them. And, following his client's instructions, he laundered dirty money until it was so clean it squeaked.

Gaudet ethics washed away as he scrubbed the dirty drug money. His new career fit him quite well, that of enabling a criminal while using his legitimate law career as a cover. He *liked* this sneaky, illegal stuff, and he was *good* at it.

He especially liked getting rich.

*

Clive LeBlanc somehow slipped in the communal shower room as the end of his final year in prison approached. He fell onto a shard of broken glass lying on the floor. It pierced his eye and penetrated his brain, killing him. In the roomful of men, no one witnessed the fall or saw the broken glass lying there. LeBlanc's demise was logged as an accidental death.

René's golden goose died, but he didn't cry about it. He'd had to smuggle five pounds of choice drugs into the prison, but felt no remorse for the death of a criminal. It was a troublesome bit of business, but he jumped into the breach and took over LeBlanc's business which, by then, he knew completely. No one ever learned who'd actually killed LeBlanc and no one really cared, including René Gaudet.

Concurrent with maintaining a career on the right side of the law, Gaudet put a handful of new men on his payroll who ruthlessly eradicated his competition in the drug business. His men kept the street dealers in line, driving out any opposition and the ambitious wannabees. Gaudet's organization took control of the city block by block until he became known as the drug kingpin of New Orleans—the man who controlled cocaine, fentanyl, and heroin through the Port of New Orleans from all over the world. Dealers who didn't like it could either leave—or die.

A network of associates helped distribute bulk imports of narcotics using the interstate highways across the southern states. No one would ever eliminate illegal drugs, Gaudet believed, so why *shouldn't* he benefit? It took big *cojones* and a loyal team of well-paid enforcers to keep his dealers in line, and he had all of that. If there was bloodshed, so be it. It wasn't *his* fault when people didn't follow orders.

Chapter Fifteen

Gaudet should've gone home right away, but it was too late now. It was part of his policy of self-preservation to have a corrupt, highly-ranked city policeman on his payroll. He learned quickly about important police activities, especially when a problem might affect his business. The alarming call tonight to his personal prepaid phone meant more than a mere problem. This stank to high hell, and he had to get to the bottom of it as soon as possible.

René prowled his swank office wondering if what he'd just heard was true. What happened to Barley and Cecile? He worried at his lower lip and paced, his agitation becoming frenzied. How should he to handle this situation? His fingers curled around one of the presidential miniatures displayed behind his desk. He bounced it in his hand, testing its weight. Feeling his impotency, he hurled it at the wall, embedding chunks of plaster in the pecky cypress paneling, obliterating the plaster president. He put his hand on the expensive wall.

It made no sense. Why kill Barley? Why did *Cecile* have to die, too? He must have misunderstood his cop, but the man wouldn't call again—too risky—and René certainly couldn't call him.

He had gone to great lengths to shield Cecile Forest from his illegal activities. He warned the other employees to keep their mouths shut. She was smart and well-informed except for her ignorance of Gaudet's drug trafficking. She was the *only* lawyer in the firm other than Gaudet himself. He stopped pacing and stood thinking, plaster-dusted fingers fisted at his sides. Feeling angst was a waste of time. Losing Cecile as a legitimate shield—if that's what happened—meant he would have to handle her cases until he found a lawyer to replace her. Substituting someone for her husband was no trouble at all. His ilk was a dime a dozen, and his predecessor as René's second in command, Jimmy Costanza, was one of Gaudet's enforcers. Jimmy could step back into his old job.

René summoned Jimmy to his home for a meeting, using his prepaid burner phone.

*

Snug in his quiet limousine, Gaudet fretted as the background of St. Charles Avenue unspooled past the tinted windows. Rush hour was over and the journey home was swift and uneventful. During this daily ride, he often congratulated himself for his meteoric rise to become a prince of commerce and material success, but he couldn't manage it today.

Today he stared at the changing scenery without seeing it and wondered what the hell had happened at Barley's house. Jimmy would unearth the facts. Then Gaudet would find out who'd had the nerve to attack his criminal empire.

Outside Gaudet's car as it rolled toward home, the lulling hum of a rumbling streetcar rose to a crescendo, then fell to diminuendo, as it dopplered down the neutral ground dividing the Avenue. Despite his anxiety, René's tension dissipated. In the sky high above the trees, blue herons silhouetted by clouds stained glorious ochre by the setting sun flew to their evening roosts. René interrupted his thoughts to wonder if the herons were headed to Lake Pontchartrain. If only *he* had no worries like the birds. What would that would be like? He grunted—*the way things were going, I'd plummet from the perch in my sleep and drown in the lake.*

The car turned past an imposing mansion of dark gray stone. Its spires and turrets poked holes in the urban sky. Glossy black wrought-iron fencing separated a verdant lawn from the old, cracked municipal pavements and the busy traffic.

Gaudet lived in a showplace, two hundred years old and originally commissioned for a New Orleans merchant prince. Its previous owners had granted the home a certain social prominence, and although its architecture warranted that *cachet* its present owner did not, because society didn't consider Gaudet to be of the upper echelon. He barely received recognition for his wealth—though the home itself scored points for its size. The mansion was indulgent, with highly polished hardwood floors covered by fine Asian carpets, topped by one-of-a-kind antiques upholstered in expensive fabrics. Fabulous brocade drapes pooled on the lush carpets. The place was cavernous for the two-man household—René and his butler—but René loved every inch of it.

René chased the last forkful of chateaubriand with a swallow of rare Bordeaux decanted from its dusty bottle. He was silent, unusually issuing not a single directive. He dined this night at a small table covered with white linen in the alcove of his opulent home office. His inscrutable butler, Cyril Smythe, stood off Gaudet's right shoulder just behind him.

After René gave his mouth a final swipe with a large linen napkin, he prepared to rise. Cyril pulled out his employer's chair with timing so perfect, it went unnoticed.

"Cyril," Gaudet said, "take the wine and a Rusty Nail into the library, and that will be all for tonight. I'm expecting a visitor, but I'll answer the door myself." The butler bowed slightly.

"Veddy good, sir." Smythe's British accent sounded like the music of wealth, making Gaudet smile. He entered the small half bath that adjoined his office using a door hidden in the paneled wall of the alcove, leaving the butler to clear away evidence of the meal.

Gaudet had dismissed Cyril earlier than usual, which was suspiciously out of character. It certainly wasn't his typical behavior, and Cyril decided *not* to retire to his quarters. Instead, he left the intercom on from the library to the kitchen, then made himself comfortable where he and his tape recorder could hear whatever would happen next.

After his first week of employment, Cyril discovered he could be a robot for all his new boss noticed. He was amply compensated, but Cyril had fallen into an extra perk that gave him an additional source of income to squirrel away, in anticipation of an early retirement.

His secret side job required him to make detailed records of his days—the comings and goings of Mr. Gaudet, who visited him, and their times of arrival and departure. This was routinely boring. Cyril had decided to take additional notes for himself of overheard snippets of Mr. Gaudet's side of phone calls as well as conversations Mr. Gaudet had with his few visitors. He recorded these electronically when he could. One never knew when one's notes might make a difference.

Chapter Sixteen

Jimmy Costanza fidgeted in the pool of light beneath the elaborate overhang of Mr. Gaudet's front door, aware he was probably visible on a monitor inside. He pressed a lighted button and heard the mellifluous doorbell. The tone sounded expensive. His mouth curled in a disgusted *moue* before he recalled his facial visibility in the house.

A short, wiry man, Costanza took pride in his inconspicuous appearance. He looked down at his clothes. He wore a short-sleeved, faded blue plaid cotton shirt and a pair of wrinkled khakis similar to a half dozen others he owned. Clothes like these, worn by many other men, provided additional anonymity in the Deep South.

Maybe he should've cleaned up before coming, not that he'd had enough time to do that. As it was, he'd answered Mr. Gaudet's summons by driving hundreds of miles all the way back to the city from his business calls in Biloxi, Mississippi.

In his birth country, Jimmy was known as José Jimenez, but he was in the country illegally and his fake name worked well for him and his boss.

He had been blindsided when Mr. Gaudet demoted him and put that Forest guy in his place as his right-hand man. The new guy dressed nice and acted smart, but he was a crooked lawyer just like the boss. Costanza kept the same pay, but the loss of that job's prestige rubbed him the wrong way. He kept his resentment to himself, smoldering, and did whatever he was told.

The footsteps inside grew louder and stopped, Jimmy assuming he was being looked at on a monitor. To his surprise, Mr. Gaudet opened the door himself, motioning him to squeeze inside. He stood, looking around, while Gaudet stuck his head out and scanned the veranda and surrounding lawn.

Jimmy rocked back and forth on the thick carpet, feeling the plushness under his toes through his thin-soled shoes. Back home, his family's hut had dirt floors covered with straw. Here in this house, wealth surrounded him from the slick marble floors to the vibrant coverings on the walls, all the way up to the foyer's vaulted ceiling.

This was his first meeting with Mr. Gaudet anywhere outside the office. He had thought Mr. Gaudet's office was impressive, but *this* place could be a museum, not that he'd ever been *in* a museum. Still, on what this house was worth, he could live the rest of his life without working another day.

Satisfied he saw no spies, René locked the massive front door and led Jimmy to his favorite room of the house.

Jimmy stood shell-shocked in the middle of a room whose four walls were covered with books up to the ceiling. He saw a ladder standing out of place in a corner, hooked to a rail. He whispered a soft "Caramba."

Hiding a frown, he realized Mr. Gaudet wouldn't offer him the courtesy of a chair. Expensive leather squeaked with his boss's flop into a chair Costanza thought was big enough to sleep in. Mr. Gaudet took a long swallow of amber liquid from a fancy squat tumbler before he asked, "What'd you find out, Jimmy?"

Costanza balanced in a wide stance and shook his head sadly, his lips turned down. "That house is wrapped in yellow plastic tape stuff, tight as a piñata. The front window glass is disappeared, blowed in. It was dark and that's all I saw. The cops did tol' me two peoples died."

"You sure about that? It was *two*?" René struggled to believe it, though Jimmy simply corroborated what his cop had already told him. He slammed his glass on the side table, sloshing whiskey out on his hand. Ice cubes flew out, scattering like startled birds. "Son of a *bitch*!"

"What the *hell* happened, Jimmy? Who *hired* that damn shooter, that's what I want to know!"

Jimmy kept his features bland as he shrugged, though he disapproved of such undisciplined behavior. All that bad language and cursing were unnecessary. The words were disrespectful, even though spoken in English. He ventured a direct look and gauged Gaudet as being irrationally angry and inebriated.

Jimmy had followed Mr. Gaudet's orders, but had he made trouble for himself? The man was so inconsistent, Jimmy never knew what to expect. He cleared his throat.

"The cops said it could be a drive-by, boss. One cop thought maybe you or Barl did it. But I don' think Barl wanted to get hisself offed, so I don' think so."

"Ya think?" Gaudet snarled and jumped to his feet, thinking as he paced. Jimmy tracked his steps and saw one of Gaudet's shoes send a melting ice cube skittering across the floor.

"Did Barley have product with him?"

"No, boss, don' think so. I saw him load it in the Jag when he left."

Gaudet groaned. "Crap, Jimmy! Another problem. Did the cops search his car?"

"No, sir. I saw it down the street, not inside the tape. They wrapped his house and the yard with that yellow tape. Nothin' on the street. That had to be his red Jag, 'cause he got a custom grille." Jimmy used his fingers to make air quotes. He added, "A chrome 'BF', for Barley Forest. Don't think they know."

"Yet," said Mr. Gaudet. "The cops don't know yet. Won't be long before they find it. Can you get in and wipe it clean before they figure it out? Without being seen?"

"Of course, boss. I'm the best!" Jimmy thumped his chest, displaying supreme confidence.

René Gaudet's only choice was to take him at his word.

Chapter Seventeen

Headache wormed through Cecile's brain like a living creature. It burrowed deep behind her eyes. She wished the deputy marshal would hurry up and leave.

What's his name? Her memory wasn't cooperating. *Is it White*? She watched as he prowled, inspecting every inch of Cecile's hotel room with some gadget—under the bed, in the drawers, under lampshades—and those pale eyes flickering in her direction every few seconds. *What's he waiting for? Me to make a break for it? What*?

She'd been at this place before with Aunt Hattie, but only as far as the lobby for high tea. The exclusive Windsor Court hotel property was secured behind a high brick wall with a wrought iron gate. The owners had attended to detail throughout, to imitate homes of nineteenth century English nobility. Until tonight, she hadn't realized the same level of decoration had been lavished on the guest rooms.

The marshal turned to Cecile as he tucked his gadget in a pocket. "Okay, you're secure. No bugs—er—listening devices." Diffident, he swept his hand toward a table in a corner of the large room.

Shrugging as if knowing she wouldn't do what he asked, he said anyway, "Try to eat," and added, "I'll be back tomorrow. I'm sorry for your loss."

"Thank you, Mr. White." *He's leaving. Finally.* She moved him toward the door, steering him by his elbow. She was still barefoot, having lost her shoes somehow.

"Gene," he said.

Confused, she hesitated. "What?"

"My name is *Gene*. Call me Gene, ma'am." He hauled out an overused old bromide. "Mr. White was my father."

"Oh. Of course." Cecile inwardly rolled her eyes and ushered Gene into the dimmed hallway, pleased to see a guard outside her room. It provided her with reassurance she hadn't realized she needed. She was reluctant to be left alone, but not enough to ask the deputy marshal to stay. She stepped back and pushed the door closed with a solid thunk.

She whispered, "Finally," slumping against the door. She engaged the safety locks and wished there were a few more, before dragging herself into a brightly lit, immaculate bathroom. Every molecule of her body vibrated with hurt and fatigue. Clothes she had worn for far too many hours chafed her skin. Grotesque bandages weighed down her head and strained her neck muscles.

Cecile opened tub faucets full strength, throwing bubble bath provided by Windsor Court into the stream. As she removed her grimy clothes and threw them into the trash, glorious hot water thundered into an enormous tub. She willed herself to ignore the mirrored wall above the vanity, not wanting to see her damaged self. She lowered her sore, naked body into the tub, and the heated water forced an involuntary groan. She felt an awful guilt. *How can I enjoy anything at a time like this?* Submerged to her chin, Cecile lay against the tub's sloping back and closed her weary eyes. Fragrant translucent bubbles covered her, vibrating with her heartbeat. A few popped with each of her breaths, raining dots of moisture on her cheeks and lifting the tension away, until finally she could think.

I wanted Barley out of my life, not dead. She felt responsible and guilt swept through her, unsoftened by the fragrant bath water.

Who killed him? And tried to kill me? Not René—he's been like a father to us. Then who? A client? Mistaken identity? Why? She felt unsteady, like sand was shifting beneath her, waves lapping it away from under her feet.

Cecile toweled dry, aghast at the mirror's pale reflection. Her head heavily swathed, she was a living Q-Tip. The two black eyes dominating her wan face under the white blob looked worse than expected, but her shocking appearance helped buffer the knowledge of Barley's violent death.

I'm taking this bulky bandage off. My boo-boo can't be that bad. Cecile picked at the gauze's taped edge, unwinding a vast length which was dark with dried blood, to a layer bright with fresh new blood. As she got closer to her scalp, she was afraid she'd made a mistake. *Too late now...*

Easing the last bit from her blood-matted hair, Cecile tossed an acre's worth of cotton into the bathroom trash and took an unflinching inventory of her bedraggled, bloody hair. The strands not pressed flat against her scalp fell lank and filthy about her face and neck, leaving pinkish bloodstains on her clean shoulders in glaring contrast to her usual gleaming tresses.

"Oh, God," she despaired, completely overwhelmed by the situation. The words *it'll be okay* nestled deep in Cecile's subconscious.

The bullet had plowed a neat, shallow furrow in her scalp. Its edges were pulled together and closed using surgical staples. The wound was punctuated in dots and dashes with bright orange iodine, all of which was clearly visible through a bumpy paper tape covering. Someone had tried to preserve as much hair as possible by shaving only a narrow strip of Cecile's scalp, but she ended up looking ridiculous. *Damn, I look silly, and damn, I was lucky*!

She eyed her reflection. Rummaging in the bathroom's tiny drawer, she found a hotel-supplied bag holding a razor, sewing supplies, and disposable scissors. *Yes! But this is going to take a while. I think I should have a drink.* Trauma called for a gulp of booze.

She covered her nakedness with a hotel robe, then retrieved a goblet of wine and the plate of croissants and cheese. Food would ease her exhaustion and residual dizziness, and the wine—well, she wanted more wine than she had, but it was a start. Returning to the bathroom with everything, she set it on the granite counter and picked up the scissors.

Cecile whimpered as the sticky strands of hair fell away until forty-five minutes later, she'd sawn off all her hair as haphazardly close as she could manage. She surveyed the damage, her eyes red and her cheeks damp. Then, tearing a plastic razor from its wrapper, she shaved the remaining stubble, avoiding the paper tape. Washing down the last dill-buttered bite of croissant, Cecile swallowed the dregs of the wine and inspected her bare scalp. *I gave myself something new to cry about.* Unrecognizable, red-rimmed black eyes, their irises murky gray, stared at her from the mirror. She removed the wastebasket's liner, half-filled with soiled auburn hair, and knotted it tightly. *Bad enough* I *know it's there. No reason housekeeping has to see the mess.*

Cecile's confused feelings about Barley were no longer relevant, resolved in the worst possible way. Her new freedom came with a healthy dose of guilt.

Let the mourning begin...

It was nearly four a.m. With the bathroom light on and the door cracked open, she headed to bed. Pillows, plumped high, waited to cradle her shorn, aching head. She ignored the chocolate candies on the bedside table next to the clock ticking toward dawn. *What a way to experience this beautiful room.*

Cecile sighed, completely spent, as she crawled under the sheets still wearing the terrycloth robe. After a few moments, she removed one of the pillowcases and carefully wrapped it against the chill of her cold, shaved head. *I won't be able to sleep* was her last conscious thought.

Her head throbbed when the bedside phone trilled and jarred Cecile awake. The dish of chocolates tumbled to the plush carpet as she groped and finally fumbled the receiver to her ear. Hardly able to speak, she swallowed and cleared her throat, her mouth dry as cotton.

"Hello?" she croaked, followed by a cough.

"Ms. Columbo?" The inquiring voice sounded crisp and female.

"What? No. Wrong room."

"Yes, you remember? You *are* Ms. Columbo, the name you agreed to last night? I'm Tammy Avenetti, Deputy US Marshal, liaison to the DEA, calling from the DEA office?" All the woman's sentences ended in question marks, as though anticipating Cecile should know her intent.

Tammy was the repository memory of the combined DEA/US Marshals initiative in New Orleans. With boundless energy, she could do practically anything and was interested in whatever was going on in her proximity. Cecile immediately visualized her type when she heard Tammy's "yat" accent—she pictured a resident of the Ninth Ward who greeted friends with "where y'at?" instead of "hello." She probably had a short, square body and a blonde bouffant hairdo to give her more height, everything finished off with a pair of retro cat-eye glasses.

The bright sunshine pouring through gaps in the room's curtains pooled on the patterned carpet, reminding her where she was, why she was there, and making her squint. Cecile managed to inhale, then a second breath oxygenated her stultified brain. Her head felt cold enough to have been packed in snow. She pushed at her hair, shocked by the stubble where her hair had been. She abruptly sat up in a move that dizzied her.

"What time is it?"

"Um, about eleven, ma'am."

"A.M.?" Cecile became more alert, shocked anew.

"Um, yeah. Did I wake you?"

Cecile trembled in the air-conditioned room. The robe she'd slept in sagged from her shoulders while she tried to concentrate of what she was being told.

"Mr. Harry—he's a DEA field agent—and the NOPD didn't find the men we think were the shooters, but they believe a third party ordered the kill." Cecile gasped when she heard the word *kill,* but the woman on the phone nattered on.

"That's who we want to find, and the money around here is positive it's René Gaudet behind it all." Cecile held the receiver to her ear, stunned. She disagreed. *They think René killed Barley? That can't possibly be true.*

Oblivious of Cecile's inattention, the Tammy person kept talking, saying she planned to go to the Octavia Street house for some of Cecile's clothes and other necessary things. She was asking her for a little guidance, like what to get and where was it kept, and the scratch of a cheap pen on cheap paper made it through the phone.

Cecile half-listened, her headache pounding steel spikes through her brain. She imagined the woman at her desk, one leg under her rear end while she twirled a pencil between her fingers. It was just another day at the office for Ms. Avenetti—perhaps more interesting than the usual day, but still part of her normal deputy marshal job.

"I'll collect basic stuff like underwear, you know, but nothing else," Tammy was saying. "No outer clothing. You have to look different now, not like you—I mean, old friends can recognize you by your clothes and style just like they know your face. I took a whole class on that.

"We conceal important witnesses like you, Ms. Columbo. Have to keep you safe until the trouble blows over. Mr. Morley from the DEA? He requested this joint mission with the US Marshals Service, which is who I work for. Mr. Morley is the AIC, the agent in charge of this mission. Remember him from yesterday? He wants you out of danger and that's the job of the US Marshals, which is why we're working with the DEA."

Cecile interrupted, distressed at her own annoyed tone. The person speaking was only following orders, and probably couldn't help herself. "Please don't call me Ms. Columbo. It's not even a good name. It's a throwback to the '60s."

Tammy ignored her. "Where in the house do you keep your clothes?"

Cecile felt violated all over again, thinking of that stranger wandering around her house, but resigned herself to staying at the hotel until Tammy delivered some clothes. *How far can I get with two black eyes, barefoot, wearing a hotel bathrobe and a pillowcase wrapped around my bald head*?

She massaged the bridge of her nose. "Can you please bring me something for this headache?"

"Sure. Is ibuprofen okay? But don't forget, Ms. Columbo, Dr. Miller will check on you. And, oh yeah, Mr. Morley and Marshal White, who you met last night, they'll see you later to bring you up to date. You have to get used to the name "Melba Columbo". That's who you are now." Tammy disconnected, leaving empty air behind.

Cecile, her injured head wobbling on her fragile neck, tried to focus on the underlying facts she had just heard.

My Marshal? It's confusing. She massaged her nose again. Jackhammers pounded in her my skull. *At least I'm alive.* She curled into a tight ball, grabbing a pillow to muffle her whimpering sobs. She seesawed from actually wanting Barley back to being relieved her tormentor was gone for good. She felt a euphoric freedom more than a sense of loss...and felt guilty about it. Beyond the guilt, she was deeply frightened—the same rudderless loss she'd felt ten years before when Aunt Hattie died.

She still missed her great-aunt, and knew she always would. *What will happen to me now, Aunt Hattie? I'm alone—again.*

Inescapable grief prodded Cecile back into the oblivion of healing sleep.

*

Tammy felt sorry for poor Ms. Columbo. She removed her headset and walked away from her desk. She leaned through Mr. Morley's office door to report that the poor woman sounded dazed and still in a lot of pain. Anyone, she was sure, would empathize with the pain and danger Melba Columbo faced.

"I can't imagine being shot and then learning your husband was murdered. Poor thing!"

"Yes, but the Agency has to take advantage of her, Tammy, for the greater good," Morley cautioned. "Remember René Gaudet is the primary target. Mrs. Forest will be his downfall when we get the man to trial. Unless we find someone else, she's the only material witness we have. She's a new widow and the jury will be sympathetic. That and our other evidence will put him in prison, hopefully for a very long time."

Chapter Eighteen

Melba was resigned to her new identity. Resigned, and ravenous. In the wrinkled white robe, a pillowcase wrapped around her naked noggin, Melba consumed the eggs Sardou and lagniappe rasher of bacon set before her on a gold-rimmed plate at the little table. An insulated pitcher of café au lait sat beside a large coffee cup. The ladylike Cecile might not have ordered—much less eaten—so much food, but each new meal cleared her foggy thoughts a little more.

A loud bang outside made Melba drop her fork with a clatter and duck, screaming, before she realized it was a noisy garbage truck dropping a metal can back to the ground. She waited for the trembling to ease, then left the table, struggling to put a new twist in her thinking.

This playacting could be fun, she thought, practicing a wry smile. The brief smile was the only attempt she'd made to adjust to a new persona. *Who am I fooling?* Her mouth drooped as reality intruded. Melba pulled back the heavy brocade curtain to gaze down at the office buildings of her beloved New Orleans.

The sunshine of October's first day streamed across the vibrant reds and golds of her suite, filling it with a rich, warm light. Despite the awful circumstances, Melba liked the room. In the outside world a half block away, a man wearing a white coverall was strapped in a safety harness, swiping a squeegee back and forth across a window. Very Zen. A few levels below him, someone in a floppy, broad-brimmed straw hat tended a terrace garden. As Cecile, Melba knew the owner of that garden. *Everything has changed. Why hasn't the rest of the world stopped going about its business?*

Cecile's sadness returned. She crawled into the rumpled bed, the events of the previous night repeating on a mental loop. *Why did Barley die? Who wanted us dead?* A thought of her elderly neighbor followed. *Poor Odette must have seen it all from her porch. She must be scared to death. Will either of us ever feel safe again? I don't understand why I'm going through all this. Why will I have to testify? I don't know anything.*

⁂

Melba's eyelashes brushed uncomfortably against the privacy peephole. She blinked rapidly in order to view whose staccato rapping had disturbed her sleep. It wasn't housekeeping or Dr. Miller, she knew. They had already come and gone, so the petite woman she saw who was weighted down with bags might be from the government.

> "Yes?" Her hoarseness surprised her. She cleared her throat, and tried again. "Yes?"

The answer was staccato, much like the knock had been.

"Tammy Avenetti, US Marshal's office, Ms. Columbo. May I please enter?"

Melba recognized those flattened, drawn-out syllables. She had heard them over the phone earlier in the day. She gave a tentative smile as she unlocked the door and opened it, raising her eyebrows in surprise.

The young woman juggled several bags, speaking as she stepped in, even before she looked up at the taller woman. She wore a no-nonsense, long-sleeved white shirt and a pair of conservative belted black slacks. Stopping abruptly, she gasped, her mouth open. In her strong New Orleans accent, she blurted, "Oh, my Gawd," and stumbled back, shocked. "I...I...knew you got hurt, but I didn't think you were this messed up. You got two huge shiners, Ms. Columbo."

Catching herself, Tammy blushed when her manners caught up with her surprise. She apologized, "Sorry—but you look awful."

Melba had to smile, motioning her into the room and locking the door behind her.

"Yes, I surprised myself when I looked in the mirror this morning. My eyes look even blacker today than they did last night." She pulled the pillowcase off her head and pointed to her wound. "And no, I'm not always bald. I cut off my hair because it was dirty and nasty and full of blood. The gash from the bullet that almost killed me meant I couldn't wash my hair, so I got rid of it." She pointed to her scalp. "See that tape? What's *under it* is what really hurts."

"Yikes." The girl's lips twitched, trying hard not to laugh, though Melba realized it was a surprised reaction to a weird bald-headed woman with two black eyes. She patted the younger woman's arm in a way that accepted her response, though there was nothing remotely funny about being shot, being bald, or being cut and bruised.

"Don't worry, Marshal. Just because *I* don't think it's funny, doesn't mean I can't see why others might laugh."

In the flesh, Tammy wasn't what Melba had expected. She was petite and about half the age. She exhibited a feminine style in things like hoop earrings that gave her a sexy little flash. An unobtrusive necklace peeked out of the "Vee" of her uniform's shirt collar and she embellished her pretty smile by wearing a soft rose lip color.

She had left her brown hair color alone, which was smart, relying on an excellent haircut. It swung, soft and shining with health, around her face, always settling back into its place.

Melba made a mental note to ask the marshal about her beautician. When—if—she came home, *if* her hair grew out, she would give them a try. She thought sourly, *how can I think of hair at a time like this?*

"*You,* Marshal, on the other hand, look completely different from what I imagined," said Melba. "I tried to picture you when we talked on the phone, and I got it all wrong."

"Yeah? How did you think I looked?"

Melba hesitated. She wanted to be diplomatic here. They would have to get along, and there was no benefit to rudeness and ill will.

"For starters, I saw you as a blonde wearing your hair twisted up, and older. I figured you might wear cat-eye glasses. It was just conjecture, me painting a picture in my mind."

"Conjecture?"

"You know. A guess. I was trying not to think of yesterday's awful things that happened."

"Funny thing is, I have a cousin looks just like what you just said." Tammy's wide brown eyes and shy smile revealed her as quite an attractive young woman. She leaned in and whispered, "My cousin colors her hair, but's really the same brown as mine.

"I was so glad to go to the mall today for fun stuff? You have a great house, too?" Her face reddened and she stopped abruptly. "I mean, don't get me wrong? I'm sorry you got hurt and your husband got shot and all?" The rising inflection at the end of each sentence made Tammy's comments into questions that hung in the room. It was a disconcerting habit Melba would have to get used to. "Just sometimes I get so bored at the office I go off to la-la land and zone out half the time, you know?

To Melba's astonishment, the young marshal paused, looking panic-stricken. "My words aren't coming out right."

"I understand, believe me," were Melba's reassuring words. "My work gets boring, too." She reached for the bags Tammy still carried, dismissing her embarrassment.

"Want some coffee? Or a Coke?"

"Thanks, I better not. I'm so fumble-mouthed right now, I'd slobber all over myself."

"I'd even *wear* one of those bags I'm so sick of this robe."

"I'm surprised you notice what you have on, after what you've been through."

They took the bags and emptied them on Melba's coverlet, which she'd thrown back over the sheets. Several practical slacks, blouses, and dresses exhibited lovely patterns and soft colors, as far removed as possible from Cecile's typical staid and conservative lawyer duds. Tammy apologized for the low-to-middle-class area that would be Melba's new location, explaining that her bosses didn't want Melba to draw notice to herself. Melba smiled acceptance, knowing these new clothes were meant for the life she would live only briefly. She liked Tammy, and wanted to reassure her.

"I love all of them," said Melba, holding a pale yellow blouse against her chest. Melba began trying on the clothes and saw that Tammy had a remarkable instinct for the colors that flattered Melba's fair complexion. "They're so pretty, all these bright colors and floral fabrics. I've always *wanted* clothes like these. They weren't practical in my old life, but they're perfect now. You did a wonderful job, Tammy." She leaned over and gave Tammy's arm a warm squeeze.

Trying on clothes had tired her and that horrible headache wouldn't go away. Melba had never been that attached to clothes. She wore whatever felt appropriate to the occasion, nothing more than that, but she kept that tidbit to herself. Tammy returned her squeeze, but still frowned.

"Well, that's a relief because I worried whether they would fit. How does everything feel?"

"Perfect. Can you stop calling me Melba, please? The name doesn't fit me at all. I hate thinking I'm stuck with it."

"'Fraid you are stuck with it, though. Melba is Mr. Morley's mother's name, so he thinks it's pretty special." Tammy reached into her pocket. "I brought your new driver's license and social security card. You'll get some other things tonight."

Melba sighed, wrinkling her nose and reluctantly taking the cards. "Thank you."

The likeable Tammy was just the messenger, following her boss's orders. Melba wouldn't make life difficult for her sweet new friend. She checked the photo on the driver's license, unsurprised the picture was from her former life. The feds seemed able to secure whatever they needed.

"And you brought me a new purse to hold everything. Thank you for that, too, Tammy."

Tammy laughed. "Mama always said a woman should have a red purse and red shoes, so I figured the DEA could at least buy you a red purse. You can't touch your old cards and stuff, either, in case the bad guys see what you're doing. So you have a new bank account, too."

She gave Melba an impulsive hug, satisfied with her work. Everything fit Melba well enough. Clothes completely wrong for an Uptown New Orleans lawyer were the perfect attire for the Melba Columbo persona that lived in a modest neighborhood. At least, she had her familiar bras and panties, and Tammy had thoughtfully included her pajamas, adding the makeup, toothpaste and toothbrush she'd found at the Octavia Street bungalow.

"You look like you're feeling better." She giggled. "Still bald, but better. Guess we took your mind off your problems for a while."

Melba's nose reddened as she whispered her thanks, hugging Tammy and clinging a bit. She wished Tammy would stay a while longer. She felt like a newborn baby chick must, imprinting on the first warm body it sees.

Those feelings came across somehow, because Tammy's expressive forehead furrowed, showing her concern. She said, in her distinctive yat accent, "Pretty ladies like you should never be sad. I know you're gonna miss that gorgeous house and your beautiful life. But don't worry—we'll take care of things for you. Now lock your door and stay away from the phone. I'll check on you soon."

Tammy's genuine thoughtfulness and concern nearly undid Melba. She managed to hold her emotions in check until she locked the door. Then, she squeezed her eyes shut and stumbled to a chair, oblivious except for a kaleidoscope of thoughts. *How can I ignore my real self? I'll always be Cecile Valois Forest. I need to know why Barley died and who did it. Yes, he was a cruel man, but did he deserve to die? And who wants to kill* me*? Why isn't the NOPD handling this*? *Why did the DEA and the Marshals Service barge in and take over?*

Chapter Nineteen

Another evening approached, and once again dusky oblong shadows stretched out. In Melba's suite, dust motes swirled in shafts of dimming sunlight over a sleeping woman. A repetitive, strident ringing roused her to an insufferable headache. Almost exactly twenty-four hours earlier, she had bumped her hip through a swinging door, carrying a tray of food and drink. And a few minutes after that her life changed forever.

She answered, her throat again raspy and sore. "Hello?"

And again, it was Tammy on the other end of the call. *Déjà entendu*. Her sweetly nasal voice elicited a smile that twitched the corners of Melba's mouth.

"Did I wake you again?" Her dismay sounded genuine. "You need as much rest as you can get. You sleep all day?"

"Maybe. I don't feel at all well." Melba was horrified to hear herself whine, on the verge of tears. *My husband was killed, and I think I'm still in shock.* Quaking shivers forced her head back onto the pillow as Tammy spoke.

"Girl! Call room service right now for a pot of tea and something sugary. Drink and eat it all. I'm not giving you much notice, Melba, but the boss and Mr. Gene will be there in about an hour. Everything is set up."

For what? That sounds scary. "What happens next? Did y'all find Barley's killer?" Melba's voice slid into a quaver. "Aren't *you* coming, too?"

Tammy ignored Melba's questions and said, "Remember, if you act calm, it'll help you *feel* calm. I was not told to be there, but the three of you will talk about everything—including funeral plans for

Mr. Forest, so be prepared. Wear something comfortable, like your new sneakers and that green warm-up thing.

"Did Dr. Miller visit?"

"Yes, mama," Melba answered.

Tammy teased, "Don't get smart with me, but I'm sorry—sometimes I get a little bossy."

"I *need* a boss. Dr. Miller says I'm doing well, but—like now, I'm starting to shake for no reason at all. I hope I can pull myself together."

"You're probably still in shock. Order that hot tea as soon as I hang up. Add lots of sugar—drink all of it. That will help you calm down."

Melba peeked at her bruised reflection, glad her matted hair was gone. Her naked scalp made her look like that Irishwoman Sinéad O'Connor. She had disregarded Tammy's recommendation of green warm-ups and chose an unremarkable pair of dark brown slacks paired with a subdued blue blouse. She had, however, added a hint of color to her lips.

Dusk had fallen without the benefit of twittering birds or the noise of home bound traffic. Nothing penetrated the hotel's thick walls. The room was so quiet Melba could hear her own breathing. She felt her head wound pulse, reminding her of yesterday's trauma. She couldn't anticipate what would happen next, and apprehension tensed the corners of her mouth.

Melba distracted herself with TV news while she ate the delicious evening meal that had just been delivered. She'd tried to keep the previous evening's nightmarish events at arm's length, but that changed when an excited news anchor dramatized Barley's sensational murder, then cut to a reporter in front of her house, bringing everything painfully into focus for a second day. A tape from the previous night showed two gurneys loaded with body bags bumping down her brick front steps before they were loaded into hearses. "Cecile" was one of the bodies zipped in thick black plastic, and knowing that left Melba feeling violated, nauseated, and dirty. Her life—her "death"—had been in the hands of a voyeuristic cameraman, one who shared her trauma with the world without her ever knowing it.

She was sniffling when she unlocked the door for Steve Morley and Gene White. Both men caught sight of the newly bald Melba at the same time, their reactions dramatically different. Without the distraction of her auburn hair, Gene seemed enthralled by her face's soft, feminine planes and her lovely eyes.

Morley stopped short, obviously dismayed by Melba's shaved head and thinking the woman looked like a freak. He blinked at the purple bruises which ringed her amber eyes and the gaudy iodined staples zippering her bare scalp. An explosive reaction blurted from deep in his gut before he could stop himself.

"Whoa! What the hell happened here? Run into a buzz saw?"

Morley fell into a chair at the table and motioned Gene and Melba over. Unwilling to waste time, he held up a hand directing Melba not to answer his question. He wanted silence and her attention.

"First news first, Ms. Columbo. Our agent, Rick Bernard, and his partner, Harry Smith, saw the entire thing. Harry chased the shooters. Rick called me, then ran inside your house—without backup, I might add. Harry called in later, after the chase," Morley's hand landed heavily on Gene's forearm, "but it was Gene's friend Rick who gave us the chance to keep this quiet."

As she learned more about the event that had catapulted her to a seat at this table, Melba was transfixed. And her trembling started up again.

"Bottom line is, we still haven't caught whoever allegedly shot you and your husband, but we will."

Melba's head bobbed. "Allegedly?"

"You know what I mean. Gotta be careful these days," said Mr. Morley.

The lawyer in Melba wanted answers, but there were too many unanswered questions, and the physical cues from these two men continued to distract her. *Mr. Morley has a tic. He scratches his head when he talks, like he needs to activate his tongue, not to mention his brain. The other man, Gene, looks like he's not thinking at all, only daydreaming. So far, Tammy seems to be the only normal person in their office. How can she stand being around these odd people?*

Morley droned on, in love with his own voice. Marshal (or was it Agent?) White stared at her, so unfocused he scarcely blinked. Both men made Melba squirm.

"Harry saw the gun thrown from the suspects' van at Lee Circle. He abandoned the chase but wasn't able to find the gun. Not sure I would've handled it that way. Somebody would've picked it up right away if people in that neighborhood saw it get thrown. We're offering a nice reward if someone turns it in. Money talks.

"Here's the bottom line, Ms. Columbo. We believe your boss, René Gaudet, ordered the hit."

Melba blanched. "That's impossible. It can't be René. We're like his family. Why do you think it's him?"

"It's not impossible, Ms. Columbo—it's *probable*." Morley slammed the tabletop with his open hand for emphasis, startling Melba and Gene. Disliking interruption, he cleared his throat and picked up the thread of his narrative.

The more Morley enjoyed the sound of his own voice, the less Gene listened and the more he scrutinized Cecile—no, Melba—who sat across from him. Jolted back to attention, Gene realized Morley and Melba were looking his way, waiting for a response. Caught immersed in a daydream, he wiped his damp hands on his khaki thighs.

"Huh?"

"Pull out the documents, I said." Morley was frowning irritably. "Ms. Columbo needs to know what comes next—where to go, what to do, how long she has to stay hidden."

He showed a remarkable lack of empathy when he turned to Melba and said, "While he's doing that, did you make a plan for your and Barley's funerals?"

The question appeared to stun Melba and she covered her face with her hands, her body shaking with more sobs.

"Hiding won't make this go away, not in this lifetime, Melba." Morley maintained his control of the meeting.

"Come on, dammit. We don't have all night. Didn't you even think about the funeral, Melba? Do you, or do you not, know how you want this to go? We *can* take over, you know. Is that what you want?"

Melba's subdued voice leaked between her fingers. "I don't know. Yes. No—wait, please. I need something to write with." It took her quite a while, as confusion warred with loss. She looked agonized, shaking her head, writing and re-writing until she found words that were acceptable.

The sham funeral plan tucked in his folder, Morley described Melba's agreement with the DEA. Melba would receive a monthly allowance as long as she remained hidden. She would keep her location secret and contact with her former life, in any way, was expressly forbidden. Morley had decided the government's expense was worth every cent if her testimony helped put that criminal Gaudet out of business and behind bars.

"Okay, gal, let's recap." Morley took a deep breath.

Melba's mouth tightened at the demeaning way Morley addressed her, but she said nothing. Gene admired her restraint.

"You're gonna hide until Gaudet goes on trial. The US Marshals are the agency that handles witness protection, and they will take you to Texas for safety, but as close to New Orleans as possible. Nobody ever heard of you *or* Gaudet in Puebla, Texas."

Morley indicated Melba's face. "Okay, you can't leave the house until those bruises fade. Once you *can* go out, wear something to cover that bald head. Don't draw attention." He flicked a glance at her head, where a dark auburn stubble had already emerged, rough as an emery board.

"Gene here will drive you to Puebla and take your daily phone checks. We want you inconspicuous, so you won't have a fulltime guard, but I'll send Gene for a weekly visit. Memorize his cell number for emergency purposes. Our liaison in Puebla will keep the place stocked with food. You'll be comfortable. Don't want you drawing any attention, so no car."

"Can Tammy get me a wig and some hats?"

"Yeah, why not?" Morley gestured at the marshal. "Gene'll ask her if she can manage it. And gimmie that folder, Gene."

Gene pushed the requested file across the table to Morley, who removed a thin stack of cash, scooting it to Melba.

"You won't need more than this for a while, but there's money in a new bank account for you. I'll hold the checkbook until your bruises fade. No shopping for now. Do not—I'll say it again—*do not* access your old Forest bank accounts. You may think they're private and secure, but they aren't. We—I'm talking about us in the government—arrest hackers every day. Gaudet has contacts everywhere, even if he doesn't have a hacker on his staff. If you access any of your old stuff, he'll know it. Don't forget we want you to look as dead as your husband—"

Distressed, Melba blinked rapidly and recoiled as though slapped, but she shed no more tears, already becoming hardened to Mr. Morley's boorish behavior.

Morley kept talking, unfazed, "—but you have to help us. Gaudet is a sociopath. He may think you're dead now, but he's no dummy, and he'll keep some kind of tickler hack out there. You could be a big problem for him. If he learns you're alive, he'll find you and kill you."

Morley gauged the debilitated, wounded woman in front of him. "But—you're smart. You can handle it."

Gene raised his eyebrows at Mr. Morley's patronizing words. Melba didn't respond, probably because she had no choice, Gene thought, but she might not know whether she *could* handle what Morley asked. He cleared his throat. It was his turn to speak.

"Cecile, er—Melba, I'd like to leave tomorrow right after morning rush hour. It's a long drive, and I don't want to stop any more than necessary. Pack all your things tonight and eat a big breakfast tomorrow. We'll leave the hotel the same way we came in, through the service entrance. Too many people in New Orleans have seen the news and you are well-known. Somebody could recognize you if we're not careful."

Chapter Twenty

Melba watched the slanted early morning sunlight bump across her motionless knuckles and quietly waited for whatever would happen next.

October. How quickly the world spun and my life changed.

Sleepless through the night, she'd groaned herself out of bed and ordered a large pot of coffee along with breakfast, then washed down two of Dr. Miller's painkillers before room service arrived. She looked worse today, if that was possible—the skin around her eyes an ugly, sagging purple with a yellow-green tinge at the edges.

She had buttoned on a collared red polyester shirt, so dark it was nearly black, and tucked it neatly into a pair of sharply creased black slacks. It was the closest she could come to the somber black of widow's weeds. Black low-rise boots waited beside her on the floor. Her other new clothes sat on the rumpled bed, folded neatly and stacked in bags. *What's my driver's name? White? Yes... Gene White.*

Not that there was ever a good time for such a thing, but the shooting had come at the worst possible awful time——just when Cecile had gathered enough courage to leave Barley and take control of her destiny. Instead, Fate had muddled her future, leaving her with an aching, bald head (half of which she'd done to herself). She was back to being frustrated and under someone else's control—*again*—though she had already tried first thing this morning to thwart those DEA plans.

She had ignored Mr. Morley's orders and decided to call her lawyer, the man she'd always called Uncle Karl, but she heard no dial tone, only a hissing sound, when she held the hotel phone to her ear. She hadn't believed him when he said the line was blocked, thinking surely they trusted her not to call anyone, but she discovered the DEA had left nothing to chance. Melba knew the DEA had contacted Karl Schmitzer to handle the funeral arrangements and it pained her that creaky old Uncle Karl had to shoulder the burden. *That gives me something else to feel guilty about. He deserves to know I'm alive, and somehow I'll make sure he finds out.*

❋

US Deputy Marshal Gene White was looking fresh and quite ordinary in a neatly tucked, dark blue Polo golf shirt, khaki Dockers, and wearing a pair of topsiders. His blue seersucker jacket was wrong for the autumn season, but he wore it anyway to conceal his holstered weapon.

Melba had consumed an entire pot of coffee, used the bathroom twice, and stared in the mirror at her denuded skull numerous times, by the time he tapped at her door. Every one of her caffeinated nerves jangled. She wanted to leave immediately, but Gene held out a small bag.

Melba peered into the bag, startled to see a ball of fur. Holding it at arm's length, she said, "What *is* this? A hamster?"

"No, Ms. Columbo," Gene chuckled. "It's the wig you asked for, compliments of Tammy and the DEA."

She was touched that Tammy had acted on her request, wondering how she accomplished it so early in the day. The small mound of synthetic coppery hair was even close to Melba's own unusual hair color. A roll of double-faced tape to secure the wig to her shiny scalp was in the bag, but Melba needed help, at least this first time, to put it on her head.

"The best light is in the bathroom, Mr. White. Will you help me, please?"

"Call me Gene," he answered in an embarrassingly high-pitched voice. "Of course I'll help. And hurry—we have to get on the road." Gruffness compensated for the sound of his voice, as sweat popped out on his upper lip. He'd never been alone in a bathroom with a woman.

Gene maintained his serious expression, covering Melba's stitches with strips of paper tape. His fingers trembled whenever he touched Melba's warm skin.

"Are you all right?" she asked. He nodded, not speaking, his neck flushed and hot as they carefully straightened her wig.

"Can you give me a minute alone in here?" she asked. He nodded and stumbled from the bathroom while Melba checked her reflection. Not surprisingly, Tammy had chosen well. *Not quite the same color, but close enough*. Melba, the woman she would see until Barley's killer was arrested and imprisoned, stared back at her, the transformation from Cecile complete.

Could René have wanted to kill us? I don't see it, but Morley has made up his mind. I'm sure René's not guilty of anything, much less of shooting me and killing Barley.

When Melba emerged from the bathroom, Gene's hands were clutching the handles of most of her bags. She dropped a few dollars on her pillow for a tip and gathered up her red purse and the remainder of the parcels, then checked the room one last time.

"Don't leave that money." Gene's request sounded like a demand.

"I always leave a tip for housekeeping." Surprised, Melba's eyebrows drew together.

We discourage it." He came across as overly patient, as though he was speaking to a very young, not particularly bright, child. "If you leave money, they'll remember you."

"They'll remember me if I don't."

Gene plopped the bags on the bed and swept up the money, crumpling the bills into his pocket. Grabbing the bags, he growled, "Come on, let's go," leaving Melba open-mouthed.

Melba's only sign of irritation was her stride out the door. She was annoyed, but this small struggle of wills was not a hill she wanted to die on, and the hushed atmosphere of the immaculate hallway helped defuse her anger. Even the air smelled expensive.

"Hold up, Melba." She heard another reproof and couldn't help snapping back at Gene.

"What!"

"Wrong way. Not using the guest elevator, so turn around. We leave the back way, like hotel staff." Embarrassed, her face flamed as she did an about-face to march the opposite way.

In a hidden alcove, Gene punched the call button with his elbow. He stood against the door, and when it slid open, Melba meekly shuffled past, eyes downcast. She saw his mouth twitch. *Let him have his way—for now. This won't last forever.*

A brisk autumn breeze kicked up yellowing leaves and stinging grit outside the hotel's service entrance, and they leaned into the refreshing gusts. The cool penetrated Melba's thin blouse and roughened her skin with goose bumps. She shivered. *Ironic—the cool weather I've been waiting for arrives just when I have to leave.* She hurried toward the warm car, her unwelcome guardian loping ahead as a gust flapped his jacket open. The sight of his gun reminded her this was a deadly serious business. *I have a bad feeling about all this.*

Chapter Twenty-One

Blurred concrete railings and giant green overhead signs zipped past as they left New Orleans. Gene White was behind the wheel of a basic four-door sedan that performed no better than Aunt Hattie's Buick and wasn't nearly as well maintained. It rocked alarmingly from side to side as it sped, bouncing with nauseating regularity on the rough roadway. Beside the car, the upper floors of office buildings flashed past the elevated freeway. Mesmerized, Melba watched other cars ebb and flow around them like a conveyor belt of cold metal formed from a river of molten steel.

Gene's hands rested on the steering wheel and his mouth stayed shut. But for the noisy ventilation and the tires skittering under them on the highway, the car was quiet and its passengers mute. Melba and the man driving watched the road.

Her wig was an improvement, though it itched. Minimal communication worked fine for Melba. She worked hard to keep her mind blank except for superficial thoughts. She observed the river's broad expanse far below the suspension bridge that exited the city. The Mississippi was greenish-brown or brownish-green, more than just the muddy water that people read about. Its color would come across better in small batches, Melba thought, maybe in the iris of an eye. It was less lovely seen in the unstoppable tons of moving water. Still, she thought of it as *her* river, one she didn't want to leave.

However the day ended, Melba knew she'd been lucky to escape with her life. And to think only two days ago the confrontation she wanted with Barley had frightened her so much. She still trembled at the thought of it.

They traveled an interstate highway system designed to deploy military vehicles. Today it was appropriated bumper-to-bumper by cars and 18-wheelers. Fascinated but alarmed by the behemoths, Melba watched Gene squeeze around the huge trucks that often created massive rolling blockades. At times her foot pressed an imaginary brake pedal, but she had a growing appreciation for Gene's competent driving.

Thinking she might as well behave, Melba made up her mind to be pleasant to her escort. Clearing her throat, Melba said, "You're a good driver." They were the first words she'd uttered in several miles.

With a quick glance at her, he said only, "Thank you," but Melba smiled and thought he seemed gratified by the compliment.

Gene visibly relaxed at the sound of Melba's husky contralto voice. His grip on the wheel loosened slightly and he settled his shoulders with a deep inhale. Contented, he thought how nice it was to be alone with this woman, despite her wigged-over bald head. He often sneaked looks at Melba that made his body tingle, so that he squirmed and had to refocus on his driving.

Melba noticed how her meager compliment affected the poor man. *He's not that bad-looking, if he would act more normal. That looks like the first nice thing he's heard in his whole life. I'd better keep up the positive reinforcement so Gene will be my friend.* It was self-serving, she knew, but it was a matter of survival. What *didn't* matter was that he gave her the willies.

As the miles unspooled, Melba sank into gloom, leaving the home she loved for an unknown future. Her law practice was gone and she worried about her clients, feeling added guilt.

Jan kept her files current, which meant another attorney could step right in. Melba missed her wonderful paralegal. Jan could probably handle most of the open files, but Melba's personal relationship with her clients was another matter. Her clients were like family members, filling an emptiness in her life. There was the young couple victimized by identity theft, for example, and she couldn't forget Mr. Taft, the wealthy widower who never saw his children though they lived right there in New Orleans. His new trust fund bypassed that thoughtless generation. Mr. Taft continued to call with questions. Melba realized he was lonely, and it was easy for her to drop in for a brief welfare check as long as Barley knew where she was going. Mr. Taft's comfortable house was on her way home. She'd miss her chats with the old man.

It makes me crazy that I can't talk to Jan about what's happening. She thought of their extraordinary bond dating all the way back to Jan's first job interview. Jan had been tentative and awkward that day, but still showed her determination. Melba had said nothing when Jan daily wore the same green suit, only changing blouses but she was pleased when the green suit finally disappeared after a couple of paychecks and Jan's wardrobe began to grow.

After seven years of working together, Melba and Jan were a smoothly running team. Jan was fiercely loyal to the woman who'd given her a new career. Melba knew that Jan was aware of everything that went on in René's firm, but she'd never said a word about René breaking the law. She would've told Melba, wouldn't she?

Melba promised herself she would learn the answer.

The firm must be a mess with both of us gone—Barley dead, and me pretending to be dead. If the DEA arrests René and gets a conviction, the firm will collapse. Jan will lose her job unless I can get back to New Orleans in time to help her.

But, René? I cannot believe he tried to kill either one of us. There was only that one time, the day I was shot, that he was anything but gracious to me, and Barley is—was—even closer to him. It makes no sense. René had nothing to gain. It's not him.

She forced herself away from that line of thinking and grabbed her water. Drawing deeply through the straw, Melba returned to the exotic panorama outside the moving car.

The tangled traffic around Baton Rouge and the state capitol held them captive until the highway spat them onto the elevated expressway over the Atchafalaya's exotic swampy terrain. Here, the law forced the behemoth trucks to reduce their speed and stay in the slow lane, much to Gene's relief.

Melba relaxed to the driving thuds of oil well pistons that occasionally penetrated their car windows. She drowsed until the itching heat under her wig disturbed her. Picking at the tape along an edge, she peeled it back, getting immense relief.

Gene noticed and said, "You can take off the wig, but put it back on if we have to stop." His lips thinned and he patted her arm.

Melba flinched and rolled her eyes, thinking *Don't touch me, mister. And I didn't ask your permission.* She dropped the wig into the purse at her feet. *The darn thing itches more than poison ivy.* She sighed with pleasure as she scratched near her sore wound. *It hurts so good.* Already growing, bristles of hair jabbed her fingers. She envisioned her head looking like a giant five o'clock shadow. *I would've yanked off the darn wig whether he agreed or not, but I won't act rude. Aunt Hattie taught me to stay quiet if I can't say anything nice. I'll keep the peace. No reason to offend "the bodyguard."*

Outside the car, cool weather dropped down from the north and chased them through the miles of spectacular and eerie cypress swamp that flashed past the elevated freeway.

Delicate flame-colored cypress leaves hung above the rippling marsh waters, testament to the approaching autumn equinox. Shorter days cloaked the feathery foliage in the new season's russets and browns. The desiccated leaves would soon fall, sinking into the rich black mud to slowly disintegrate, absorbed as part of nature's miraculous cycle of life. The sculptural cypress trunks would remain bare until the next springtime had cloaked them once again in green.

A magnificent white egret slid across the steely sky and Melba daydreamed of being carried to a hidden world, her cheek cradled on the bird's soft feathers. Below its outstretched wings, mallard ducks flapped, skidding to warmer waters, having left the northern feeding grounds to winter in the South. Hunters would soon target them for delicious Cajun gumbos.

Turtles laboriously hauled their enormous shells from marshy waters onto fallen logs, and lined up in rows nose to tail to absorb a last blast of sunshine before shorter days buried them deep in a muddy semi-hibernation. Mesmerized by the hypnotic peacefulness, Melba half-dozed, determined to ignore her trauma.

"See those birds, Mr. White?" An arrowed grouping of flapping herons paralleled the causeway, flying level with their speeding car. Though the birds were soundless through the closed window, she imagined their midflight conversations, communicating as they flew.

"Yeah, I see. What about 'em?" Birds, to Gene White, were life forms that flew through the air—nothing more, nothing less—ones that spattered white gunk where it was least expected.

The car barreled ahead, its wheels humming. The sun tracked its passage, lagging, then overtaking them and leading the way west, shadows shortening, then lengthening, as the hours ticked by. In her side mirror, Melba observed the sky behind them darken, relieved whenever the car's GPS announced they were ever closer to her new home.

She sank into silence, returning to her thoughts. *Barley. By the time he died, there was no love left, if there was any to start with. He was so mean—a bully. And he hurt me—but what could I do? He was my husband.* She sniffled, not quite sure why. She suspected it might be a new unresolved guilt because she felt a euphoric freedom.

As he drove, Marshal White's thoughts were dispirited. He hated being assigned to work on this joint task with the DEA. *Mr. Morley has led this poor woman to believe she'll be in Puebla for only a month or two. I've never seen the government move that fast, and it probably*

won't happen now. That's a terrible thing to do to a woman whose husband was murdered. Her defenses are down. And she trusts the government—go figure. And now I have to make this miserable trip every week until they arrest Gaudet and put him on trial.

Although—it works to my advantage in a sense because I like Melba—a lot.

RIO FRIO

Chapter One

Faint shadows thrown by the dim street lights obscured a cracked, narrow sidewalk running between an unremarkable stucco house and the uneven street. Tall, narrow windows flanked a weathered wooden door fitted with metal hinges. There were Aztec carvings on the rafter tails that jutted over the pavement and supported the roof's curved clay tiles, giving the place an exotic air. Despite its embellishments, this looked like an average house on an anonymous street in a poorer neighborhood.

The car cooled at the curb, its metallic ticking sounding like gasping breaths. Melba stared at the house, her lips pursed. *This is it? An earth-colored Mexican adobe hut*? Her fingers twisted at her loose blouse. She turned to ask for a ride back home, but Gene was already halfway out of the car.

She squinted, trying to see through the shadows. The house crowded the sidewalk so that not even weeds could push up between them. There was no yard to keep up, but there were no trees, either. Sidewalks stretched straight and empty in either direction down the skinny street. It was as sterile and featureless as any place she'd ever seen.

A scrap of paper scratched down the sidewalk on an errant breeze. This was a neighborhood where people worked and had no idea how to play. Folks came home to eat and sleep before they repeated the same pattern the following day. With sudden insight, Melba realized that's how she'd been living her life for the past ten years. It'd be different now.

Her thoughts curdled with exhaustion. *Why do I care if the neighborhood is scruffy? It's for only a few weeks*. Her head hurt after bouncing around all day, pounded and tenderized like a stringy piece of tough, raw meat. Melba was hungry and she ached for the pain pills in Dr. Miller's medical supplies. Hopefully a decent bed awaited, but she worried it might not be. *An Army cot? Maybe a sleeping bag? Cobwebs in the corners of the room? Worse—spider-webs?*

"Here's your house key, Melba. You unlock the door and I'll get the bags." His long face looked gray and dog-tired. *The poor man. He looks worn out. I hope he doesn't plan to stay here for the night.*

She took the key and took a moment to stretch her cramped legs. She smelled something different, foreign, in the air. She sniffed loudly. *What is that? Chili powder? Cumin?*

She caught Gene watching her, wearing an odd expression.

"What?"

He shook his head, blinking. "Nothing. Unlock the door."

Gene had stretched across the width of the car's back seat for the last bag when he heard Melba's gasp. He backed out, the back of his head taking a blow from the door frame. He ran in a crouch to Melba's side, his gun drawn, cursing and in pain. With his weapon aimed at the ground, he gritted out, "What's wrong?" In his twelve years with the Service, this was the first time his weapon had been unholstered outside target practice. Its substantial weight was almost unexpected.

"How did you do this?" Melba looked at him, delighted. "This place is gorgeous."

Gene shrugged, thinking *fool woman*, relieved there was no danger. The room he saw looked like any one of dozens just like it, maybe newer, but that's all. He rubbed the bump where he hit his head and stormed back for the bags, eager to get inside out of the dangerous darkness.

Melba hadn't moved from the doorway, taking a good look at the interior. Loaded with bags, he waited impatiently, churlish and put-upon, and in no mood to waste time. He added headache to the list of his aggravations.

"I have to get back on the road." Irritation roughened his voice. He brushed past and piled the bags on a chair.

"Everything you need should be here, but call me if it's not and I'll take care of it." He puffed an exhausted, spent breath, then checked the rest of the house thoroughly.

Melba gently tapped his arm when he rejoined her, and said, "I'm so thoughtless, Gene. I haven't thanked you for your help."

Her gentle gesture, with all the possibilities it held, traveled at warp speed to his brain. His grouchiness vanished without a trace. He licked his lips, clearing his throat.

"Doing my job, that's all. If you want me to, I can stay," he offered, his eyes gleaming with hope. He pushed down the errant thought of his boss's reaction if he stayed the night, but she shook her head, backing away.

"Oh, no, no. I'm perfectly fine. You'd better get going...it's a long drive back."

His shoulders sagged, the rejection painful. Gene's energetic eagerness extinguished, his crushing exhaustion returned.

"I'm outta here." He sighed, thinking of the long drive ahead. "You've got my card – with my numbers, right? Have your new phone? Is it charged? Do you have your charger?"

Nodding assent, Melba edged him outside, promising a call if she needed anything. Throwing the dead bolt closed behind him, she yanked off the itching wig and surveyed her new home.

Its warm palette echoed Melba's beloved Octavia Street home. She noticed touches of red in a pillow here and a small vase there. Aunt Hattie had used red that way, too. She saw enough books lining one wall to satisfy a voracious reader. The inviting room enveloped her like a comfortable cocoon. *I can see Tammy all over this. She must've taken photos at my house and zipped them to a decorator here.*

Kicking off her shoes, she wiggled her toes in the lovely fringed rug which centered the living room. Exhaustion temporarily at bay, she explored the small house, quickly reaching the master suite.

A carved four-poster bed sat against the honey-colored back wall oozing comfort and relaxation. A faint calming scent hovered in the air. Melba made a note to call Tammy tomorrow with her thanks. But now Melba forgot hunger, forgot a bath, and even forgot a pain pill. Fully dressed, she crawled onto the bed's duvet and was instantly, blessedly, asleep.

Chapter Two

In the name of safety, the US Marshals Service had discarded the option of housing Melba in the French Quarter since René Gaudet had eyes and ears everywhere in the city. Mr. Morley, in charge of the DEA's pursuit, couldn't take the chance that Gaudet would find their star witness tucked away. When he presented it to her, Melba accepted Morley's rationale.

Texas was a good alternative for the two government agencies—the DEA and the US Marshals. The pleasant hacienda in Puebla was frequently used to hide important DEA witnesses—but the solution was a lonely one for the new widow.

⁕

Melba woke, her stomach rumbling, still exhausted from her injuries and the long drive. The oversized bedroom clock showed nine o'clock in large red numbers, which was much later than her normal wake-up time, not that she had a schedule anymore, much less a "normal" one. She planned to fill the hours searching for the killer who had put her life in danger.

Uncomfortably aware she had slept fully dressed, thinking, I slept like this? Isn't *that* special! Melba looked for the bathroom and took advantage of the very well-equipped one she found.

Refreshed and squeaky clean, still barefoot but wearing a clean new green boat-neck knit shirt and comfy jeans, Melba rummaged in the kitchen. *Ah, there it is—not the dark roast I love, but it'll do. Any port in a storm.* With a pot of coffee burbling and dripping, its delicious aroma filling the kitchen, she turned to the fridge, where she found a supply of yogurt and assorted fruits, flaxseed bread, and enough butter to last her for months. She bumped the door closed, leaving bacon and a carton of eggs languishing in the cold, and set her choices on the counter. A cup of coffee would come first, in hopes of ridding herself of a niggling headache. Then she would feast.

Cradling the large cup filled to the brim with hot coffee, she inhaled its scent and sipped, praying the caffeine would ease her throbbing head. Dragging closer the bag of medical supplies Dr. Miller had provided, she rummaged for another pain pill and found a card with the U.S. Marshals' office phone number.

I should check in. A glance at her new cell phone showed it carried enough charge for a brief call to Tammy, which was answered in a cheery voice on the first ring.

"How you doin' this morning, Melba? I'm surprised you're not in bed." After a few comments, she dove right to business. "We don't have Barley's killer yet, girlfriend, but traffic cameras tracked the van, unmarked and unbelievably dirty, for miles, but we lost it after it crossed the river. We have a partial license plate ID, so techs are cross-checking numbers with vehicle types. That takes a while."

Melba didn't like hearing "Barley's killer" and she *hated* being called "girlfriend," but what could she say? She gritted her teeth and let it go without comment.

"I hope that's legal."

"Completely legal. We do it all the time. You want to know who these guys are, don't you?"

"I want to do my part, too, Tammy, but I *can't* when I'm so far away."

"We do want your help, since we plan to interview everybody at your firm. What we need is a list of questions—whatever might be important—and we thought you'd be good at that. Will you do that, and text it to my cell?"

"Of course, but you're wasting your time. Nobody there would hurt us."

"Maybe, maybe not. We'll see."

When Tammy paused, Melba asked, "When will you question the staff? I want to be sure Jan is all right." Her gentle secretary must feel at a loss, the same way Melba did. Neither of them had a companion to provide loving comfort.

"Mr. Morley asked me to question Gaudet's staff, including René Gaudet himself, but these're my first real-life interviews. I haven't done any outside a classroom, but it can't be that hard if I have a list of good questions. I'll start tomorrow, but we don't really have anything to go on. We suspect *who* ordered Barley's death, but we can't prove it yet."

Tammy prattled on, giving Melba time to digest the information. *Gosh. They think a brand-new interviewer working alone will get them their answers?* Melba experienced a black, sinking feeling and made no comment. She knew René had nothing to do with Barley's death, but she'd love to see Barley's case files, especially the cases he'd lost. The killer could well be a disgruntled client, based on the scruffy types she'd occasionally seen with him.

"By the way, we found Barley's car, almost by accident. It took a while because he parked on the street and the team didn't recognize it. Once they searched it, it was already clean as a whistle, not even a gum wrapper inside, much less anything incriminating. Somebody jimmied the lock during the night and sanitized the whole thing, including the trunk and the engine block. A sniffer dog alerted to drugs, but we couldn't find a thing."

At her end of the conversation, Melba felt flushed, thinking she could have volunteered the Jaguar's location had she been asked—but she was unconscious at the time.

"How could they tell someone cleaned it?" she asked.

"By scratches around the lock, and every surface of that car inside and out had been wiped clean. The dang car smelled like a bleach factory. The techs found one single smudged fingerprint on the entire car, and that included the trunk. Somebody who knew what they were doing wiped it clean. That told us we're on the right track, but there's no way to tie Gaudet to that."

Melba's phone beeped, about to lose power. "I'm about to get cut off, Tammy. Listen, I'm stashed so far away, how can I help find Barley's killer? I should be closer. I'm comfortable here and it's beautiful, but..."

Tammy interrupted, "You feel helpless, right? Leave it with us, honey. We're the experts, Melba."

"Mr. Morley promised..."

"That's why you're getting this update. I know you must be frustrated." Melba rolled her eyes, wondering how Tammy could possibly know how she felt. There was a huge difference between being told someone was shot, and being the person who was shot in the head.

"I have a question, Tammy. If everyone wants to keep me safe, where's my guard?"

"That bothers me, too, but Mr. Morley said nobody but us knows you're there. He thought a guard would draw too much attention, but I scheduled a tech to check your security system today. Grit your teeth, girlfriend. If you need us, you have my number. Gene will be there in a few days to check—"

Melba's phone went dead, cutting off the end of Tammy's sentence, the power depleted before they could say goodbye.

With her phone on the charger soaking up power, Melba explored the house she now called a hacienda. Behind the bedroom curtains, she found a row of French doors, beyond which was a brick patio that spanned the house, leaving a postage stamp-sized grass yard. She stepped outside barefoot on the cool bricks, rubbing her arms in the crisp October air. From somewhere out on the street, two loud voices argued back and forth in rhythmic, rapid Spanish. *I'm stuck here. The DEA should use me as bait, instead of hiding me.* Intense homesickness washed over her. *Useless. Shake it off, and let's see what we have out here. That's enough pity party. I'm injured and already homesick, but I'm standing above ground and that's a good thing.*

The Marshals Service had lent her an extraordinary refuge. A small table sat on the patio between a green chaise and two comfortable-looking chairs, all strategically positioned under a security light secured to the stucco wall above them. The small yard—patio, grass, no trees or flowers—was enclosed by a cedar privacy fence. The scent of new-cut grass mixed pleasantly with aromatic whiffs from the raw, unpainted cedar. She unlatched a gate that opened to a pathway down the side of the house to the street. Beyond the opening, she saw only asphalt. Already aware she had taken the lush flowers and foliage of New Orleans for granted, Melba gave an audible sigh.

Her sore head forced her to turn her back to October's cool, bright sun, and she trudged inside where she heard the peal of the doorbell. She ran down the hall to the door and peered through the peephole.

"Who is it?" She sounded thin and shaky, quite unlike her usual calm competence. *Dammit, Cecile, er, Melba. Hold yourself together.*

"I'm here to update your security system, ma'am." The man's Texas twang was clearly local. "I'm Adam, ma'am.

"Can I see some ID, please?" *Tammy told me to expect someone.*

The tall uniformed man, very young, wiggled a wallet from his back pocket, flipped it open to his license, and held it up to the peephole. *How'm I supposed to know it's real?*

She shrugged and opened the door. Adam's eyes widened at her black eyes and bald head, but he said nothing. Standing just inside the door, he shuffled a large pair of cowboy boots and flipped through yellow, white, and pink papers on his clipboard with a moistened fingertip. "I brought an old schematic, 'cause you ain't gonna want me around all day."

Melba swallowed hard. "You'll think this question is weird. What *is* this address?"

Adam gave her a speculative stare, then checked the card clipped to his papers. "Could be I'm at the wrong place. What's your name, ma'am?"

Sweat formed on her upper lip, and she struggled to remember. "Uh, Melba Columbo."

"Yep, that's right." He snaked a finger up under his cap and scratched. "Don't run into many folks don't know they own address. That cut musta messed up your mem'ry some. This here's 2812 Rio Frio Street. Named, I guess, for that Rio Frio River over yonder in the hill country." He repeated "Rio Frio" several times. "It sorta rolls off the tongue, don't it?"

"I remember now," she stammered. "I'll stay out of the way, but can you show me how to set the alarm when you're finished?"

"Yes, ma'am. This setup is super confidential. It links to us and another number, you know, but headquarters handles that part."

"Nooo... I didn't know." *Was he supposed to tell me that—who's the second number—the killer? Does he already know where I am?* Fear pricked the stubble on her scalp.

"Yes, ma'am. Some Louisiana exchange. It's written right here." His knuckles lightly thumped the card. It was the same number she'd called earlier, for the joint DEA and US Marshals Office in New Orleans.

It was late afternoon by the time she waved goodbye to Adam, having fed him lunch, learned all about Puebla's attractions, and thoroughly entertained herself. A realization suddenly hit her. *Wait! Barley was buried today. What kind of rotten person am I? I should've ignored everything else but him.*

Despite the relief of being rid of her tormentor, a contradictory feeling of loss dampened her eyes and she gave herself a mental slap. *Stop—your life has changed, but quit with the pity party, remember*?

She wasn't the only new widow in the world. Yes, she had no support system, but she would pull herself together and find out who killed Barley and tried to kill her.

Chapter Three

Frustrated, Melba was chomping at the bit to get outdoors. Safely buffered from Melba's irritation by their Skype connection, Tammy could view Melba's fading bruises with surprising clarity from her desk in New Orleans.

"This is taking forever, but I have to admit I like this short hair, Tammy. I watched that old movie *South Pacific* on TV the other day, and I promise Mitzi Gaynor's hair was shorter than mine is now. I think it's long enough to stop with the wig."

"Honey," Tammy soothed her, "you're not quite there. Under your eyes still looks yellow. You want people to remember your bruises? No, you *want* to be invisible, right? Give yourself at least another day."

Stuck in the house on Rio Frio Street in the small city of Puebla, Texas, Melba kept grousing.

"I'm tired of being cooped up. I need exercise and a change of scenery. Did I mention I miss my friends and my work, and how can I help you people find Barley's killer from way over here?"

"Let me remind you—again—you *are* helping by analyzing the interviews. I'm transcribing them now so I can email them to you." Still chafing, Melba told her to hurry up so she could get to work.

*

Melba squeezed her eyelids shut, her overworked eyes stinging with eyestrain, and pressed against her forehead, hoping to ease her headache. The niggling pain interfered with her capacity to analyze information, but even so she could tell Tammy was not a seasoned interviewer. Neither the initial questions, nor the answers and follow-up questions put to the staff at René's firm, shed any new light on the search for Barley's killer.

A few answers did raise questions about René's other activities, however. How, exactly, *did* René—or Barley, for that matter—spend their days? Had she unknowingly worked with a criminal for *seven* years? *Seven years*? Worse, had she idiotically *lived* with a criminal for the past *ten* years? Melba punched speed dial for Tammy.

"Hey, girlfriend," Tammy answered. After chatting briefly, they got down to business.

"You get the interview transcripts I emailed? Anything catch your eye?"

"Yes. I may be a total idiot, but I *don't* see evidence of a killer." The difference in diction between fast-talking Tammy and Melba's slow, refined Southern cadences was mindboggling, given that they had both grown up in New Orleans. Each of them struggled to understand the gist of the other woman's sentences.

"Idiot? I doubt that. Why do you say that, Melba?"

"Because—which you already know—nobody admits to knowing what work René or Barley did during the day. But that's not what we're looking for, is it?"

Tammy took a breath, ready to admit the DEA very much wanted to know how René spent his days, but Melba kept talking.

"We're looking for Barley's killer, and I have a question. I didn't see the interviews with either René or my paralegal. What about those two?"

"Actually, I think I missed three, including René. Who's your paralegal?" On Melba's phone screen, she watched as Tammy retrieved a pad, moistened her forefinger, and flipped some pages.

"Jan Yokum is, was, my paralegal."

Melba, hearing an uptick in the wind outside, stood and separated the slats in the blinds shading the front window. Raindrops made tiny pings against the glass. Outside, rainfall bounced off the barren concrete street, an unusual rain in this dusty place. With a grimace, she let the slats clatter back in place as she listened to Tammy from across the room.

"Hmm, I'm looking. Oh, here it is.

> "Jan Yokum called in sick that morning, nauseated with a migraine. Others on the staff

said the poor girl went into hysterics when she heard about you. We'll catch her the next go-round. There's no real rush."

Appalled, Melba stopped walking. Her thoughtless agreement with the DEA had caused Jan's tears. It would be a long time before she forgave herself for that rash decision.

> "Where was René during all this? I couldn't find his interview either."

"He wasn't there that day, but we weren't ready to interview him, anyway. We know he was at home and that Jimmy, the one who took over Barley's job, was with him."

At the mention of Barley, Melba looked pained. Tammy rushed to add, "I probably shouldn't tell you this, but we're following Mr. Gaudet, and we pretty much know where he is almost all the time.

"Oh, and we have a little change this week, Melba."

"What is it?

"I'm taking Gene's place tomorrow. I'll be the one driving over to see you. We can talk face to face. Won't that be great? I'll say goodbye for now and I'll be in Puebla tomorrow."

A big smile on her face, Melba said, "That's terrific, Tammy. I'm always happy to see you. Drive safely."

Tammy disconnected, then said into dead air, "This time might be the exception, girlfriend."

Chapter Four

What a sad little neighborhood, Tammy thought with dismay. Melba must have culture shock, coming from Uptown New Orleans. She pressed Melba's Rio Frio doorbell and waited, bouncing on her toes and listening to cars zoom past on the street behind her during the noon rush hour. She was plenty nervous about today. She had some serious business to discuss.

Melba opened the door, her smile welcoming. "I'm so happy to see you. Come in." Beckoning the petite US Marshal to enter, she then impulsively hugged Tammy. "It's great to see you in real life, after all our computer calls."

Startled by Melba's hug, Tammy responded and patted her on the back. "Mmm. It smells deliciously like chocolate in here." *Okay, now I feel terrible. I do like this woman, so I should relax, but she may not like me by the time I leave.*

Tammy had ordered the work done on the Rio Frio location to prepare it for Melba, but she hadn't seen the final results. The place was stunning. Her limited funds had gone a long way toward creating an extreme contrast between the neglected neighborhood outside and the attractive interior of Melba's safe house.

"This is so much like your New Orleans home. The decorators did a great job," Tammy said, noting the colorful throw pillows, wall art, and candles that warmed the room without compromising its efficiency.

"They did, thanks to you. How are you, Tammy?"

"I'm good." Tammy took a deep breath, asking, "What is that wonderful smell?"

"You'll just have to wait and see," said Melba, teasing.

Like old friends, the women conversed easily. Though they spoke daily on Skype, this was only the second time they'd visited in the flesh. Tammy set her bag on the sofa, tossing her pumpkin-colored sweater next to it.

"Let's eat while we visit." Melba directed her to the table where a light lunch salad of greens, farmer's cheese, blueberries, nuts, and strawberries waited.

"This looks so delicious. I didn't expect a meal, but I'm starving," said Tammy, smiling at her hostess. She began to eat as soon as Melba picked up her salad fork, making happy little sounds.

They cleared the table of empty salad plates and the crumbs of warm brownies. Only then did Tammy pull her tape recorder and notebook out of her bag onto the table.

"What is all this?" asked Melba.

"We have to interview you, too, of course," said Tammy in an apologetic voice. She pressed the recorder's "on" button. "We need everything you can recall."

"I didn't realize I'd be questioned too, but that's fine with me."

Tammy quickly went through the preliminaries, asking a few innocuous questions. She shifted her posture, telegraphing the introduction of more serious topics. Melba, the more seasoned interrogator because of her law practice, smiled at Tammy's physical "tell."

"When I interviewed Mr. Gaudet's and Mr. Forest's secretaries, I learned a few new details." Tammy watched Melba closely as she talked.

"Okay..."

"Can you guess what those might have been?" Melba cocked her head to the side with a puzzled expression.

"I don't have a clue. Details? What kind of details?" Melba showed no hint of trepidation, looking merely curious. *Either she's the best liar in the world or she's telling the truth. Oh, boy. I hate this. This is going to hurt her bad.*

Tammy cleared her throat and swallowed. "Independent of each other, those two secretaries gave us the same information."

"Uh huh...and..."

"Your husband apparently was having an affair."

Melba gasped. Her pretty face paled to a bluish-white, except for patches of bright red on her cheeks. Her eyes seemed to bulge, the lashes fluttering. Her tongue licked across her lips before they clamped tightly shut.

Tammy reached across, covering Melba's hand with her own. She thought it curious the woman didn't react with anger, showing nothing but dismayed surprise.

Melba finally squeaked a question. "Somebody at the office?"

"No, but this was nothing new. Mr. Forest was having the affair before he started working with Mr. Gaudet.

Now Melba became more animated. She wailed, "Oh, my God! That was seven years ago."

"Both secretaries knew the woman's name. We tracked her down and interviewed her at her apartment, which is in Mr. Forest's name, by the way. She filled in more of the blank spaces for us. Mr. Forest had supported her with a monthly allowance for the past ten years."

The remaining color drained from Melba's face. The skin around her mouth was dead white, her whole body shook, and her amber eyes shone with unshed tears.

"That's as long as Barley and I were married. We just—ha! Not celebrated—marked our tenth anniversary. Do I know this...this person?"

Thinking the light in the room had dimmed, Tammy felt nauseated, sorry she'd eaten that second brownie. She closed her eyes on a deep breath, hating this part.

"Yes, I'm afraid you do. This is awful, I know. The woman says you know each other very well, Melba. Her name is Fitch—Mary Ann Fitch."

Shocked, Melba gaped, then collapsed without warning, falling from her chair to the floor with a tremendous noise, like a bag of sand plummeting off the top of a building.

Tammy jumped to her feet, horrified by the sight of someone dropping unconscious right in front of her. It happened so fast she'd had no time to react. She dropped to her knees beside Melba, praying she hadn't broken her neck in the fall. To her lasting shame, her first thought was that her boss would fire her when he found out about this.

Kneeling alongside the crumpled Melba, she found a reassuring pulse in the unconscious woman's neck. As Tammy wondered what to do next, Melba's eyes fluttered open. Her breath remained shallow, but her color improved. She lay without moving for long minutes, staring fixedly, before she spoke.

"Did I black out? I'm making this a rotten habit."

She turned her face into the hardwood flooring, saying thickly, "Mary Ann is—was—my best friend." Her shoulders shook with smothered sobs, the sounds of an innocent, bruised heart breaking.

"It's my fault, Melba, my fault. We should've moved to the sofa, but I had no idea this would happen. Are you okay? I mean, I know you're not okay, but did you break anything?" At Melba's negative head shake, Tammy scrambled up, feeling shaky herself. "I'll get you a pillow."

Melba's voice shook. "No. Just help me up. I need to hear what else they told you."

"The only place I'll help you to, is bed. After that, I'll decide whether to keep talking." Melba used Tammy as a crutch to walk to the bedroom, crawling onto the duvet. Once she was settled against the pillows, Tammy retrieved her tape recorder and resumed her story.

"Mary Ann said you two met at Café du Monde the day Barley died, and she asked about your marriage."

"Yes, I lied. I told her Barley was wonderful to me. Driving home, I decided it was time to ask him for a divorce. I had no idea my husband and my best friend...cheated on me."

"She told you the father didn't know she was pregnant. That was a lie, too. Barley *did* know. She told him everything you said, and demanded he do something because he would soon be a father."

Melba closed her eyes, exhausted and hurt. "I'm such a fool. I was so worried about her."

Tammy gauged Melba's behavior. She could be lying, but she didn't fake that faint. Obviously, one of them—Mary Ann or Melba—had played some kind of role in Barley's death, but for the life of her, she couldn't figure out which one. She'd recommend both women be treated as suspects, but take no other steps now, knowing neither woman was going anywhere in the near future.

Chapter Five

Melba opened her bedroom curtains to the morning light and stepped barefoot through the patio door. The pleasant mixture of newly cut grass combined with an occasional whiff of fresh-cut cedar hung in the air. She rubbed her arms against the morning chill, obsessed with thoughts of her difficult task, unused to feeling at a loss.

I can't help find that cheat Barley's killer when I'm stuck here, not that I care about him. No, I'm worried about the killer coming for me. The DEA should use me as bait, instead of hiding me away. Or do they only want to snare René and don't care about Barley...or me? That disturbing possibility nestled close to the surface of Melba's thoughts. *Of course, I* could *set myself up as bait, couldn't I?*

Intense homesickness flooded her thoughts. Back home, the neighborhood ghosts and goblins would soon be trick-or-treating and she wouldn't be there to hand out candy and act afraid of their scary getups.

Confined to the house, Melba had read close to a novel a day while she healed, doubling up late at night when sleep was hard to come by. She was sick of watching TV. Other than the TV's electronic noise, her house was disturbingly quiet during daylight hours, with only an occasional rumble from a passing truck, but that was it. Home on Octavia Street, she could always hear something—a slamming door, a mother calling her kids. Cars that revved their motors as they left, returning at the end of the day. Tantalizing odors drifting in the air. The aroma of seafood gumbo, or a mouthwatering hint of grilled steak, floating across her yard and through the windows. Not here, though. Not inside this sealed house, the air artificially monitored. She might as well be on the moon.

Stop being so whiny, girl. Shake it off, and let's see what's next, now that my bruises have faded away. Tomorrow, I'll pull on that itchy wig and walk around the block. If I don't get some exercise, my muscles will melt into a very unappetizing jelly.

Chapter Six

"Look on the bright side, girlfriend," Tammy had giggled during their Skype call. The young woman, Melba had learned, was a determined optimist, especially when it came to keeping up Melba's spirits. "You already have a cute butch haircut *and* a skunk stripe to go with it."

Melba walked at a good clip, familiar with her path and still thinking of yesterday's conversation. Her lips twitched in a slight smile. The most important thing about the call, as Tammy had pointed out, was Melba had made no mention, cheating or otherwise, of her husband. No Barley Forest had intruded in their call.

It felt wonderful to stretch her legs on a vigorous walk. On a whim, Melba crossed a busy street into an unfamiliar section of Puebla where there were store fronts and commercial businesses. A modest sign which proclaimed "Library" brought her to an abrupt stop. *Hmm! I wouldn't mind being a volunteer. I should have enough hair in another week not to embarrass myself.*

Gene wore a deeply creased, shiny navy-blue suit when he arrived for his weekly visit. His white shirt gaped between its buttons under its solid black tie. Melba shook her head at Gene's less than successful attempt to imitate the clothes-horses Melba had known back in the city, though Gene imagined himself quite put-together and dapper.

Melba gave him the same gracious greeting she gave everyone who entered her house, especially those she already knew. She had set aside her saggy warm-ups and stepped into a pair of skinny jeans, adding a fitted, untucked, blue and white checked shirt. Her cheeks wore a little blush, and, by his expression, Gene approved. Her bruises had faded. Her face looked fresh and lovely, and her fuzzy chia crown of wavy auburn hair gave her an unaffected gamine appearance.

Typical of their weekly visits, Melba offered her guest a delicious meal. This time, she'd experimented with trout amandine and sautéed green beans, duplicating one of the meals she'd enjoyed at the Windsor Court hotel.

The glass of wine Gene allowed himself relaxed him and made him talkative, though he chewed with his mouth open, which was not a pretty sight, and gestured with his fork. Melba ignored his shortcomings and they talked about happenings in "the city" as they called New Orleans. He wasn't well-informed, but Melba managed to pay attention. *He must sleepwalk through his days. All I hear is 'I don't know' or 'I didn't notice.' Frustrating.*

To hopefully wind up the meal—and the visit—Melba placed a healthy slice of homemade rum cake garnished with strawberries and whipped cream in front of Gene. He blushed to see her innocent flash of skin as she leaned over. Not speaking, he smiled his thanks, a flake of fish at the corner of his mouth.

The minute Gene lowered his dessert fork, Melba pushed her chair from the table and stood.

"It's so late," she exclaimed. "Look at the time. You'd better get back on the road for that long drive home, friend."

Caught off guard, he rose without comment, but he hovered as though loath to leave.

"Thanks for another delicious meal, Melba. You're a great cook." His words trailed off. Melba knew he would linger with the slightest indication she wanted him to stay. He was to be disappointed, and finally said, "I'll call when I'm on my way next week."

"Thanks for coming, Gene," she said at the door, a consummate hostess trained to be polite. "See you next week."

Once the door closed, Melba breathed more easily, the difference as physical as cloudy weather to a sunny day. She didn't want to offend Gene, but his increasingly obvious romantic attention was a slight problem that seemed only to be getting worse.

Now that he had driven away, she planned to walk around the block while the weather was pleasant, this time visiting the small library she had discovered. If the DEA wouldn't let her help search for the person who shot her, why shouldn't she do something else to pass the time? Wearing the proper clothes for an informal job interview, Melba smoothed her dark gray flannel skirt and straightened her teal funnel-neck sweater.

Chapter Seven

René Gaudet, shorthanded, found it difficult to hide his business from the DEA. The merchandise currently stored in a bulging warehouse deceptively named WickerGoods had to be moved. For now, the warehouse sat unnoticed in the middle of thirty corrugated tin buildings that looked almost exactly like it. Barley Forest had managed all the drug distributors before he died and Gaudet still hadn't decided on his replacement.

The job required someone unscrupulous. Barley, while bent, had been a smart man. Stupid happens if a dumb guy gets in the mix and screws up things. Where *had* the overworked, underpaid lawyers disappeared to? René couldn't find a single one, and until he did, he would have to juggle a legitimate law practice with one hand and a drug operation with the other. *It's a miracle the law isn't on me yet.*

René employed many people of the thug variety, but negotiators were hard to find. He'd returned Jimmy Costanza to his former position, not convinced the man could be a competent manager. He found himself back where he had started—dealing with street-level distributors. He was in the crosshairs of the federal authorities—right where he didn't want to be.

René heaved himself to his feet, breathing heavily. With Barley gone, he now helped launder money and deliver product to the middlemen. His fastidious appearance had become a bit disheveled, a tad wrinkled, and he looked a great deal more exhausted. With end-to-end encryption on the Internet and using banks in countries like Canada and the Philippines, paying his suppliers was the least dangerous part of his business. *Collecting* payments, however, took some of his valuable time. He needed to relax, but knew not to sample his products, restricting himself to wine and spirits once home. Remaining cautious, he was run ragged as he struggled to return to lawyer-mode after his long hiatus.

René was astonished at the number of clients Cecile Forest had developed. Her cases were time-consuming, but not difficult because Jan Yokum, Cecile's paralegal, was exceptionally competent. Jan handled most of the work without bothering René. He reviewed her work and signed the papers she set in front of him. With every day that passed, he was reminded he had once been a decent lawyer.

One morning he eyed the woman and asked, "Jan, you okay?" The question was out of concern for himself, not for Jan. He eyed the paralegal, standing in front of his desk with a sheaf of papers. Dark bruises made half-moons under her eyes. They accentuated her pallor, her thin body shrunken inside clothes billowing about knobby elbows and knees.

"Sure, Mr. Gaudet. Just—you know—I m...miss Mrs. Forest. She was like my family." Her eyes glistened and she wiped the tip of her reddened nose with a wadded tissue.

On the list of Gaudet's dislikes was the sight of a crying woman. He pushed away from his desk and left his office, leaving Jan irked and dejected. René knew his painstaking façade of a law practice might collapse, exposing the actual source of his wealth, if he lost Jan, too. Hopefully, she would soon snap out of her mournful funk. He felt his entire life lately was constructed mostly of hopes and prayers for good luck and a return to better days.

René Gaudet was *nowhere close* to being safe. On the contrary. Steve Morley and the DEA had convinced a judge to sign a surveillance order, and they'd bugged Gaudet's office. One night after the cleaning crew departed the Gaudet & Authement firm, technicians had planted cameras and microphones the size of pinheads on the walls and ceilings. Morley's personal favorite was the sensitive mike hidden just under the edge of René's desk surface. The raw data from the devices was funneled like sweet sugar crystals into a windowless room one level below René's private office.

The building management had thought it odd when their newest lessee wanted a specific room, on a certain floor, at the end of a hall. They were told it was for information storage, but money was money, and who were they to judge. The new tenant was quiet and the rent was paid on time.

Morley issued strict instructions. "Do not act on any data not pertinent to our investigation. Delete it. We don't want extraneous information to screw up our case." DEA agents collected René's activity on thumb drives that recorded crystal-clear audio and excellent video.

Most of the agents had law degrees, which kept them interested in the legal work they saw and heard, but most tantalizing were the snippets of illegal transactions they glimpsed despite René's efforts to be circumspect in his conversations. The DEA had all the time in the world to collect René Gaudet's slips. All crooks made mistakes, and Gaudet was no exception.

Evidence against Gaudet began to accumulate. However, if he had been responsible for Barley Forest's murder on Octavia Street, the DEA never heard a word about it.

*

Back at the DEA, Steve Morley's impatience became monumental. He paced, listening to Cyril Smythe, Gaudet's English butler, as he nattered on. Though paid to spy, so far Smythe's reports were useless, as frivolous as Morley's children's wash-off, temporary tattoos.

Cyril had a unique dual citizenship by virtue of his birth in the United States to British parents. René Gaudet's house was the fanciest place he'd ever lived. He already earned good money working for Mr. Gaudet when the DEA approached him. Cyril's life was good and became even better financially once he began gathering information for the feds.

His accounts contained a gold mine of minutiae, but nothing of lasting value. Mr. Gaudet spoke freely over the house phone, many conversations which Cyril heard over the intercom system. True, he heard only one side of the conversation, but that yielded helpful tidbits. René became more nervous after the Forest murders, but remained cautious. Even Cyril wondered if the DEA was getting their money's worth.

"These reports get me nowhere, Cyril." Morley's flat vowels and nasal voice contrasted with the modulated deep tones of Smythe's diction. "Doesn't anything ever happen in that house? Get back to work and find me something."

Morley was sick of his stalled investigation and Gaudet's pointless phone calls. The butler had a prime position, and nothing was coming of it. Cecile Forest would be a valuable material witness if they could ever get to court. It was more apparent than ever that he would need her help to take down René Gaudet's drug empire.

If they solved the Forest murder in the process, it would be lagniappe, but it wasn't important in the scheme of things.

Morley wouldn't break his neck trying to find the Forest man's killer.

Chapter Eight

What a find! The library Melba discovered on one of her earliest walks had exercised an irresistible pull on her. The first thing she had noticed was its highly polished signage reflecting the bright sunshine and highlighting the words Puebla Community Library. Melba, silently laughing at her pun, thought it must be a "sign".

She checked that she hadn't been followed before she stepped inside and paused to survey her surroundings. Immense, it was not. The library building was a long, narrow structure, not overly deep, shoehorned between two larger buildings. The interior lighting was poor and the bookshelves looked rickety and unstable. *Maybe it's not a perfect gem of a library,* Melba thought, *but close enough. Of course, I think all libraries are close to perfect.* Before she lost her nerve, she approached the front desk.

"Excuse me," she whispered. The busy librarian looked up and answered in a normal voice, not whispering, still arranging books on a rolling cart.

"Yes?"

"I wonder if you want volunteer help." *I sound so tentative. This is harder than I thought it would be.*

The librarian looked up, startled. "Ma'am? *Unpaid*? Um, I don't know. There's really no time to train you, Ms..."

"Melba...Melba Columbo." Relieved not to have stumbled over a name that didn't roll easily off her tongue, she gestured toward the street. "I live a few blocks away for the next couple of weeks, and training's not an issue. My major was Library Science. I'd like to volunteer my help...free. I won't be in Puebla long, and I'm looking for something to do with my hands. You'd be helping *me* more than

I'd be helping you." Left unsaid was Melba's hope that the constant fear for her life might recede if her mind was occupied with enjoyable work.

The busy librarian surveyed the pale, pretty woman standing in front of her. Frozen in mid-task as she absorbed Melba's offer, the busy woman's frown was followed by a thoughtful expression, which then settled into relief.

A shy smile transformed the librarian. Brushing a lock of crinkled dark-brown hair off her face, she extended her hand. With a start, Melba noticed the woman's clothes looked quite similar to her own, the ones Tammy had provided. *I'm blending in*!

"Nice to meet you, Melba. What a unique name! I'm Glory." She gestured toward the books stacked around her. "I want to say yes because I'm swamped, but Joyce isn't here today, and we make decisions together. Can you wait until tomorrow for an answer?"

Melba returned Glory's smile. *Everyone I've met—okay, only two people so far—seems nice.* "I'll get out of your hair for now and come back tomorrow."

Buoyed by conversation with an adult not part of that mess in New Orleans, Melba practically skipped out the door. Her headache and the itchy wig were discarded history. Her head wound was mostly healed, leaving only a stubby streak of white hair.

Life was looking up.

Melba clicked the library thermostat completely off. Expensive electricity strained their paltry budget, so the last staff person to leave turned off the heat, knowing the place would be cold by the following morning.

Pushing her arms into a new brown microfiber coat and tugging on a purple knit wool hat to match her purple gloves, all provided courtesy of Tammy and the DEA, she was ready to step outside.

She had been nervous as a cat when she began working at the library six weeks ago, always alert to possible danger. At the end of each day, she had hesitated at the door, working up the courage to leave.

Joyce, a clone of her twin sister Glory, finally asked about Melba's behavior, calling out from the book stacks. "Whatcha doin', girl? You a scaredy cat?" Melba jumped, caught peering into the winter darkness.

"Uh, no." She laughed nervously. "I guess I've been this way since I was widowed." That was the truth, but not the whole truth.

"Aww, I'm sorry." Joyce came over to throw her arm around Melba's shoulder. "You hafta nip that in the bud. Don't fix it, and before you know what hits you, you be holed up in a stinky old room 'fraid of everything you see."

Melba leaned against Joyce, enjoying the warm bulk of the other woman. It was the first womanly hug she'd felt since her Aunt Hattie died. A wave of homesickness hit, making her eyes glisten.

Glory and her sisters had enriched Melba's life with their upbeat, irreverent approach to life. It started the first morning she reported to work. When she walked into the library, Glory sat unsmiling behind the desk.

"Am I late?" Melba asked. She didn't want to be thought an unreliable volunteer.

"Follow me." Unsmiling, Glory slid from the tall chair and walked to the back wall. Behind the last book stack, she sat with her sisters at a small table. Impassive, they stared at her.

Melba sucked in a breath, feeling herself begin to sweat. Had they discovered her secret? Cecile had tried to be Melba, but she was a terrible actress. Her shoulders sagged, but suddenly all three sisters stood up and began making a loud racket with jangling bells and blowing whistles, yelling hooray and yay and thank God you're here.

"Ahh!" squeaked Melba, stumbling back. "Wha...?"

Joyce pulled the white sheet off the cart behind her to reveal steaming cups of coffee and a pyramid of assorted doughnuts. The three sisters meeting Melba talked nonstop and gave her bear hugs. Melba, almost completely alone for weeks, experienced a strange, unexpected happiness.

"Look at Melba's expression," Glory chuckled. "We got her good." The three sisters high-fived each other.

A woman who could've been Joyce's clone elbowed her way to Melba's side.

"Melba, I'm Rejoyce, Joyce's twin sister. Joyce calls herself being in charge, but *that* stopped when she hired me an' Glory."

Glory and the twins were to enrich Melba's life with their carefree approach to life. Melba was folded into the happy-go-lucky group and was quickly accepted as the fourth sister in their rowdy family. It was a rare weekend she wasn't being thoroughly entertained by one of the sisters and their families. They worked hard in lives that had little money to spare—painting, cleaning, washing cars for each other—but fun prevailed. Their way of living was new to Melba.

She loved being part of a happy group of women.

Chapter Nine

Melba knew she was an emotional wreck and wanted to feel normal, so she searched online for the reason. After the library closed each evening, she walked the few blocks to the place she had begun to call home and opened her laptop. Eventually, she navigated from "bad marriages" to "marital communication" and finally landed on the subject of spousal abuse and its effects on its victims.

Employing the same methods she'd once used to build legal arguments, Melba analyzed everything she could find on the topic, dismayed to recognize herself multiple times.

Unable to act independently—check. Insecure—check. Belief the abuse was her fault—check. Afraid the outside world was worse than the hurtful world she lived in—check.

Melba sat back, pinching the bridge of her nose. Her research brought new recognition of the person she'd been throughout her marriage. She had denied the abuse so long, she had no longer been able to recognize it.

There was a new twist, however, and that was her own culpability. Melba learned for the first time that her passive behavior, dating to her childhood, had enabled the long-term abuse. When her family died in Indonesia, she'd done whatever she was told by her great-aunt to keep herself safe.

Poor Aunt Hattie. I must've dragged at her like an anchor.

*

Melba's natural optimism gradually returned. She slept well under her comfortable covers and sang along with her Pandora music as she scrubbed her kitchen clean. Her intense desire to return to New Orleans faded, and she discovered a new enjoyment in her volunteer work at the cozy library and in the easy companionship of those who worked there. She had chosen her college major well and was thrilled to put her knowledge to such good use.

There were times when Melba, staring at her ceiling and waiting for sleep, imagined herself a lone tree quivering in a vast field, every leaf gone, plucked from her branches, drawing sustenance only from her roots. Breezes murmured their doubts she'd ever bloom again, but she knew her juices would flow in the spring sunshine, if she could just hold onto who she was.

Joyce, Rejoyce, and Glory had become close friends who treated her more like another sister than a friend. They appreciated her presence and often told her so. Something about having these new friends added buoyancy to her mood and made routine things—simply getting dressed and putting on a pair of shoes or brushing out her hair—as enjoyable as it had been before she married.

As upbeat as she became, Melba hated that every day she was living a lie—about her fake name, her real career, how her husband died. She wanted to blurt the truth and yearned to say she missed her law practice and Jan, her assistant. She liked the people of Puebla, but she acknowledged she was in an artificial, contrived situation.

She was concerned about her friends in New Orleans and her home there. What would her bungalow look and *smell* like after months away? Homes left empty soon deteriorated. Too, there were things she *didn't* miss—one was her former best friend Mary Ann, who'd betrayed her.

Frustration and impatience were difficult to keep under control, but the friendship and laughter with Glory, Joyce, and ReJoyce helped her feel normal. *Calm acceptance? No, more like suspended animation. Thank goodness for the library, her friends there, and Tammy Avenetti, or I'd be a basket case.*

⁎

The Puebla bureaucrats paid little attention to the inconspicuous Rio Frio library, though it provided impressive services to the underserved area. The promises of enough funding always ended up stuck in the sludge at the bottom of the political barrel. The library had three paid employees, one volunteer, and not much else. As chief librarian, Joyce tried everything she could, but nothing worked.

Melba chafed at the indignity of the situation until she realized she could capitalize on the situation, maybe even kill two birds with one stone.

She bundled up for the short walk to work against a morning chill unusual in south Texas. In her arms, she lugged a heavy white box snug against her midsection.

With her new habit of vigilance, she peeked in all directions while pulling on her gloves. She snickered, knowing how ridiculous her swiveling head must look, but she didn't care. Though remote, the possibility of danger was impossible to ignore. As she trudged along, Melba laid the foundation of her plan. She resolved to leave her old insecurities behind and make her own decisions.

True, she enjoyed her volunteer work and her new friends, but that poor library existed on a shoestring—one that didn't include a restroom. The store next door had made their facilities available to the library staff and patrons, calling it a community service.

Nevertheless, the library *needed* its own restroom, and Melba made that the basis of her plan. She had an idea that might solve more than one problem—the library's lack of a restroom, yes, but also uncovering the identity of Barley's killer—if the DEA was correct about criminal hacking abilities.

She had to overcome her fear of an unknown killer, while she engaged in some intensive research. Only after those things were done would she be willing to break the DEA's cardinal rule.

The trick was to not lose her life in the process.

*

She knew the terms of the maintenance trust Great-aunt Hattie had set up for her, but not the value of its assets. On Melba's thirty-fifth birthday, the trust would be liquidated and delivered to her. Since Barley died, she hadn't touched a cent from the trust's monthly distributions, which were managed by Karl Schmitzer ever since Aunt Hattie's death. The unspent distributions might be enough to build a restroom for the library.

The moist, cold air left her shivering, and rouged her cheeks a ruddy red as she speed walked, taking surreptitious glances all around as she went. Caution, always a good thing, was now her normal behavior.

She blinked as something struck her eyelashes. *Is that snow*? *In Puebla, Texas?* A few flakes drifted from the sky, melting as they landed. The delicate scent of petrichor, that earthy aroma, tickled her nose, and she inhaled deeply. She tried to catch a snowflake, juggling the box she held. Snow was a rarity this far south, and Melba wondered whether enough white stuff would fall to cover the ground.

Through the glass door when she reached the library, she saw hazy figures swirl. *What the...?* She pushed inside in an envelope of cold air, to the sound of laughter as the three sisters bumped each other and called it dancing.

"Good morning, you silly things," she said. "It's snowing out there! Did you know that?" "And I brought non-caloric chocolate doughnuts for our skinny lattes."

"Snow and doughnuts," someone said. "A perfect combination."

Glory, Joyce, and Rejoyce jostled, acting like their sisterly selves. Joyce's staff was a family affair, and all three were trained librarians passionate about books. They treated Melba like another sibling, with offhanded loving gestures and playful insults, accepting her story that a car accident had made her a widow, and giving her their unquestioning sympathy.

During the rare times the library was empty, no topics were off limits, especially sex. The sisters talked frankly, making Melba's face flame with embarrassment, which made the sisters hoot gleefully. They relished sex with a capital *S*, and loved talking about it. They enjoyed the physical things Melba remembered as uncomfortable and hurtful. It boggled her mind that there was such a disconnect about sex between their experiences and hers, so much so that it made her squirm. She managed to laugh with them, but she refused to comment. Melba kept her private life private. *They'll think something is wrong with me, and maybe there* is, *or maybe I'm weird. I'll just keep quiet...like I've done for years.*

It was safe to talk about doughnuts. That was something they all had in common.

This morning Joyce chuckled, licking the chocolate off her fingers. "Melba, honey, you're gonna make me fat. I'm gonna get a potato peeler and skim off about thirty pounds any day now."

Glory, hands on hips, looked skeptical. Showing attitude, she looked Joyce up and down. "I hate to tell you, big sis—I wouldn't even notice those thirty pounds."

Rejoyce, quiet only because her mouth was full of doughnut, crinkled her eyes and nodded in agreement.

"You can't be cruel to your boss, girl." Joyce lunged, but Glory dodged out of reach, grazing Melba's elbow. Melba snorted and steadied her sloshing hot coffee.

"My Charlie likes me this way, and everybody knows it," said Joyce. "But looka there at our movie star."

She pointed at Melba. "Skunky has a perfect body and a skinny white streak in that funny color hair, and she works for free. On top of that, she brings doughnuts. Only thing missing is a man." She wrapped Melba in a mighty hug, getting a squeeze in return.

"Tonight Charlie's making chili." She gestured at her sisters. "They coming. Their families, too. And I'm asking you. You coming?"

"I'd love that, thanks." Melba wasn't just saying that. Dinner with these friends and their families would be fun.

She'd have to leave the sisters behind once Barley's killer was found, but she'd stay in touch. She could never leave this precious new friendship. Squeezing Joyce, she breathed in her fresh, clean smell. That same scent clung to all three sisters, the scent of starched clothes hung outdoors to dry. Their houses, she'd discovered, sparkled the same fresh, clean way except when the air smelled of delicious food.

Joyce whispered, "You know I'm teasing, right? You ain't got nothing missing."

"Cut it out. You just want more doughnuts," Melba teased. *If someone asked me two years ago where I would be today, I wouldn't have dreamed I'd be in a library with three hilarious, no-holds-barred sisters.* "I haven't laughed this much since grammar school, but y'all are definitely more fun, because my teachers were some serious nuns."

Things quieted when a library patron walked in. Melba pushed up the sleeves of a turtleneck the color of autumn leaves before settling down to re-shelve returned books, the sounds of compatible women working together a pleasant undercurrent to her day.

Her bladder signaled she needed to run next door before she started her next chore, and to make it snappy. She *had* to fix the awkward bathroom problem. The library would be more comfortable and pleasant, and it would make a wonderful Christmas present for everyone, herself included. Melba smiled at the thought. She appreciated the gift of unconditional friendliness she received every day and she longed to reciprocate. The perfect time to put her plan into action was when things quieted down for the holidays, and that was right now.

Chapter Ten

Seventeen-year-old Tremell Williams sat in a far corner of the library, his gangly, jean-clad legs stretched out, his nose buried in a textbook.

Tremell found refuge in the Rio Frio library as often as he could when cold winter weather sagged south into Puebla. He was on the cusp of a handsome manhood. His full lips smiled readily, white teeth gleaming, and his dark brown eyes shone with intelligence. A high school senior, he starred on the varsity track team. He was also homeless, though he never thought of himself that way.

He thought his parents had been stoned again, that day they'd told him to pack because they were leaving Puebla. No way were they serious.

He replied, "Yeah? Whatever. I'm not leaving," and he hurried off to class. After athletics practice, he found his belongings stacked at the curb and the house padlocked, an eviction notice on the door. He couldn't believe his parents had actually left town without him. What kind of people were they?

He knew they were addicts, but they'd always managed to keep him alive. Sitting at the curb beside his things, Tremell had to rethink his future outside of sports for the first time. One last childhood tear slid down his cheek, which he wiped away with a sniff and a heavy sigh. He eyed his rusty old truck parked nearby, the only thing of value he owned. Maybe he could sell it. He certainly couldn't afford to keep it.

He had six months of high school left before graduation, and his dream of college was fading unless he could score a track scholarship. That would be a godsend. Until then, school served free breakfast. Ditto a hot lunch. He could survive on those two daily meals during the week, but he needed shelter, somewhere more comfortable than his cramped truck.

Tremell was tough enough anyway, to manage life on his own. Because his parents were addicts, he'd been self-sufficient for years, and he was determined to make his own way. He admitted he was a little heartbroken, but he'd get over it. He'd been disappointed many times. This might be different, but it was really nothing new.

*

"Tremell?" He looked up, blinking to refocus on the woman smiling down at him.

"Ma'am?"

Melba motioned toward the front of the library. "I brought you doughnuts and a latte." His wide smile lit up his face. Offering his enthusiastic thanks, he dropped his book on the table and headed straight for the food.

Melba and Tremell had developed a bond. Both were emotionally adrift and living out singularly unlikely scenarios. Melba's circumstances had developed out of violence, but she had lived a life of plenty. Tremell's circumstances weren't as clear-cut, but he always, always, looked hungry, and spent way too much time in the library. His clothes were faded and wrinkled, but clean. He would often discuss his schoolwork, and his friends on the track team, with great enthusiasm. Still, he never mentioned home or family or where he lived.

Melba habitually sent Tremell for burgers and fries in the late afternoon toward closing time. After only a few bites, she would ask him to eat the rest, feeding the bottomless pit of a hungry boy's appetite. She couldn't quite put her finger on the reason why, but Melba recognized a loneliness in the teenager which was similar to her own.

*

Tremell slouched in "his" corner of the library, frowning into the pages of a textbook, papers and pencils scattered nearby.

"Want help preparing for the SATs, Tremell?"

Surprised, he studied Melba.

"What you know about SATs?" he asked. He doubted someone old as Ms. Melba knew anything about SAT scores needed to get into college. Amused, she cocked her head.

"I'll have you know I needed good SATs to get into college, too."

Their friendship deepened as cold weather encroached on the South. The sisters, each with their own household, included Tremell in their family invitations, and the more they studied together, the more Tremell and Melba enjoyed each other. She helped him with school work whenever she had free time. A good SAT score would win him an academic scholarship and relieve the pressure for an athletic scholarship to get him into college.

He swallowed the last enormous bite of Melba's "unwanted" hamburger, washing it down with a gulp of a sweet, icy drink.

"Can I ask you something, Miss Melba?"

She eyed him suspiciously. "Can I stop you?"

He looked confused until she added, "I'm messing with you, Tremell. Of course you can ask."

"I have to sell my old truck, but I don't know how."

Melba raised her eyebrows, amazed. "You have a truck? It's your name on the title?"

Mildly affronted, Tremell answered, "Of course, but I can't afford to keep it."

Impulsively, Melba blurted, "I've been looking for a better way to get from place to place." Here was an opportunity, dropped right in her lap, even though the DEA had cautioned her not to acquire a car, telling her that driving made her discovery much more likely.

Heads close together at the library's computer, Tremell and Melba checked his truck's appraisal value online and Melba agreed to a generous price. She typed out an act of sale, pretending to copy from the internet, though she'd done many such forms in her law practice. Tremell drove them to her bank to have it notarized. She withdrew cash, handing the money to him and accepting his keys in exchange. Though Tremell signed the title over to Melba, she didn't legally transfer it at the courthouse or get insurance, keeping it a secret for now.

Tremell taught Melba to drive using a clutch and manual gear shift. It took a few days to master the concept, but she enjoyed the challenge. She found an excellent shade tree mechanic to check the little truck and take care of the deferred maintenance.

Melba hadn't planned to acquire a vehicle or to keep such a purchase a secret from Gene or the DEA or the US Marshals. With her growing assurance and independence, she nevertheless decided it was none of their business.

So, keep it a secret she did, occasionally moving the parked truck from one spot to another on the street.

*

Melba cocooned, warm and dry, made sleepy by the whisper of falling rain. She moved the window covering to check on the newly purchased truck sitting in front of the house. She should move it—later. Dropping the shade, she completed a rough simulation of the library dimensions and surrounding structures. It was rudimentary, but might be enough to get a plumbing contractor to estimate costs. That completed, she emailed Tammy, with a request for help locating the owner of the library building—probably the city of Puebla—and the bureaucrat responsible for decisions concerning the library.

Tammy wouldn't answer until after the weekend, but Melba grew anxious as her self-imposed deadline approached. What she planned was a long shot, but there was no downside, and, if it worked, the library would get the restroom it needed.

Daylight hours shortened and average temperatures edged down. The library was less used during cold weather, except by die-hard bibliophiles and by Tremell. During chilly weather, families hunkered down, reluctant to leave their warm homes, and checked out their reading materials online.

Melba worried about Tremell's welfare during the coldest nights.

She might not know about Tremell's nights, but he knew about hers. Out of curiosity, he had once followed her home. It was odd, he thought, that she walked to work even after she bought his truck. He wanted to know why, but asking her seemed an invasion of her privacy. He was surprised when he watched her unlock a carved wooden door in a downtrodden neighborhood only a few blocks down the street from the library.

"Hunh," he said aloud. Her house was nothing fancy. The honey-colored stucco structure had the undulating, terra-cotta tile roof typical of the surrounding rundown neighborhood. The next afternoon at the library, he mentioned he'd seen her there, asking if that was where she lived.

"Why, yes, it is," Melba answered, alarmed that she hadn't noticed Tremell, but his comment gave her the opportunity to question him in return.

"Where do *you* live, Tremell?" He dropped his eyes, remaining silent. She touched his arm lightly.

"I worry about you, Tremell. Aren't we friends?" He nodded, but didn't look up. "Why can't you tell me where you sleep at night?"

Embarrassed and angry, he blurted, "Cold, hard church pews, all right?" He sniffed, emotional. "My parents left without me, but I'm fine. I'm fine." His voice hitched. "Why?"

Melba's soft heart broke. This boy had been abandoned, left behind by his parents. She struggled to keep her own voice steady.

"I wondered, that's all. But I have a proposition."

"I said I'm fine. Just let me be."

"Wait, Tremell. You owe it to me to at least listen and hear me out. I'm alone, too, and I'm frightened in that house by myself." *Little white lies can be all right, can't they?* "I can hardly sleep, I'm so scared.

"I've been wondering how to ask you this. Would you be willing to stay at the house until you graduate? I have an empty bedroom. It's only for a few more months, but don't say yes if you don't want to."

Tremell's liquid dark brown eyes looked directly into Melba's amber ones, searching for pity and not finding it. He pointed first at her, then at himself.

"So *you* need *my* help?" She nodded. Tremell closed his eyes and Melba watched as the strain under his eyes relaxed. His breath whooshed out in a great gust as he shook his head. His shoulders dropped, releasing a tension he hadn't been aware of.

Starting that night, Tremell slept, warm and comfortable under sheets in a dry bed protected by a roof over the honey-colored stucco walls, while in her big bedroom not far away, Melba dreamed of home.

Christmas arrived and Puebla celebrated the holiday season with Hispanic joyfulness.

*

Tammy had answered all of Melba's questions concerning the library, though she had no idea why those answers were necessary.

Walking home and nodding at bundled-up neighbors, visible puffs of warm breath trailing behind, Melba considered the best means of implementing her idea. *It's time to be assertive. I can do this.*

Her preoccupation did little to interfere with her enjoyment of the colorful neighborhood. Melba had met her neighbors. She knew most of them by name, and everyone was comfortable enough with her to follow their normal outdoor routines. They said *hola* and waved as she walked by.

She spoke to Maria Gomez, who sold homemade tamales from a small window of her house, the best tamales Melba had ever eaten. Rhythmic salsa music often floated in the air, sending her shuffling to the beat. Crows flapped off the overhead electrical wires and rode the breeze as she walked below. Safely out of reach, they cawed rude insults down on the busy people.

Melba looked far different than the bruised, wounded woman who'd first walked through her Rio Frio door less than three months before. Her short, dark coppery hair, now more cordovan than not, contrasted with the narrow white streak tracking exactly the width and length of the bullet's path. She'd discarded most of the timidity foisted on her by the abusive Barley, gaining in confidence as the weeks had trundled by.

Melba remained wary, even among her new friends. She constantly searched for strangers, fearing discovery by whoever had tried to kill her. Whether or not the DEA believed René was responsible, Melba was certain he would never harm her.

This afternoon, Melba would test her own belief in René. She planned to ignore the DEA's rule and contact someone from home to help her friends and hopefully flush a killer out of hiding.

Melba rode a blast of chilly air into the house. Tremell looked up from his homework, faking a shiver as he smiled. His presence there provided a peace of mind Melba hadn't realized she needed so badly. There was a synergism that couldn't be denied between the two of them. Tremell was not only comfortable on Rio Frio, he liked knowing someone cared about his days. They shared all the household chores and talked about their daily lives. No one in

Puebla, not even Tremell, knew the burden of Melba's secrets, but those warm friendships lightened her life.

After ten miserable years, she had begun to laugh again, and that made her next decision an easy one.

That night after their evening meal, Melba excused herself to Tremell and called Karl Schmitzer, her lawyer in New Orleans. As Aunt Hattie's special friend, he had always been a constant presence in her life, even before he handled Aunt Hattie's petition to become her niece's legal guardian.

Chapter Eleven

"Ms. Columbo? This is Karl Schmitzer. How can I help?"

The familiar, warm, courtly Uptown New Orleans voice strangled Melba with emotion. She hesitated as his kind face materialized in her mind at the sound of his voice, almost a tangible presence. The old lawyer waited patiently for her to speak. He would be upset with her, when he learned she had deceived them all with her false death. She struggled with her words.

"Uncle Karl?" Melba was tense, and she thought her voice sounded childish. Had she not been so nervous, she might have been annoyed at herself. "This is Cecile. Cecile Valois Forest?"

To her chagrin, her voice quavered. Her lips trembled and tears trickled down her cheeks with relief, at last reconnecting with someone she loved. Schmitzer didn't seem to have a strong reaction, waiting until she regained control. She would shortly learn why, but though unsurprised he was thrilled to hear her familiar voice.

"Cecile! Finally back from the dead? How's my girl?" He sounded pleased, but not startled.

"You don't sound at all surprised to hear from me, Uncle Karl."

"That's because I'm *not* surprised. Not at all. The DEA man, Mr. Morley, told me your secret, that you were alive. Hidden and safe, he said, and he told me why. Those words healed my broken heart.

"Tell me everything, child—from the beginning. Start with the day you left home."

The floodgates opened and Melba poured out everything that had happened, from the moment she and Barley were shot, living with a new identity and a new life, and ending with the wait in Puebla until she could go back home.

Her voice trembled when she spoke about her fear of being hunted, and worse, the fear of being found. Karl Schmitzer listened, never interrupting and not commenting that Cecile only once mentioned Barley, in her recital.

"The DEA foisted this gosh-awful name, Melba Columbo, on me, Uncle Karl, and Mr. Morley said I'd be home soon, but that was months ago. It's taking too long."

Her tension dissipated as she talked. Melba had been numb until now to how truly frightened she had been during the past months. The weight of a good-sized mountain lifted from her chest, allowing her lungs to expand with relief. *Dear Uncle Karl—he makes me feel safe.*

Schmitzer occasionally tsked, commiserating with her story. "I didn't know your new name, or where you were, but I knew you were alive and under DEA protection. Mr. Morley explained his reason for this charade." The old attorney, usually nonjudgmental, shocked Melba when he described her old boss as an ill-mannered, underhanded, so-called lawyer who sullied the hallowed halls of the law.

"Gee, Uncle Karl, why didn't you say something seven, almost eight years, ago?"

"What was I supposed to say, Cecile? I didn't know you'd joined Gaudet's firm until after you'd already signed your contract. After the fact, just like your impulsive marriage to Barley Forest.

"When Mr. Morley said the DEA suspected Gaudet was a dangerous member of the underworld, it hardly surprised me. Then, when he told me you—a lawyer yourself—were one of his targets, I was appalled." He conveyed the distinct impression it was almost too much to bear. The emotion she heard in his voice warmed Melba's heart and made her smile into the phone.

After a few false starts, Melba—the former Cecile—explained what she wanted. She could hear Schmitzer open a drawer, followed by the rustle of paper. She imagined him moistening a fingertip, flipping to a fresh page of a yellow legal pad, and selecting a freshly-sharpened pencil from those lined up and ready on his spotless desk. She pictured his flowing cursive penmanship and his notes, which were always beautifully legible. As a child sitting beside him, waiting to be collected by Aunt Hattie, she'd spent many hours at Uncle Karl's feet, hidden under his desk while she scrawled on one of his yellow pads with a similarly sharp pencil, listening to his rumbling voice and pretending to be a lawyer.

Melba outlined the project she visualized to benefit the Puebla library, and how she planned to implement it. Her only question was whether she had enough money for the project to be feasible.

"Are Aunt Hattie's trusts still viable? Has enough ready cash accumulated to pay for the project since I've been gone?"

Schmitzer laughed. "Yes, there's enough. We folded the unspent dividends back into the principal after you left. And remember, Cecile. You're about to celebrate a birthday that will get you the rest of the assets from both trusts. We'll talk about that another time, but yes, you have plenty of money."

Happy to be working together, the two gifted lawyers crafted a specific, anonymous, grant that, once accepted, would construct two new restrooms at the Rio Frio Street Library in Puebla, Texas.

The little Puebla library would welcome her gift and she would be there to see the faces of her friends when they learned about it. She felt a satisfaction she hadn't experienced in many years. Her gift would fill an important need, and be damned if there was a personal danger to herself. She was counting on the bad guys to discover her through her actions, whether or not the DEA and the Marshals Service wanted it.

Pensive as she later curled deep into the hollows of her squashy sofa cushions safe in her stucco bungalow, Melba cradled her cheek in her hand. She wore a faint smile, happy that her dear Uncle Karl, in addition to the DEA and the Marshals, knew she was among the living and not the dead.

*

The day before Christmas, Joyce took a routine call from Puebla's mayor that she believed expressed season's greetings, following which she stumbled from her broom closet office and called the staff together for an announcement.

Looking shell-shocked and bemused, she said, "Listen up, everybody. The strangest thing just happened."

Glory said, "Well, spit it out. We got work to do."

"Somebody, I don't know who, gave us money for restrooms."

"What! Why don't you know who?" They shared astonished looks before Joyce gave them the few details about the anonymous grant.

"That's wonderful," Melba said, "and great timing to find out the day before Christmas."

Joyce agreed. She had a good feeling, but reminded them that the suspicious Puebla city lawyers had to study the grant's terms. Only after it passed their inspection would it be accepted. What a great Christmas gift from some generous soul.

New Year's Day came and went before the dedicated funds appeared in the library's bank account. All the staff and patrons celebrated, Melba included, knowing they would soon have the facilities they needed. More than anyone else, the anonymous donor was jubilant, secretly humbled by the meaningfulness of her gift.

Chapter Twelve

Billy Fortier was a hacker who thought of himself as a cyber-warrior.

The Authement & Gaudet law firm had hired Billy at the age of fifteen to work part-time because of his computer skills. Now nineteen years old, he affected the unwashed, shoulder-length hair of his early teens, but now sported three self-designed Star Wars-themed copycat tattoos. His clothes were the same every day regardless of the season—droopy jeans that bagged at the butt, worn with a festival of faded concert T-shirts.

His employer paid for Billy's IT classes, but he greatly preferred to exercise his skills on the job. Any success, small or large, gave him a thrill. Researching a target, then following up with a subtle undetected hack, exhilarated him. Once he set up a file, it was simple to track. It wasn't *his* business how Mr. Gaudet handled the results.

Billy heard the rumble of rumors, though, and had twice recognized in online obituaries names he'd passed along.

He'd personally hooked everything up in his cramped office to make it feel like a command center. Electronics hummed on three consoles, giving Billy the heady feeling of flying a starship from his captain's chair in front of multiple screens. A flashing red light and a bleating sound alerted him whenever a target generated activity.

That was exactly what happened one evening when Billy arrived at the office after class—bleating, blinking lights drenching the room with a sound and light show.

Billy threw off his backpack and plopped his ample rear into his captain's chair. Lightning-fast fingertips blurred across the keyboard until a blinking cursor revealed Karl Schmitzer's electronic instructions to Cecile Forest's bank for a wire-transfer from her trust fund to an account in Puebla, Texas. This was the first-ever alert on the tags he'd set up months ago on Barley and Cecile Forest.

The husband and wife had been lawyers at Authement & Gaudet, but they were murdered. Why Mr. Gaudet asked Billy to monitor stuff for people who were dead was a mystery to Billy but he didn't ask questions, he just followed orders and put traces on all the Forest records he could uncover, including bank accounts, tagging them with his automatic alerts. He figured that was the end of it.

Those alarms would remain silent forever.

And he now had proof René Gaudet was a friggin' genius. Billy scratched his itchy nose and templed his fingertips at pursed lips while he studied the details of the alert. The delightful alert was juicy, dealing with finances, his favorite thing. He lived for this stuff.

Fingers flying over the clicking keys, Billy followed the electronic trail, his nose stud mere inches from the screen. His eyes widened when he uncovered the recipient.

"Well, hello-o-o there," he breathed. "Gotcha!"

Digging his cell phone from his pocket. Billy punched in the number for his boss's burner. Exhilaration had him trembling as he waited for his call to connect.

By the time René answered Billy's call, he had made copies of the information—where the money came from (the Cecile Valois Trust), the dollar amount, and who initiated the order. He tracked the account the money was transferred into and for what purpose (a construction grant), and that the donor was to remain anonymous. Had someone raided Cecile Forest's dormant trust fund under cover of a construction grant?

Billy excitedly reported his news, causing René to pause with his tumbler of whiskey halfway to his lips.

René cleared his throat.

"I want to be sure I didn't misunderstand you, Bill. Repeat what you told me, but more slowly this time." Taking a deep breath, he listened intently to Billy's recitation, then complimented him, saying, "This is good stuff. Good job. Tell you what—type it out so a yoyo like me understands it and shoot me an email. Then take the night off...and add a two hundred dollar bonus when you turn in your time sheet. Tell 'em I approved it."

"Great, boss. Thanks a lot. You'll get it in a sec."

Billy sent the consolidated document on its way and left for his favorite hangout, never considering—or caring—how his research might be used.

Ensconced behind the opulent desk of his home office, René stared at Billy's document. How could this transaction occur? Cecile's relatives were deceased. Was it remotely possible she was alive? He raised his snifter of Courvoisier for another sip, surprised to find it empty. Curiosity overrode caution, though he wondered briefly if he was about to blunder. He *had* to know whether Cecile was alive, and if so, why she had gone into hiding. Forced into action by his uncertainty, he called his fixer, Jimmy Costanza. René knew Jimmy would follow the plan he had in mind.

Chapter Thirteen

A false spring descended on New Orleans as the New Year started. The doomed buds of Japanese magnolias along the Avenue swelled into pink and maroon glory at the tips of bare winter branches. Night fell early during the winter months and ragged clouds dimmed the effect of a full moon, but clouds weren't able to diminish the harsh artificial light from a solitary window. That specific opening pierced through the pre-Civil War brick wall of a graceful edifice on Lee Circle.

Within the building, the light illuminated Karl Schmitzer's offices, where he shook hands after-hours with a visitor. Karl enjoyed the law, even after practicing it for so many years; he'd forgotten how long ago he'd passed the Louisiana bar. It had been a busy, tiring day and Karl wanted to go home.

René Gaudet, the man who occupied the chair across the expanse of his desk was not a new client, and Karl knew him only by his questionable reputation. He heard what the man had to say as though through a sound-dampening fog.

"I'll come straight to the point," Gaudet was saying. "You may know that Cecile Forest, who was killed, worked for me. Now I hear street rumors that she may still be alive. Can you confirm that?"

Caught off guard by Gaudet's direct question, Schmitzer pushed his leather chair back from his antique desk to gain time, flicking away an imaginary piece of lint with an elegant finger.

"Do you expect me to answer that?" Schmitzer's suit was too heavy for today's weather, and tonight it was intolerably warm. It was right for the season, but the March day had been unnaturally warm. His neck felt uncomfortably damp under his starched collar, the discomfort mostly caused by the man who stared at him across the desk.

Gaudet, too, was dressed well, but his appearance did little to reduce Schmitzer's discomfort. The man had asked an unexpected question. *This man is asking me to divulge confidential information. Why, of all the attorneys in New Orleans, does he think I know anything about Cecile Valois Forest?*

"Even should this Forest person be my client, Mister Gaudet, as an attorney yourself, you know I cannot divulge confidential information. Why are you asking this question?" Schmitzer demanded, trying to go on the offensive. To avoid showing his discomfort, Schmitzer used his most supercilious tone.

"I see," Gaudet said, his expression thunderous. He rose, thanked Schmitzer for his time, and left the old man's office. He forcibly slammed the door closed behind him, dislodging flakes from the antique brick wall. Schmitzer's obvious discomfort confirmed Gaudet's suspicion that Cecile Forest was alive.

Gaudet's visit rattled Karl. He gripped the arms of his chair and took deep breaths until his heart rate slowed. Pulling his neatly pressed handkerchief, he mopped his damp brow and neck. He should call the DEA. They wouldn't be happy to learn of Cecile's earlier call to him, but that couldn't be helped. What could they do, anyway? That Steve Morley fellow who headed up the investigation had shown no interest in solving Barley Forest's murder, so why should he care whether Gaudet knew Cecile was alive?

Karl decided to go home to his dog and his cognac where he felt more at ease. He didn't like the idea that he might've been outfoxed. He grabbed his fedora from the hat rack, thinking he'd call the DEA from home.

To be on the safe side, Karl asked the security guard to escort him through the darkness to his car. He sat behind the wheel, his hands unsteady as he fought to fasten his seat belt. Gaudet's unexpected visit left him upset and in need a strong alcoholic antidote to the odious man. He headed home, where his favorite antidote awaited.

During his drive, he decided a call to the Bar Association to complain about Gaudet's attempted abuse of attorney-client privilege could wait until morning. He should maybe sleep on that one.

Safely inside his comfortable penthouse, Karl double-checked both locks and made certain the safety chain was engaged in case he'd been followed. He poured three fingers of Hennessey cognac to settle his nerves, then sat in the buttery leather chair bought by his beloved Hattie. Reviewing the meeting with Gaudet, he reached for his phone.

With one foot planted in a more genteel age, Karl Schmitzer had no understanding of today's underworld, of its danger and how lightning fast things could happen in this modern time. The elderly lawyer had outlived most of his generation—the greatest generation—including Hattie DuMond, the only woman he had ever loved—Hattie, who was Cecile's guardian and her great-aunt. Karl would give anything if Hattie were there to give him one of her warm hugs.

Had he realized modern criminals were opportunists whose success depended on their rapid reactions, Karl would have called the DEA before he drove home, but he was oblivious to the danger Gaudet posed. His procrastination gave a head start to a deadly threat, and danger barreled west, unchecked, on the highway to Puebla. Its eventual destination: a small stucco house on Rio Frio Street.

Melba had broken the DEA's cardinal "no contact" rule. An inevitable convergence of events had begun.

*

Steve Morley twitched, surfacing from deep sleep to the sound of his electronic ring tone. He fumbled with the lamp and removed his cell phone from its charger. His wife gently snuffled and rolled over, before subsiding back into sleep.

A male voice rasped, "This is Karl Schmitzer. I hate to bother you at this late hour, but this is important. I had a visit from René Gaudet tonight. He demanded I tell him if Cecile Forest is alive."

Disconnecting after their conversation, Morley in his striped pajamas sat on the side of the bed in deep thought, looking at a midnight-dark window. Schmitzer had finally informed him of Melba's earlier call to him that she'd made before Christmas. Morley was aghast, and he struggled to keep his temper in check. Schmitzer, an ordinary citizen, had no legal obligation to report a contact from Melba, but why hadn't he called? Was his careful plan to snare Gaudet coming apart? Could it be salvaged? Could this wait until morning?

Steve Morley lay down, pulled up his covers, and closed his eyes.

*

Furious over how badly he'd handled the Schmitzer meeting, René Gaudet slammed into his house, rattling a few windows. He should've known the old goat wouldn't straightaway give him any answers. Yanking his burner phone out, he summoned a reluctant Jimmy Costanza to his house.

"Come on, boss," Jimmy whined. "It's late. Do we have to do this? I'm with my girlfriend."

"*You* have a girlfriend? Tell the woman good night and make it snappy. I'm not kidding, Jimmy."

When Mr. Gaudet laid down the law like that, Jimmy had no choice but to obey.

*

Cyril had the night off. Before leaving for the French Quarter, he'd checked the voice-activated tape recorder, placing it on the table directly beneath the open intercom in his quarters. He returned after midnight, inebriated, and fell into bed fully clothed.

Early the following morning, bleary-eyed, Cyril reviewed the tape of René's conversation with Jimmy Costanza and became instantly alert. Alarm prickled his scalp and tingled all the way to his fingertips. He felt horrible that he hadn't been there to report right away, but his dismay was mixed with excitement. He was agitated the entire time he spent serving Mr. Gaudet his breakfast, because he couldn't call the DEA until after the man left the mansion.

"You have a little hangover, Cyril? Rough night out?" Mr. Gaudet acted surly.

"Sir? I'm sincerely sorry, sir," he apologized. "I misbehaved a trifle, I'm afraid."

He pulled himself together, straightening his sleeves and concentrating on the job at hand, sighing with relief once Mr. Gaudet stepped into his limousine.

His surging adrenaline made it difficult for Cyril to speed dial the DEA, but he finally relayed the gist of the tape to Mr. Morley. Cyril prayed Morley would overlook his delay and focus instead on the emergency he had on his hands. He had no idea Karl Schmitzer had already alerted Steve Morley, and that Morley had made the decision to sleep on the information.

René Gaudet had ordered Jimmy Costanza to kidnap Melba—and Cyril had the recording to prove it. Costanza had a head start because he, Morley, had taken several hours to act on the information. If Gaudet's man was caught doing something illegal—and would admit his boss's involvement—it might help the DEA's case, but there was a problem. Neither Gaudet nor Costanza had mentioned drugs, and that was Morley's main interest.

In the morning, Morley took care of another bit of business on his way to the office by leaving a message for Tammy Avenetti.

"Take Cecile Forest's name off the suspect list for Barley Forest's murder. She had nothing to do with it. But keep supporting her."

Steve Morley returned to his thoughts after he disconnected, realizing his tardiness might've jeopardized his sole chance to arrest and question Costanza, a man close to Gaudet's illegal drug enterprise. Had his poor reactions ruined the whole pursuit? If Gaudet's goal was to eliminate the Forest woman, had Morley waited too late to mount a counterattack? They knew her general location—Puebla, Texas, and anyone with half a brain could suppose the quarry was connected to the library and start by looking there for her.

A question remained. How had René Gaudet discovered the secure location?

Morley checked his watch, which showed it was still early morning. Morley believed he had plenty of time, thinking Costanza wouldn't leave for Puebla until today or tomorrow. If he reached Puebla before a DEA team, it would take time to find Cecile Forest under her new name of Melba Columbo. Doubtless, Costanza could find the library, but he couldn't know whether she spent time there, nor could he know where she lived. There was no record of a Cecile Forest who lived in Puebla.

If Costanza found Cecile's home, maybe even discovered her new name, a sophisticated alarm system protected her there, but it wasn't enough. Too late, Morley realized he should have had a warm body guarding his witness. He'd been dismissive of her importance and now the predator was stalking the prey.

He resented having to scramble to protect Melba, since it was *she* who broke the cardinal rule of witness protection and called someone from her past. Morley's view was that Melba's actions made her fair game and he wanted to make the most of it.

Morley assumed he knew all the facts, leading him to believe there was enough lead time to snare Costanza without endangering Melba. Once the man was in custody, he would certainly flip on Gaudet, but they had to catch him first. If Morley raised the alarm, and Melba acted frightened, it would spook Costanza and the DEA would lose its advantage...but, if Morley left Melba dangling as bait....

He decided not to alert Melba yet. No sense in unnecessarily frightening her.

⁕

Morley strode into the conference room, where a small operations squad had assembled in uncomfortable chairs for an emergency briefing. Much as he loved his PowerPoint presentations, Morley hadn't had time to produce one this morning, for which the squad was grateful.

The required boxes of doughnuts and chicken salad sandwiches dotted the large table, interspersed with Styrofoam cups of half-drunk institutional coffee. Large commercial coffee dispensers, more Styrofoam cups, stirrers, a plastic jar of Coffee Mate, and colorful papers of sweeteners sat at the end of the room, along with cans of carbonated drinks screwed down in a bowl of ice.

Morley's bureaucratic process was painfully slow, cumbersome, and not at all intuitive. Every extra minute spent today was a precious minute of advantage gone forever. While Morley talked, Jimmy drove on, ever closer to Puebla and the library on Rio Frio Street.

The DEA chief twisted his wedding ring on his finger while relaying the latest developments in the Gaudet case.

Looking at each person, he said, "You are our most experienced team, which is why you're here. Take today to assemble your gear, eat a good supper, and get to bed early. You'll meet here tomorrow at dawn, say 0500 hours. You'll drive two vans to Puebla." His men were astonished by the delay in their departure, but there was a collective groan at not being able to sprawl in the no-knee-space vans.

Morley said, "It's not that bad, folks. Listen up. Your primary assignment is to protect Melba, but I want you to arrest Jimmy Costanza and return him here to me.

"We want Costanza to flip on his boss with enough evidence to dismantle Gaudet's drug empire and put him behind bars for a long time. Without Costanza's help, we'll have to keep plodding along."

Chapter Fourteen

Jimmy Costanza knew the early bird caught the worm. His success as a criminal had proved that.

After he left Mr. Gaudet's fancy house, Jimmy caught a few dreamless hours of shut-eye at home, departing for Puebla just before dawn. Sometimes he went for days with very little sleep. Today would be one of those times and he hoped to travel across Louisiana before

18-wheelers clogged the roadway.

Proud of his efficient advance preparation, Jimmy was good to go at a moment's notice, but he took a minute to go over everything in his mind. A packed bag of clothes sat in the trunk of his car. It rested on a rubber mat that concealed an arsenal of weapons hidden in the trunk's locked false bottom.

Jimmy wore typically anonymous clothing of khaki slacks and a blue plaid long-sleeved shirt under a lined, zippered jacket. His sneakers were dark and rubber-soled for stealth. Six-packs of water and a box of junk food, chips, and candy bars (glove purchased) sat in easy reach on the passenger seat of his meticulously clean vehicle. He snapped on a pair of surgical gloves and wiped down the car's interior, then put on leather driving gloves. Before he left the city limits, he refueled his inconspicuous beige turbocharged Chevrolet Malibu, then swerved up an access ramp onto I10.

In the past, Costanza had proven he was an excellent sleuth. He could ferret out Cecile Forest's location without breaking the law—at least, not right away. That skill was another reason he considered himself the best at his job.

As he approached Puebla, Jimmy fully appreciated the exuberant lavender-and gold-tinted clouds reflecting the early morning sun as it rose behind his car. He squinted against the brightness that escorted

Texas drivers on their daily commute, scrabbling in his glove box for his Polaroid sunglasses.

Taking the first exit into Puebla, Jimmy became one of the hundreds of fast-food customers that day, but he ignored the drive-through. Stiff after his long drive, he flexed his knees a few times and torqued his spine until it cracked before he pushed the door open, walking directly to the restroom.

He then placed his order, but not wanting to sit down, he took his breakfast outside where he ate a pretty good egg and sausage muffin and drank a cup of hot forgettable coffee while leaning against the hood of his Malibu in the bracing mid-January morning. Vehicles swished past on the nearby street. Customers thunked their car doors shut and he clearly heard the tinny voice of the drive-through clerk. Jimmy enjoyed the rush of a new operation, stoking his body with the fuels of food and caffeine. His brain revved to hyper-alert anticipation, and in his mind, he bulked-up like the Hulk, his muscles tense, inflated, and super-sensitized.

Like a good citizen, he tossed his debris in a trash receptacle, then punched the Rio Frio library address into the Malibu's GPS and swung out of the parking lot, driving just below the speed limit. He encountered little traffic, traveling against the flow of commuter traffic most of the way until he reached Rio Frio Street.

He missed the inconspicuous place on the first two passes, finding the narrow building on his third try. *Libraries are big buildings. What kinda place* is *this*? Jimmy climbed out of the car and dropped a quarter in a meter. *Parking is cheap here.* Trying to get a feel for the place, he poked around the plants of a landscape and flower business while he scoped out the library across the street. These plants were so different from the scrub brush in his native country. In New Orleans, he had planted colorful flowers and fruit trees, and here he saw more interesting varieties of vegetation. He debated the merits of buying a few of the more unusual ones and maybe a few hollies, but when a salesperson approached, he turned away and left, jaywalking across the street and casually sauntering inside out of the breezy day.

Glory had the first shift at the reception desk that morning and greeted Jimmy with a dazzling smile. "Can I help you find something? A video, maybe? A book or a magazine?"

Jimmy forced his mouth into an awkward smile. "No thanks, ma'am. Can I speak to Cecile Forest for a minute?"

"Cecile Forest?" Glory looked confused. "I'm sorry. Nobody by that name works here. And it's just me an' Melba, er... Miss Columbo this morning."

At that moment, less than twenty feet away Cecile Forest appeared like an apparition from between two bookshelves. Jimmy immediately recognized Cecile as the supposedly dead female attorney from Mr. Gaudet's law firm.

Jimmy hid his surprise and stuttered, "M-my mistake. Let me check that address." He dropped his head and frowned at his phone, pretending to double-check the address.

Damn, that's her. The same woman. Shorter hair, a white streak. Thinner. Prettier. Younger-looking? Maybe plastic surgery? Home run... Did she see me? I'm not sure.

He quickly snapped a photo. Lowering his head, his face obscured by the bill of his cap, Jimmy got the hell out of there, leaving without another word.

Glory frowned at the receding figure as he crossed the street. She scooped a stack of books, tucked them to her ample chest, and took them to her coworker. It was Melba's job to reshelve the books this morning.

"You know better than to carry such a heavy load, Glory," said Melba, in stern mock anger. "Use the cart. You'll hurt your back, girl."

Glory ignored her and gestured at the door. "Did you see the man who just walked out? I could swear he snapped your picture."

Melba jerked, her eyes wide. "Really?" Fear spasmed across her nerves, but she managed to laugh it off.

"Oh, I doubt that, Glory." Hyper alert to anything unusual, the tiny hairs on the back of her neck tingled. She looked in the direction where Glory's finger pointed, but there was nothing to see. Melba grimaced, wondering if someone had uncovered her through that call to Uncle Karl. If so, good. She had made herself the bait and things were finally moving. Should she wait a while to see what happened next, or should she call Tammy?

Glory was talking. "Funny, huh? And another funny thing. He was asking for somebody named Sybil—or something—Forest. I told him she didn't work here, so he left. Didn't even say thank you." Stunned speechless, Melba shook her head, her ears red and hot.

Jimmy slammed the car door and drove several blocks before circling back to park within sight of the library door, but far enough away that he couldn't be easily seen. Welcome warmth streamed through the windshield, predicting the coming spring. Jimmy texted his photo of Cecile Forest to Gaudet and waited for his next orders. Jimmy knew what *he* would do, but his boss might have other plans for the woman.

He checked out his location and found his surroundings acceptable. Shade trees overhung the recently swept street, always a plus this far south where falling leaves could be unsightly. This might be a nice place to goof off for a few days.

His girlfriend would like Puebla. Jimmy relieved his boredom with thoughts of reserving a nice hotel room for a surprise getaway with Jan. His mouth twitched into an unaccustomed smile, still dumbfounded that a classy woman like Jan Yokum found him attractive.

His phone buzzed, shaking Jimmy from his torpor. The name Gaudet flashed on the screen. He hit the *on* button and started talking without bothering to say hello.

"Boss, Barley's wife is alive. She changed her name, got a white streak in her hair. But it's her. What you wanna do?"

"Oh, man! I knew it." Jimmy heard Mr. Gaudet's obvious agitation, with maybe a little apprehension thrown in. Completely unlike his usual tough guy persona.

"You did some fast work there, Costanza. Great work, too," he said. "Stay out of sight for now. Find out where Cecile lives, and keep an eye on her. I need to think about what to do. If she went to all this trouble, maybe she's working with the feds. We gotta be careful here. I don't know what she knows, but she knows something. That idiot Barley musta blabbed." Mr. Gaudet's voice clicked off.

Disgusted at Mr. Gaudet's language, Jimmy tossed his phone onto the growing mound of empty candy wrappers on the passenger seat. He hated to hear people talk bad about the dead, but this was a job he needed, so he kept his mouth shut.

He made himself comfortable and settled down to wait until the library closed and he could follow "Melba Columbo" home. *That name. Caramba!*

He wouldn't risk leaving the stakeout, but it wouldn't be much of a loss not to drink more of the brown water Puebla called coffee. In New Orleans, Jimmy drank a strong brew, a real coffee you could nearly cut with a knife. Soon enough, he'd deliver the woman back home and he'd be able to drink all the coffee he wanted.

He periodically reloaded the parking meter, listening to the coins jangle in place, before resettling behind the steering wheel to watch the library door. He wasn't positive his prey would leave that way, but it was a chance worth taking. During his few moments inside the place, he had seen no other exits.

Jimmy Costanza had a prodigious brain, one that should've been put to use in more productive ways, but unlawful behavior had run in his family for generations. His father and his father's father were criminals, so that became Jimmy's goal, too. It was all about the family tradition.

Chapter Fifteen

Melba stood partially hidden to one side of the library's glass door, hoping to see the man Glory had described. *Who was he?* Could he be Barley's killer, and had he lingered? She saw nothing suspicious. Was she being overcautious, thinking he might be trouble? Maybe not. Should she tell Tammy, or wait? After five months, the DEA hadn't developed any suspects in her injury or in Barley's murder. It had become apparent to her that their bureaucracy was not geared to quick solutions. *That* was the problem, as Melba saw it, and that's why she had taken matters into her own hands. Now she was beginning to think she'd outsmarted herself.

Briefly alone, she called Tammy's number, happy when her call was answered on the second ring.

"It's Melba."

"Hey, girl. How you doing?" Tammy's voice reflected her big smile. "You caught me just in time. I'm leaving for more interviews at your office."

"Good. Listen, Glory told me a man came to the library this morning and took my picture. It worried me."

"Worried you? Who's Glory?"

"Glory is a librarian. That's not important, Tammy. This stranger said he was looking for Cecile Forest. Glory had no clue what he was talking about, but she watched him take my picture with his phone."

"No!" Tammy's voice squeaked. Her concern, though real, was staged. "Are you scared? I can call someone to guard you right away. Get off the phone and be careful, Melba. Where are you now?"

Melba's became the third call reported to Morley about the same issue. He had now heard from Karl Schmitzer, the lawyer; Cyril Smythe, the snitch butler; and now from the potential victim, Melba Columbo, via Tammy Avenetti. Steve Morley knew Melba's location had been discovered, but he had chosen to keep her uninformed, still dangling her as a temptation to René Gaudet.

Without being told, Melba knew it was her call to the man she knew as Uncle Karl that had instigated the stranger's visit.

⁕

Jimmy's main concern now was to remain alert after no sleep the night before, which he'd spent driving. He was a pro who had managed many sleepless nights. It came with the job. He shivered, but refused to run the car's heater, knowing the chill air helped him stay awake. He sang tunelessly with songs on the radio, blowing into his cupped hands to warm his nose. When the parking meter clicked its red 'expired' tag, he fed it more coins. He didn't care if he was seen.

Jimmy wasn't breaking the law, and he doubted anyone had noticed his behavior. If they did notice, the car had stolen Ohio plates that couldn't be traced to him, and he would be gone in a few hours. He scrabbled in his cardboard box for his favorite snack, Cajun-seasoned beef jerky, then tossed its empty wrapper on top of the others. Unlike most people, Jimmy enjoyed surveillance. It gave him the perfect excuse to eat the junk food he otherwise denied himself.

Twilight arrived so gradually, it took Jimmy a while to notice. With the advent of dusk, he began to get nervous, wondering if he had missed other exits. On the verge of giving up for the night, he saw the library employees emerge, his quarry among them. She wore a red coat and a dark knit cap. It surprised Jimmy to see someone who was hiding wear a noticeable color, but there was no doubt it was Barley Forest's widow. The bright scarlet would make her easy to track.

She looked at home in her surroundings, turning into the wind and walking the same direction Jimmy's car faced. Tucking her chin, she took long brisk steps, leaning forward with her shoulders hunched. Before stepping from the curb to scurry across the open intersection, she checked both ways, then continued along Rio Frio Street.

Jimmy gave the energetic woman a long head start before he pulled into the street. The red coat made a visible beacon in the distance. Melba covered a lot of ground, which helped Jimmy's pursuit, since his car could travel fast enough not to attract attention. He saw her flinch as two teenage boys came from behind and ran past her on the sidewalk, which made him believe she might be hypervigilant.

Jimmy nearly decided to drive past into the next block when Melba stopped at a small house, but he lifted his foot from the accelerator and eased to the curb instead. He watched as she unlocked a substantial-looking door and saw her glance back as though she felt herself being watched. Then she picked up some kind of dead plant by the entrance, and reached up to the wall just inside the dwelling.

He recognized the move, as her gloved hand stretched toward an alarm pad, and he chuckled to himself. No security alarm posed a problem for a master criminal. A couple of hours after she doused the lights, he would cut the electrical power to the house.

That would solve the alarm problem.

In the trunk of his car, Jimmy carried a set of universal keys with his other tools. One of them would unlock Melba's door. Now satisfied, he looped twice around the block, checking for indications of a posted guard. Seeing no one, he parked directly across the street from her door behind an old Dodge hazed with undisturbed dust.

He could see where automated street sweepers had swerved multiple times to avoid the derelict vehicle. There were no parking meters here—another plus. No trees, either—so different from the graceful arboreal tunnel he'd found at the other end of this same street. There was hardly any foot traffic in this neighborhood, though the weather was pleasant enough, just chilly.

Jimmy maintained his vigilant watch until he felt certain the Forest woman was in for the night, before leaving for a badly needed pit stop at a fast-food joint. Then he got back in his car and joined the drive-through queue to order, rather than eat inside at a table where his face might be remembered.

Returning to Rio Frio Street, he took it as a good omen that his former parking spot was still open, and pulled in to unwrap and wolf down a surprisingly delicious meal.

Chapter Sixteen

The shears severed the thick wiring, sparks illuminating the dark night air and making Jimmy squint. At a less tense time, he would've enjoyed the spectacular, dangerous arcs. The work was simple, really, much easier than less well-informed folks imagined. Clamping the heavy shears between his knees, he grinned, happy with himself as he shucked a pair of protective insulated gloves, stuffing everything back into his oversized backpack.

Only one insulated line, now cut cleanly in two, had provided power to the house. Its location, only a few dark, undetectable steps down the side stucco wall, made the line easy to reach. The lights were off and the security alarm was now neutralized. Jimmy's gleaming Cheshire cat grin was invisible in the darkness. Next up—ten seconds to unlock the front door. *Think deadbolts stop me? Not gonna happen.*

Within twenty seconds, Jimmy stepped quietly into the house and lowered his backpack to the floor, just inside the door for easy retrieval when he left. He noiselessly shut the door in case some sleep-deprived idiot walked by and noticed it open.

In one hand, he carried a heavy flashlight, the dual-purpose type used by police that could also be a weapon, if necessary. Its long, ridged, hard rubber casing made it easy to hold. Tape across most of the lens restricted light to a narrow beam. Jimmy flicked it on, holding the beam below window level. He quickly swept the slender shaft of light across the living room locating the furniture, doors, and hallway, and extinguishing it seconds later.

Carpet. Good. He padded in rubber-soled sneakers past the living area and risked a momentary flare from the flashlight, brushing his fingertips against the wall to verify his positioning. Property invasion thrilled Jimmy. He enjoyed its challenge and relished the rush he got when someone realized they were in his control, at his mercy. *This "Melba Columbo" woman was in for an ugly surprise. He could hardly wait to see the expression on her face.*

Chapter Seventeen

Melba's eyes snapped open, shaking off the remnants of a bad dream in which Barley raised his fist to hit her in the face. He meant to kill her this time. The room was pitch dark.

Where's my clock? What time is it? Dense blackness enveloped the room and she couldn't see the clock's large illuminated numbers. Her nose felt cold and she didn't feel the usual warm breeze of the heater blower. Wait—she *did* hear something—but it was the ticking metallic sound of the heater as it cooled. Melba, groggy, snuggled under the covers, feeling the unyielding protective bat she kept as a weapon in the bed beside her. *The power must be out, but it'll be on by morning.* She hoped Tremell was warm enough.

An unexpected scrape brought her fully awake. *Is that Tremell?* She patted the bedside table, feeling for her phone, before recalling it was on the kitchen counter being charged. She relaxed, thinking her guest was walking about for some reason—too sleepy to be frightened. *Did I see a light outside my room?*

Melba listened, frozen, as the opening door bent the carpet fibers, making them whish faintly as they rebounded. She swallowed a scream that bubbled at the back of her throat. Her fingers found the safety of her bat handle, gripping it tight as she eased off her covers. A *frisson* of alarm tensed her body. *Oh my God, they* did *find me! What can I do?* She slipped to the floor, dragging pillow and bat with her.

Terrified, she prepared for battle, realizing her weapon was useless in the dark. *Who is it?* Melba crouched, blindly held the bat in front of her with both hands, and began to scream.

*

Jimmy Costanza planned to sneak up on Barley's widow in her sleep. He would pin her with her covers to control her until he taped her mouth shut. He was annoyed that the boss wanted her returned uninjured to New Orleans for questioning. He could've questioned her right there in her bedroom. But now she was awake and his initial plan was no good. That made him furious. He had no idea how she'd heard him, but he was about to have a fight on his hands. *Nothin's ever easy. I hate fighting women. Not that it's a problem, but who needs it?* He prepared to do battle, ready for anything.

*

In the following weeks, Tremell couldn't recall what woke him. Maybe he was cold, because the ambient air quickly chilled when the heater quit blowing in Melba's spare bedroom. There was faint illumination in the room provided by the outside streetlight, but he couldn't see that well. He did remember how he'd been alarmed by the muted sounds, combined with an urge to protect his hostess.

Ms. Melba's high-pitched screams woke him completely. All he knew was he was wide awake, his heart thumping and his brain engaging in the ancient fight-or-flight impulse.

Tremell swung his legs over the side of his bed, sitting in the darkness and wondering what was going on. Did Ms. Melba have company? A scream escalated to a long shriek that abruptly cut off, followed by thumps and scrambling sounds. *That sounds bad. I ain't no hero, but I can't run from whatever this is.*

Jimmy thumbed on his flashlight and saw his target crouched screeching like a banshee in the corner, funny-colored hair all askew. Blinded by the light, she wildly swung a baseball bat, so ludicrous, Jimmy sniggered. *Like that's gonna stop me. What a joke!* He advanced inside the arc of her swinging arms and yanked the bat from her hands with a violent pull, flinging it across the room. Her weapon gone, Melba lashed out with fists and fingernails, her shrieks so piercing Jimmy was sure only dogs could hear them. He had a grudging new respect for the woman. She wasn't about to give up without a fight.

His jaw throbbing where he'd been hit and scratched, Jimmy stepped back to gain some leverage and, with his open hand he delivered a hard slap high on her cheek. It was a violent blow, sounding sharp as a gunshot, which snapped Melba's head to the side, spittle flying, and knocked her from her feet. She caromed off the wall and fell to the floor, grazing the corner of the bedside table. Stunned, her desperate screams muffled to a whimper.

Jimmy stood panting over her crumpled figure, his fists clenched, hating himself. "Just stop," he snarled. His father had hit his mother in the same way, and he had sworn never to hit a woman. *It had to be done.*

Melba cowered in a corner of the room, clad in flannel pajamas sprinkled with ridiculous candy canes, so silly-looking they made him want to hit her a second time. Her arms curled over her head for protection. Jimmy breathed hard, astonished by the fight put up by the delicate-looking female. Laying his flashlight down so that the beam shone on Melba, he pulled a roll of duct tape from a pocket. Hiking up his pants legs, he squatted by the moaning woman.

"Nobody can hear you. You might as well shut up and give me your wrists. We can do this the easy way or the hard way."

Jimmy heard the door behind him creak, but had no time to react as it slammed open. An animal as strong and sinewy as a *jaguarondi* smashed onto Jimmy's back. The blow deflected him away from Melba and jarred the air from his lungs. He wheezed, bouncing painfully on his face against the floor. Blood spurted from his broken nose. *Caramba! She had somebody in the house. This is harder than I thought.* He gathered himself, prepared to go back on the attack.

He found himself spread-eagled on his stomach before he could move, his assailant's knees pressed hard against his back. In the flashlight's long shadows, he saw a hand grab for the duct tape. Jimmy, though, was wiry and strong, and had plenty of fight left. He arched his back and bucked, getting his knees under him in a martial arts maneuver. Whoever, or whatever, clung to his back lost their grip and fell, losing the advantage, but sirens were growing louder as they approached. No way could he get caught.

Jimmy gathered himself, lurching from the shadowed bedroom, stumbling down the dark hall and flinging himself out the front door before the cops arrived to crawl unseen into his car. Fighting a strong urge to flee the scene, he waited until the responding officers entered Melba's house, then drove back to New Orleans, leaving the lights and sirens of Puebla far behind him. His body hurt all over, and now his brain hurt, knowing he'd failed because of his own mistakes. He hated to report to Mr. Gaudet, but he had to do it.

⁕

Melba cowered, curled in the corner, until Tremell coaxed her out, gently shaking her by the shoulder.

"He's gone, Ms. Melba. It's over. That guy took off like a jackrabbit." He picked up the intruder's heavy flashlight, surprised at the weight. He peeled off the duct tape that covered the lens to give them more illumination in the dark room.

She squeezed her eyes tight shut, rubbing her injured head and quaking with residual fear. "You saved my life, Tremell. Thank you. I thought sure he'd kill me. What did you do? How'd you scare him away?" Suddenly, she imagined he might still be in the house, asking, "He *is* gone?"

Silhouetted as Tremell was by the man's abandoned flashlight, she didn't see Tremell's relieved smile. "Yes. He's gone—for now, anyway, whoever he is."

Chapter Eighteen

Tammy Avenetti kicked the leg of the table where she sat, frustrated and disgruntled. She definitely didn't want to be in this damn room. She should be with the rest of the team in Puebla, not stuck in New Orleans with more interviews. Her carmine-painted nails clicked on the shiny expanse of the conference table as she waited for René Gaudet in the stuffy room. Mr. Morley's list of embarrassing, stupid questions lay in front of her. She checked her tape recorder again, for the third time. Superficially, the interview concerned Barley Forest's murder, but the far-ranging questions were designed to advance the investigation into Gaudet's illegal drug enterprise.

"Good morning." René entered the room from behind Tammy, chuckling when she jerked at the sound of his voice. He went to his customary chair at the head of the table, effectively undermining Tammy's carefully thought out plan to seat him across from her. Her ears reddened as she swiveled to face him. She was in danger of losing her control of Gaudet's interview before it even began.

Tammy lowered her pen beside her list, which now showed checkmarks beside each question, and changed her tape. The recorder's green light continued to blink, but Gaudet's interview was over, all Tammy's questions asked. She had a new appreciation for the lawyer's skilled evasions. He was a master of empty rhetoric, except for those questions specifically related to Barley and Cecile Forest.

Gaudet had leaned forward during those questions. His perplexed expression seemed to show complete ignorance about every facet of Barley's death.

Appearing completely earnest, he asked, "What the hell happened to Barley, Agent Avenetti? I still don't know. One day he and Cecile were here, and then I never saw them again. I treated them like they could've been my own children. I went to their funerals, you know."

Tammy *did* know. She had watched him weep during the burial service, and had repeatedly watched the video for telltale clues.

"I'm begging you to share any information you have about Cecile's death. She was a gifted lawyer and our office hasn't been the same since she died." Tammy thought the man was believable, catching only one suspicious glint in his eye. Either he was completely honest, or his was a virtuoso performance deserving a standing ovation. She was totally buffaloed.

"We sympathize with your loss, Mr. Gaudet," said Tammy, who was disappointed by his answers to her questions. She cleared her throat, saying, "That's the last of my questions and you're free to go." She held up her hand to stop Gaudet as he rose from his chair. "However, I want to interview the rest of your employees. There are only two left—your shop worker, Jimmy Costanza, and Cecile's assistant, Jan Yokum. Please ask Mr. Costanza to join me now."

Gaudet checked his watch, looking surprised at the time. His raised eyebrows and slack jaw showed what Tammy took to be genuine surprise.

"I'm so sorry, Agent Avenetti. He's not in the office today. Haven't you already interviewed Jimmy?"

"No," Tammy responded, her teeth gritted. "So far, he hasn't been available." Darn interviews were taking forever to finish up, she whined to herself.

"I reassigned him to Barley's job, delivering documents to one of our rural clients in the central part of the state. He won't be in today." Gaudet blinked without pause, a caution light should Tammy choose to see it.

Tammy exhibited annoyance, trying to increase Mr. Gaudet's uneasiness.

"I told your secretary—is it Alyssa?—yesterday there were three people left on my list, you, Mr. Costanza, and Ms. Yokum. She promised to have you all here for me and I'm not at all happy."

Gaudet stood, straightening his cuffs and looking at the petite blonde who wanted to make his life so miserable. He glanced at his watch, looking completely at ease again. "I sent Jimmy out, so you can blame his absence on me. Don't blame it Alyssa. I'll tell her to send Jan in to you right away." He strolled from the conference room, having regained his aplomb.

Tammy did a double take at the appearance of the woman who walked into the conference room. Could this be the same smiling person standing with Cecile Forest in the website photograph? Jan Yokum's mismatched clothes flapped around her emaciated frame. Her complexion looked an unhealthy yellowish-gray. She wore no makeup, her lips colorless. Her face was framed by oily, lank hair in need of a haircut, as though she couldn't deal with its upkeep. Above dark, bruised-looking smudges, her eyes were red-rimmed and looked hopeless.

She sat opposite Tammy, silently waiting, the corners of her mouth downturned in her unsmiling face. Tammy projected a warm sympathetic demeanor toward this grieving woman.

"Ms. Yokum—Jan. May I call you Jan?" Tammy received a silent nod in response, and gestured at the equipment on the table's surface.

"The tape recorder is on, so please give audible responses to my questions."

Jan apologized, her voice muted and whispery. "I'm sorry, ma'am. Yes, please call me Jan." Her eyes glistened.

Tammy hesitated, concerned about this latest interviewee, then ran quickly through the first innocuous questions designed to relax the interview subject, then began the more difficult inquiries.

"Jan, what kind of relationship did you have with Barley and Cecile Forest?" A flash of emotion, indefinable, perhaps fury, maybe regret, crossed Jan's face so quickly Tammy thought she might have imagined it.

"What...do you mean?" Jan's eyebrows bunched together over her nose. The corners of her mouth, clenched now in a thin line, drooped even more. Her chin quivered and her clasped hands twisted as she dropped them out of sight below the conference table top. Her extreme reaction startled Tammy into thinking this woman could know something important.

"You've worked with the Forests for several years. Did you socialize outside the office? Would you say you're friends?" Once again, she saw unshed tears gather in Jan's eyes.

Jan's voice roughened as she sneered, "I didn't know Mr. Forest very well, but I didn't like him."

She paused for several beats while she stared at her twisted hands, gathering her thoughts. "Cecile is who hired me." Tears wet Jan's cheeks.

"We were together all day every day. We became such good friends," she sobbed. "I love her and I miss her so much every day. I feel terrible." Jan put her head down on the table on her protective arms, sobbing in uncontrollable exhaustion.

Tammy was embarrassed that her questions caused Jan such pain. Sympathy welled up in her so that she went to Jan's side, pulling up a chair beside her, patting Jan's back until the poor woman's tears subsided. Tammy had no choice but to end Jan's interview for now. When she returned for the remaining interview with Jimmy Costanza, she would ask Jan the rest of the questions on her list.

Chapter Nineteen

When Jimmy Costanza cut the power source at the Rio Frio house, he had initiated a cascade of events.

Flashing red lights at the alarm headquarters signaled a power outage and pinpointed the customer's location. Three simultaneous calls followed the alert within seconds. The first call, directly to Melba Columbo's cell phone to verify the alarm, rang unanswered.

The second call alerted the police department's duty desk to order a safety check of Melba's Rio Frio house. Fortunately for Melba, this was a slow night, and two Puebla officers were patrolling less than a mile away. They made a U-turn and sped down empty streets, their siren howling and their flashing lights brightening the way.

In New Orleans, a DEA dispatcher fielded the third call just as his shift ended. He grumbled over his delayed departure, but punched in Steve Morley's code first, then Gene White's, linking the calls and automatically logging each of his actions.

Red-eyed and tired to the bone, Gene White was driving to Puebla when he received the alert from the alarm company. At that hour, he and about a thousand 18-wheelers—that's how it seemed—were the only vehicles on the interstate highway. After all these weeks traveling between New Orleans and Puebla, he felt he could make the trip with his eyes closed.

As he listened, his blood thrummed and he accelerated through the darkness. Other than the looming trucks he dodged his way through, he saw only the ghostlike shadows of trees and buildings along the roadway, appearing and quickly disappearing. Gene flipped the switch that turned on flashing lights in his front grille and back window, as he sped ahead and kept his eyes on the road.

A tripped alarm in the predawn hours was never a good thing.

⁂

The dispatcher's call dragged Morley from a dreamless sleep. Certain this concerned his witness, Morley tensed even before he answered, instantly aware he had miscalculated Gaudet's timetable. He felt concern for Melba's safety, though she'd brought this on herself.

This might be the break Morley needed—provided it was something more than the power outage of unreliable electric service in a little Texas town like Puebla. Rubbing sleep grit from his eyes, he had his dispatcher order the DEA helicopter made ready, then connect him to the Puebla PD duty officer. He told Puebla that should this be a bona fide break-in, the intruder would be armed and dangerous. He asked for more than a cursory safety check, requesting the responding officers enter the residence and be prepared for confrontation.

Struggling to get his pants on while he talked, Morley authorized the police to conduct a thorough search of the safe house and asked for a real-time verbal report from the officers at the scene when they'd secured the place.

Morley cinched his belt, then let it out a notch, pulled on a sweater emblazoned with the letters DEA, and hurried to his waiting car and driver for the ride to the smaller Orleans Lakefront Airport, where his agency helicopter waited, its rotors already spooling up.

Chapter Twenty

Melba sounded shaky, observed the officers. She struggled to find the voice she'd once used in courtrooms because she was recounting her own traumatic story this time.

She described the pitch dark and invisibility of the bedroom door as it opened. "The first thing was he said like something in Spanish, something like 'karomba.'" The officers nodded, knowing that was entirely likely in south Texas.

"I sensed that he was short, but a strong man. I can't tell you exactly what he looked like because his flashlight blinded me. I screamed until he hit me really hard. Then Tremell jumped him and pulled him away, but I never saw his face. He got away after that." She concluded her story by saying the attacker escaped out the front door.

The two police officers concentrated on her story, sharing occasional glances at each other. They remained jumpy, watching Tremell, their hands poised near their guns.

Melba touched Tremell's arm, adding, "This is my friend Tremell. He's a Puebla high school senior who sleeps in my spare bedroom. Thank goodness he does, because he's the only reason I'm alive."

Hearing her explanation for the young man's presence, the officers shifted their weight, relaxing their vigilance. One of them flicked the useless light switches hoping they would work, before finally reporting the power outage and requesting an emergency electrician.

The utility worker worked until the sun came up. Once the power was reconnected, the patrolman identified as Riley made an excellent, badly needed, large pot of coffee. After laughing off Melba's offer of help, with her permission he cobbled together a delicious-smelling breakfast of scrambled eggs, onions, and mushrooms for everyone, adding a second skillet of sizzling bacon and sausage.

Melba and Tremell sat on the sofa shoulder to shoulder, bleary-eyed in the middle of all the activity. They'd been told to sit tight and wait for the DEA, and not to disturb anything. Melba wondered how long the wait would be and Tremell was pressing a towel-wrapped plastic bag of ice against his nose.

"I think my nose might be broken. I can hardly breathe." Melba looked over and thought he was right when she saw a drop of blood splat onto his hand from the tip of his nose. Tremell was just about to ask Melba who she might be besides a librarian, when she spoke.

"You're bleeding," exclaimed Melba, looking at him and stating the obvious. "Lord!"

"It's cool, Ms. Melba. Stay calm." He threw a worried look at his friend, who was starting to turn blue around her mouth.

She was shivering despite her warm robe and candy cane flannel pajamas, apparently sliding into shock. Her speech sounded close to nonsensical babbling and her teeth were clenched tight. She held Jimmy Costanza's heavy flashlight in her lap. Melba's short auburn locks were in disarray and parted down the back of her head. Some of her hair was poking up like Alfalfa of the Little Rascals. Bruises bloomed on her cheeks and spread darkly, threatening to merge with smaller discolorations that smudged her chin.

Waves of excitement buoyed Melba enough to forget her exhaustion and her current state of shock, despite the night's violent altercation. Karl Schmitzer's meeting with René Gaudet and this encounter tonight finally exposed Gaudet as responsible for Barley's murder, which was what Steve Morley had suggested on that night many months ago. And it had taken her call to Karl Schmitzer to make it happen.

Rubbing her arms briskly as her shock began to abate, though her teeth continued chattering, Melba thought it a shame her attacker had escaped. She huddled with Tremell on the sofa and considered how she could pursue and capture him, with her final goal being his interrogation, followed by a long, long incarceration. All with or *without* the help of the DEA.

Melba couldn't care less about catching the killer on Barley's behalf, now that she fully understood their unhealthy relationship. Caring woman that she was, she'd at first worried that he'd suffered until she was told his death was instantaneous. Knowing that had left her free to worry about her *own* safety, though Melba wouldn't feel safe until the person who tried a second time to kill her was locked behind bars for a very long time.

The only question was whether she had enough courage to make her own decisions, rather than mindlessly do what someone else dictated. She'd started to make that happen. Melba bit her bottom lip and decided to forget about the DEA and follow her instincts.

Chapter Twenty One

The glittering frost on Puebla roofs and cars had slipped into the streets courtesy of a fully risen sun as Melba's handler, Marshal Gene White, pulled to the curb in front of her house. He was not at his best this morning, especially not after learning the bad guy had escaped and he'd missed the chance to be Melba's hero. Tired and surly, Gene took out his irritation by snarling at the police officers who had unwittingly usurped his role as her protector.

What made his irritability worse was Melba, tousled and looking gorgeous in her jammies, was casting a disapproving eye at his behavior from her perch on the couch. He tried to fake a sociability he didn't feel.

"How you doing, Melba?" he managed to say. "You banged up?"

She shrugged, waggling her hand in a so-so expression. "Nothing so bad that I can't manage. I've felt worse, and not all that long ago, either." Her smile was rueful. She returned her attention to a tall youth who sat beside her.

Gene bristled at the sight of Melba tending to the young man's scratches. He barked at the kid, using an officious, peremptory tone to cover his jealousy.

"Who the hell are you?" he said. "What are you doing here?"

The tall, strapping Tremell shrank back without a word. Melba immediately leapt to his defense, putting her hand on his shoulder.

"For your information, this man saved my life. You leave him alone. You've got some nerve, accosting people without getting the facts. You weren't even here, Gene." Melba and Gene stared at each other, both appalled—her, by her bad manners, Gene by a side of Melba he had never seen before.

*

Outside, a horrendous uproar penetrated the house. It brought the early morning activities of the entire neighborhood to a standstill and interrupted Melba mid-sentence. Gene and the police officers ran outside, Melba and Tremell following more slowly. A helicopter was kicking up a dust storm as it settled in the middle of the street, blocking traffic. Melba's neighbors emerged from their homes wide-eyed and stunned at the sight of whirring blades spooling down, the initials D.E.A. emblazoned on the helicopter's sides.

Before the blades had stopped spinning, one of the officers on-site requested patrol cars to block traffic on either end of the street. Steve Morley stepped onto the street, heading straight for Melba. She hadn't seen Morley since the meeting in her New Orleans hotel room. Unsmiling, he grasped her elbow and steered her back inside.

The reason Morley flew to Puebla was to transport a prisoner to New Orleans. Morley's plan, now that he was positive René Gaudet had ordered Barley's murder, was to convince the captive to cooperate during the return flight, suggesting his prison term could be reduced if he provided information about his boss's illegal drug activities.

Morley's presence and his flight were for naught because the intruder had escaped. He'd wasted his valuable time and the budgetary cost of the helicopter. He was not a happy man. Melba's location had been irretrievably compromised because she'd called her lawyer. That meant he had to start all over again with the US Marshals' help.

He started in on Melba before he slammed the front door shut.

"What were you thinking? You compromised your safety the minute you called Schmitzer. To top it off, you nearly got yourself killed."

Melba yanked her arm out of Morley's grasp, flushing a dark red. She kept her anger in check and countered, saying "Shouldn't you be thanking me instead of yelling? You're so hung up on busting René and his alleged drug business, you haven't even tried to find Barley's killer for the last five months."

At Melba's angry retort, Morley stumbled back a step, unused to criticism, especially criticism with undeniable truth, but he accepted the blame with a nod, taking a deep breath before he replied.

"We know it was definitely Gaudet who intercepted your call somehow, we know that. Equally, we know you're in more danger now than you were before.

"I'm making tonight your last night in Puebla. I'll move you to a new place tomorrow, but we need a few hours to pull everything together."

"Absolutely not." Melba looked furious, but she sounded reasonable. Her jaw was set and stubborn, not the same tentative woman Morley had first met in New Orleans months earlier.

"I'm staying here, Steve." Morley noted Melba's growing confidence, no longer using an honorific and his last name. "You can't plop me in a strange town for who knows how long. I love my friends here and I like my work." She glanced at Tremell standing on the far side of the room, his eyes wide. "Tremell can protect me. He did a wonderful job tonight."

"Tremell? This is Tremell?"

Melba beckoned the teenager to her side. Tremell carefully kept his eyes on the floor.

"Steve, this is the man who saved my life. Tremell's graduating from high school this year and he's been staying in the guest room...to... to protect me." Standing in the background, Gene White looked startled.

Morley knew he'd been remiss in not assigning someone to guard Melba. Knowing that, he felt he couldn't challenge Melba's efforts to protect herself. Instead, he whirled to confront Marshal White.

"Did you know about this, Gene?"

"No, sir." Gene planned to say more, but trailed off when Mr. Morley stopped him with a raised hand.

"Tremell can stay here, but tomorrow Gene will take you to a new place, and that's final." The brusque DEA chief turned without another word and left, boarding the helicopter for an emptyhanded flight home. Disgusted, he messaged his en route team on the highway below to make a U-turn and return to their base in New Orleans.

The DEA team aboard the "people mover" van left the interstate at the Lake Charles, Louisiana, exit, where they found a seafood restaurant offering a feast of superb Cajun seafood to fortify them before the long drive back home.

Morley's helicopter rotors pushed chilly gusts against the gathered crowd. They shielded their eyes and watched the craft levitate, becoming a small speck amid a whirlwind of Texas dust. In moments, the street returned to its usual sleepy self, leaving one anomaly—a small, decrepit truck parked not far from Melba's stucco Rio Frio house. It would soon be gone.

Morley had left explicit orders behind him when he departed, and the lives of those individuals affected would change... again.

After the DEA chief departed, Gene White stood rooted in Melba's living room in the midst of a sudden silence. He stared in confusion at Tremell, who had returned to the sofa, and whose head drooped almost to his knees.

Gene was shaken by his awareness of his deep attachment to the woman he was charged to protect. He thought about Melba constantly, with the realization that he loved her, wanted her, and had to have her. He was unshaken in his belief that she felt the same way about him.

This young man Tremell, though, had created some kind of danger to Gene. Why was Tremell here in Melba's house? She was twenty years older than Tremell, but he had the full height of a man, and he was obviously fit and looked powerfully strong. When Morley learned Tremell had saved Melba's life, he had pulled Tremell into a brief private meeting.

*

Tremell had been afraid to look directly at the man who stood in front of him, unable to gauge how much trouble he was in. The way people deferred to this guy meant he was an important man. After Ms. Melba explained the role Tremell played during the night, Mr. Morley ordered everyone to leave the room except him, and everyone left without saying a word. Tremell guessed Mr. Morley might send him to jail and that would end his dream of college.

"Look at me, son," Morley said. He had a booming voice full of authority. Tremell thought the man would make a great high school principal. He moved only his eyes, keeping his head ducked low.

"You remind me of myself, kid. Okay, you're taller and fitter and a different race—but I was like you, back in the day. Tell me your story and don't skip anything.

"Who are you? Where's your family?" Morley peppered Tremell with questions and listened until he knew a great deal about the youth's life. When the questions finally ceased, Tremell was emotionally wrung out. His painful secrets, many of which Melba had never learned, had all been scoured from their hiding places, leaving his eyes damp with unshed tears.

Morley stood with his hands on his hips, thinking hard. He placed a hand on Tremell's shoulder and told the teenager what he would like to do.

"You saved Ms. Columbo's life." Using the royal *we*, he said, "We are in your debt and we want to give you a little help." Tremell's smile grew as Morley described what he had in mind.

Dazed with his good fortune, Tremell returned to the living room and tapped the dozing Melba.

"Listen to this, Ms. M. Mr. Morley says I can stay here unless they need the house. That could be soon, but it might be never."

Melba's gentle smile lit her face as she squeezed her young friend's arm.

"That's great news, Tremell! You deserve it for saving my life last night."

"Yeah, but I didn't say anything about being terrified. That dude was really strong."

"Tell me!" Melba laughed. "I know."

Tremell said, "The DEA will keep lights and water on, the alarm, too, in case the bad guys come back for you. I have to take care of the place. The bad part is he says you have to leave tomorrow, Ms. M. And I can't talk about *any* of this until he gives me permission. What the heck is going on?"

The two friends talked for a while longer. Tremell eventually retreated to his favorite chair in the room, thrilled to the core, his exhaustion forgotten in his thoughts about his new future. Sitting quietly on the sofa, Melba contemplated her own.

Before he too left the Rio Frio house, Gene White barked orders at Melba to be ready for departure early the next morning, frustrated at being upstaged by Tremell. He delivered his words with a glower, his forefinger stabbing the air to punctuate each brusque remark. He then stomped out into the early afternoon. Melba and Tremell smiled at each other, amused at Gene's petulant behavior.

"He don't act much like a federal officer, Ms. M," said Tremell.

Melba shrugged, giving Gene the benefit of the doubt. "He's been up all night just like us, Tremell. Exhaustion changes people." She patted the sofa cushion beside her.

"Come sit with me, Tremell. You and I have something to talk about." He walked over and plopped next to his friend.

"What?" Tremell's exhaustion was forgotten in the excitement of his day, his intelligent eyes sparkling with new anticipation.

Melba said, "I'm grateful for the help the Marshals have given me, but this isn't my real life. I already *had* a life, and I need your help to get it back. I want to leave witness protection... tonight...secretly, without the DEA knowing. They don't care about finding the man who's been stalking me—the same man who killed my husband. *The DEA's* only interested in taking down my old boss's criminal drug business."

"I don't get why you can't let it alone, Ms. M," said Tremell. She nodded that she understood.

"I don't know why this is so important to me, Tremell. My husband was *not* a nice man, especially to me. Maybe it's just me thinking a wife should 'honor' her marriage. I refuse to lower my standards to the ones my husband had. I want to stand up to adversity." If she could do that, Melba thought, it would be a giant step forward in her maturity.

"The man who killed my husband tried to kill *me* at the same time. And he tried it for the second time last night. Unless he's caught, he could try to kill me again. But the DEA doesn't care about catching him, they only care that I'm alive to testify against my old boss. Finding who attacked me is secondary to their mission, but I can't accept that, and I plan to do something about it."

What Melba was saying was so bizarre, Tremell couldn't absorb the words. He sat down, his hands clutching at his short curls. "But what are you talking about? Where will you go?"

"I'll be long gone before Gene shows up in the morning. I hate to ask you to lie, but you can tell him you didn't hear a thing."

Though he begged, she wouldn't tell Tremell where she was headed because it would mean fewer lies, but she had no firm idea, anyway. She would think it through once she was on the road. She knew one thing. She had to be near New Orleans—where everything began.

Melba curled Tremell's familiar old key ring into his hand and gently pushed him to the door, asking him to park her truck in front of the house while she packed her things. She watched him walk away, already missing him, and blinked away the sudden haze in her eyes.

Tremell had reawakened Melba's capacity for affection. She appreciated his company and his upbeat, bright intelligence. Regardless how physically far apart they would be, Tremell had a forever place in her heart, and the closest thing to family Melba had had since her great-aunt died. That included her husband, who had never tried to be part of her family.

She looked around the comfortable, warm living room of the house that had served as home for so many months. She would miss this as much as the Rio Frio Library and the wonderful sisters who welcomed her into their lives. When this was over, Melba vowed she would return some day as her real self and reintroduce herself to her friends.

Sighing, she headed to her bedroom, carrying a box of garbage bags from the kitchen to use as luggage. She'd take only a few Melba-type clothes and some makeup, adding a few items from the kitchen—one fork, one knife, one plate, etc. Working as Melba Columbo for the very last time, she bent to her task.

If her goal was to be well down the road before the sun slipped below the horizon, she had no time to waste.

The setting sun would be at her back this time, the oncoming dark lying in wait.

*

During her long drive, Melba revisited her months in Puebla. From the very first, she had deplored the lack of trees and flowers, and she still did. But she'd learned to appreciate the neighborhood's spare landscape, which forced her to focus on the pleasing pastels of the stucco houses, their terra cotta tile roofs undulating down Rio Frio Street like the waves of the sea.

She had reminded the forlorn Tremell to leave a peanut butter smear on a window edge to snag bugs for the resident chameleon.

"I can handle that, easy. I'm gonna miss you, Ms. M," he'd answered. He rubbed at a speck of dust, or a lash, something that made his eyes water.

She had struggled to smile, reaching up to give him a hug. "Keep being your wonderful self, Tremell. I'll see you soon."

There were things she would always miss. Things like her Rio Frio neighbors who had gradually become her friends over the past weeks and months. Their delicious TexMex food, too. Most of all, she would miss her fun and rewarding library family—Gloria, Joyce, and ReJoyce.

Melba knew her destination for tonight. She'd searched Airbnb online at the library and had located an appealing residence in a small town within reasonable commuting distance of New Orleans. Because the place was hundreds of miles east of Puebla, her drive today would be a lengthy one.

Chapter Twenty Two

To confuse the DEA, Melba had taken modest evasive action. Driving west out of Puebla in a northerly direction toward the interstate highway, she stopped at every ATM she saw, three in all, carefully parking her truck outside camera range. At each stop, she lowered her head and withdrew the maximum allowable funds. She wasn't foolish enough to think she wouldn't be recognized, but she gained extra time and hoped a search for her would point in a westerly direction. No one would notice her absence until Gene showed up the following morning.

By that time, Melba would be off the highways and well hidden.

Melba shed more than dust when the old truck left Puebla behind. She rid herself of the Melba Columbo persona which was never a comfortable fit. Her real name, Cecile, was well-known to the DEA and it wasn't feasible to keep, but that was never the plan.

Using a pay-by-the-minute phone purchased with cash, she had called Karl Schmitzer for his help a second time a few weeks before. He was hesitant to risk DEA wrath again after his recent dressing down, but Cecile explained why she needed him.

Karl had reluctantly agreed, accepting a list that included documents similar to those the DEA used for the Melba Columbo identity. This time, the driver's license and social security card were in Cecile's childhood nickname and her father's—and her original—surname. Bank accounts were unnecessary, since she had access to the remainder of Melba's account. That and the trust fund controlled by Schmitzer were her money.

Melba had been astounded by Karl's contacts. Within days of their conversation, a package arrived by courier from one of

Schmitzer's former clients. The contents of the parcel now sped along the highway concealed in a waterproof packet under the truck seat.

Her new identity, or rather, her old one—Sunny Valois—was a perfect fit. And why wouldn't it be? It was her own name.

She was happier than she had been in years. First, she would establish a base of operations and focus on finding the killer before he found her again. Entering the Airbnb address into the phone's GPS, she sped toward Louisiana and another temporary new home.

Sunny thought briefly of her former best friend, Mary Ann Fitch. Mary Ann's affair with Barley had been the catalyst for the recent drama of Cecile's life, causing dramatic changes, one of which *ended* life for Barley and released Cecile from her misery.

Chapter Twenty Three

After his good night's sleep, Gene's morning was going very well.

He'd had a big, delicious breakfast at the motel, and now approached the day's *pièce de résistance*. He was about to drive several hours with the lovely Melba by his side, taking her to her new home in Pinewood, Louisiana, a location closer to headquarters than Puebla, Texas, thank God.

Gene spared a thought about the monster bruises he'd seen on Melba's jaw the day before. That poor sweetheart had been traumatized by her intruder, but he would teach her how to stay safe. He yearned to hold Melba's soft hand, but he had to hide his feelings.

Melba's program was unusual in many aspects, but the US Marshals Service forbade relationships between marshals and the witnesses in the Witness Security Program (WITSEC). Gene would at least lose his job and perhaps spend prison time if Gaudet's lawyer used Gene's relationship with Melba to get his client off the hook. He hated to conceal his feelings for Melba, but it was the right thing to do.

Obsessive protectiveness surged through him. She was always so docile, so tranquil, so quiet and ladylike. His every thought centered on Melba—embracing her, inhaling her perfume, imagining the smooth softness of her skin as he lay with her in a darkened bedroom.

Wait! Thunderstruck, Gene paused in the midst of his erotic thoughts. Why hadn't he realized Melba already loved him like he loved her? She smiled, happy every time he showed up. Every week, she cooked and served special meals and great desserts. She listened to his every word, laughed at all his jokes, and waited on him. Before he walked out the door for the long drive back to New Orleans, she always touched his arm and hugged him goodbye.

It's fated. Being together is inevitable. Gene's relief scoured away all the months of tension that had built up. The way ahead was clear.

He pulled to a stop outside Melba's Rio Frio house in his freshly washed and vacuumed car. He checked his teeth in his car's clean side mirror, then jumped out.

Yep, all good. Let's get this show on the road.

OAK ALLEY

Chapter One

In Louisiana, spring brackets parts of May and June, lasting approximately a month. No one can predict the day summer slams the door shut on spring, but once that happens, the long sizzling days are "large and in charge" for six months or more.

⁕

The old truck shivered and wheezed, its brakes squealing as it vibrated to a stop. Sunny Valois stretched and yawned a tired, careless yawn that caused her to yelp and cradle her tender chin. She fussed, laughing at herself. The intruder's hard fist had frightened her and slugged her silly no more than a day ago.

She rubbed her jaw, and through her bug-spattered windshield she scrutinized a picturesque house that seemed to pop straight out of a fairy tale.

Wow! This hits the jackpot if it's the right place. The house nestled deep in a dappled glade, flanked by greening grasses, immersing Sunny in a welcome world of natural beauty. Unlike the Rio Frio house that opened onto a city sidewalk, this place sat at the end of a meandering drive among shrubs and trees covered with tender new chartreuse leaves.

In a Tudor style reminiscent of old English architecture, the steep-pitched roof rose above a door sheltered by a cantilevered canopy. A whimsical stone griffin perched on the eaves to guard the house. The building's exterior was half gritty old stone and half thick lap siding the particular shade of damp moss after a gentle rain. The shake roof had aged to a charcoal color that went well with the dark gray trim and the winding brick walkway that ended at three wide brick steps up to a generous landing.

The front door was a glossy pumpkin color. The knocker featured the brass head of a lion holding a ring in its mouth. Fizzing flames flickered in the oversized brass lanterns bracketing the door at eye level. *Charming. Best of all, it's close to New Orleans. How sad to have to experience this all alone.*

She shook out the kinks in her legs and hauled the first bag up the brick steps, feeling a cool spring breeze bite through her clothing. Had her breath left a dissipating cloud behind? Doubtful, not this far south.

Sunny stood, listening to rustling leaves on the verge of being replaced by spring green. She shivered. What she would give to share such things as wind through the branches with someone she loved. The trees murmured a muted welcome to a visitor who believed trees were her talismans. She inhaled fresh country air and her loneliness floated away as she renewed her faith that the trees would keep her safe.

Following instructions, Sunny found the iron filigreed key hidden behind a shoe scraper on the brick landing. The key turned easily in the oiled lock.

Oak Alley had a history. In the early 1800s, an itinerant blacksmith collected acorns as he traveled. When he returned to his log cabin, he and his old mule plowed shallow black furrows along the dirt path and he dropped in the acorns. Copious Louisiana rainfall and hot summer days encouraged the tender acorns to sprout and grow. Tall and strong years later, their branches stretched over the well-trodden path, now turned to road, and their shade cooled parched, dusty travelers. Many years later, the village could hardly name itself anything other than Oak Alley.

As lovely as the village might be, Sunny's plans would allow her to spend little time in the pleasant place.

*

Sunny stepped through the door onto gleaming wide plank floors, pausing to absorb her new surroundings. Her fatigue evaporated as she looked around the pleasant room.

A conversational grouping of club chairs upholstered in hunter green linen clustered near a stone fireplace that anchored the front wall. A brocade of English fox hunts covered the sofa, its front edge on a fringed Oriental carpet. A large oil painting of a country landscape hung behind it, flanked by small portraits. On the antique chests used as end tables, tall lamps cast strategic pools of light. The magical impression of the exterior flowed right into the house.

"Beautiful," Sunny breathed. She set her burden down, pushed her short dark auburn hair with its white streak off her forehead, and went back for another load. She could explore the place later.

Several trips later, twilight had faded to full dark and Sunny had hauled the truck's contents into the house, including the extra items she had purchased on her drive when she had spied a large electronics store and a Dick's Sporting Goods sitting side by side.

She hunched over, exhausted, to stretch her back, facing a towering mound of boxes and bags. Nothing had made it past the front room yet, but she had only enough energy to ignite the fireplace's gas logs.

Patting herself on the back for buying a burger and milkshake on the way into Oak Alley, Sunny sat cross-legged in front of the glowing fire and devoured her meal and milkshake. Tomorrow, on what she laughingly called her first day out of captivity, she had big plans.

Her hunger satiated, Sunny sank onto the sofa and stretched out for a brief rest. Staring into the fire and gathering together the threads of her thoughts, Sunny decided to explore her new home...in a minute. Her eyes closed to the lulling patter of rainfall on the roof, blinking awake with the rising sun, roused by the flickering of the gas log fire. She had a painful crick in her neck and her mouth was cottony dry.

She stretched and looked for a bathroom, then wandered from room to room, reminded of her bungalow in New Orleans. Alone again, she yearned to share this latest adventure with one of her friends, but until she found Barley's killer and saw him punished and herself free of fear, she was on a mission.

It was a singular task, best undertaken on her own. No husband, no family except Odette and Uncle Karl—who weren't really relatives. No friends here in this town, this clump of houses in the country, nobody at all. The thought sobered Sunny, but her self-assurance had grown over the past months. She would manage, even if she had to wrestle each day from a monster fear. Aunt Hattie's voice was loud in her ear, saying take life each day as it comes.

Chapter Two

In the DEA spy center just below the Authement & Gaudet law offices, state-of-the-art communications equipment hummed to life. René Gaudet steamed in his office as Jimmy Costanza tried to excuse his botched assignment.

"They knew I was coming, see? This huge gorilla of a *hombre* hid in Ms. Forest's closet. He nearly killed me before I slipped away. I hurt all over."

His job had been a simple one: capture Cecile Forest, who was pretending to be somebody else, and bring her back to New Orleans. She should be at René's warehouse this very moment, waiting for René. Gaudet wanted—no, needed—to know why Cecile had faked her death and gone into hiding. Exactly how much did she know about René's illegal drug business?

René was nervous about Jimmy's ruined task. Preoccupied, he barely noticed the rain pelting his office window as he stared through it. Copious annual rainfall in New Orleans left the city feeling greasy and slick, bruising the ubiquitous magnolia blossoms, but he had more important things on his mind. René twisted his lips to control his temper in front of the sagging Jimmy, managing the feat only with effort. He'd shown an extreme lapse in judgment when he lambasted Jimmy for making a mess, yelling at him until his ears were as abused as his sore body.

The more René talked to Jimmy, the more the DEA eavesdroppers, clustered in their hot, cramped room, had high-fived each other. They heard as Gaudet ordered his car and slammed from his office, leaving a demoralized Jimmy behind.

Their target had openly admitted an attempted kidnapping, and so had his henchman, Jimmy Costanza. Whether or not Gaudet revealed a scintilla about criminal drug activity, once Costanza was under arrest, he would tell the DEA everything he knew to avoid a long prison sentence.

⁕

When Steve Morley stormed back into the DEA office, his staff viewed their boss with alarm. The pouches under his eyes were darker and growing baggier as his troubles mounted. His material witness had vanished from Puebla. Gene White had discovered Melba Columbo's disappearance only when he arrived to escort her to a new safe location.

Gene had rung the doorbell several times before a sleepy Tremell padded to the door, barefoot and shirtless.

"What you want, man?" The teenager had slept hard, exhausted by his exertions of the previous sleepless night.

"Where's Melba? It's time to go."

Tremell shrugged, stepping back as Gene pushed past to look for his protectee. He approached Tremell, his fists clenched with a menace that put the teenager on the defensive. Tremell's voice shook and he was on the verge of tears.

"I don't know where she is, Mr. White. I didn't hear nothing." Melba was gone, having taken some clothing but very little else.

Time and Gene's heart stuttered to a stop before he shook himself back to life and called the DEA office. They could run a search that might uncover Melba's escape route.

⁕

She had withdrawn funds from three separate ATMs in Puebla within minutes of each other sometime before daylight. Each terminal captured a fuzzy image of her face. Gene wondered how she was traveling, because she didn't have a car and no vehicle was visible at any ATM.

A check of all the car rental companies came up negative. Nor could anyone tell in which direction Melba fled, but the locations of the ATMs trended westerly. If she made it to Houston, she was likely lost to the DEA.

Steve Morley was stymied. Melba's escape—what else could he call it—was unexpected. It made him first frantic, then furious. Morley's staff heard him moan, head sunk in his hands, when they passed his door.

The chime of an incoming email forced his eyes up to his computer screen, where he saw a message from the snoop crew at René Gaudet's law office. The disheartened man read the cover message, which gave his eyes a new sparkle. He clicked the attachment, which was a surveillance file of Gaudet's conversation with Costanza. Morley realized this changed everything.

His grand plan to catch Costanza kidnapping Melba in Puebla had been torpedoed, shot out of the water. But the tape of the overheard discussion with Gaudet when Costanza returned gave the DEA probable cause to arrest both men. Alone in his office, Morley laughed out loud, his pudgy midsection quivering. His careful plans, years in the making, had finally trapped his prey. The DEA had benefited from Melba's meddling after all, and the payoff was worth every second, all the work, and all the patience.

Morley celebrated, but he would have to run it by the prosecutors to be sure his case was airtight. It might be too soon to arrest René Gaudet. He leaned back in his chair, hands behind his head, and daydreamed of shrugging on his holstered gun and taking a team to make an arrest.

Gaudet's head would snap up to see a vaguely menacing, rumpled figure wearing a dusty-looking hat as Morley pushed his door open.

"Get outta my office," Gaudet would say. "Who the hell are you?"

Morley would snort. "I'm your worst nightmare, that's who." And then he'd say, "René Gaudet, you are under arrest..." The rest of the words would sound jumbled and the picture would blur as Gaudet stared down a long, dark tunnel. Morley would reel off the crimes Gaudet had set in motion over several years and, in some cases, committed himself.

They would leave the mansion by the front door, to give gawkers a chance to see the billionaire hauled off to jail.

There would soon come a time to arrest Gaudet, who was the worst of the bad guys. Morley could hardly wait. Like his TV hero Columbo, Steve Morley would have the bad guy in a corner. It would be time to write "The End" and roll the credits.

Morley surfaced from the daydream, his positive frame of mind restored, ready to search for Melba.

She was the material witness whose testimony could cement the guilty verdict when Gaudet went to trial. She was smart enough to realize she'd been dangled as bait without being told and she was frightened and angry because of it, knowing whoever tried to kill her was still out there, looking for her. The DEA had better find her first.

Chapter Three

The law discovered Sunny in an unexpected manner on only her third day in her new home.

The day before, after wandering the rooms of her compact Oak Alley house, Sunny had written out a list of her goals and a plan she hoped would achieve them. She knew this written plan, made with the help of a map of New Orleans streets, would almost certainly change as the days passed. Night came, and after a light dinner and a glass of white wine, she tumbled into her comfortable new bed, still feeling bruised, and still recovering from the fright she experienced back in Puebla.

On the morning of her third day, Sunny woke refreshed and took the time to savor an aromatic cup of coffee while she sat barefoot out on the kitchen steps. Wisps of morning fog draped, curling through the tranquil trees crowding the dewy grass. How any homeowner could leave such beauty was beyond Sunny's comprehension. The snug house nestled into the surrounding trees, its large windows so private they needed no coverings. She was grateful for that, loving the seclusion. Smiling, she relished the serene world glinting in the dawn.

Although reluctant to abandon her peaceful vista, she at last made her way inside to scrub herself clean and review her plans. She would drive into the city and observe René's office while remaining unobtrusive, hoping for any kind of break.

By the time she towel-dried her hair and pulled on a lightweight beige sweater and cordovan twill slacks, her thoughts were organized. She pushed into comfortable brown shoes, ready for her drive into the city at the end of the morning rush hour.

The obscenely loud doorbell rang, making Sunny jump. She ran to the door, choking down the last bite of cream-cheese-slathered bagel. Through the peephole she saw a tall, uniformed policeman pinching the bridge of his nose. She dabbed the corners of her mouth and opened the door, realizing too late that the impulsive action was incautious.

"Can I help you?"

The man was about her age. When he first saw Sunny, his eyes widened, then crinkled in an attractive, pleasant smile. His light cologne preceded him across the threshold. Mmm, she thought.

His taupe uniform, crisply pressed, covered a toned physique. The officer's shirt sported a gleaming metallic shield and, behind him, an official-looking police cruiser was visible at the foot of the steps. He blinked, and Sunny realized that her appearance was a surprise to him.

"Just checking in, ma'am. The homeowner asked me to welcome you to town. Make sure you got in okay. Told me you'd be here for a while." He was uncomfortable like it was an interruption to his day, which it most certainly was.

"Thanks," said Sunny, thinking *his ears look red. Is he blushing? How cute.* "Nice of you both. I'd offer you a cup of coffee, but I'm running late. Have to get to the city," attempting to send the man on his way. She kicked herself for blurting any information to this stranger, regardless how handsome he was. Perversely, she thought the man could be an ax-murderer for all she knew. She stepped back, but he spoke before she could shut the door.

"Ma'am?" His hand moved toward his gun. She gulped, the hair on her arms stiffening, then felt foolish, annoyed with herself when he retrieved his wallet and removed a card. He held it out to her.

"My card, my numbers. You can always reach me. I live close by and I'm the one-man Oak Alley 24/7 police force whenever I'm needed."

"Thank you." Sunny took the card, looking up. The man's smiling brown eyes and lean, suntanned face made it difficult to look away.

Taller than average, he had pleasant, regular features. His easy smile caused the skin at the outer edges of those hazel eyes to crinkle. Sunny, widowed less than a year, was appalled by her visceral reaction to the stranger. She mentally regrouped. She had to concentrate, get on the road.

Once the door closed, she checked the policeman's card. The name read David Kelley, Chief of Police, Village of Oak Alley.

⁕

The monocular Sunny had bought in the hunting department of the big Academy store she'd discovered, had proved handy on more than one occasion, when she'd sleuthed in the right place. Like now. Hidden behind overgrown azaleas across the street from her old law office she saw her former paralegal, Jan Yokum.

Jan, magnified by the monocular and looking very thin, surprised Sunny by kissing a man before she entered the building. The way the man moved seemed familiar somehow, but Sunny didn't recognize his face at all. Sunny hadn't been in New Orleans for several months and she certainly hadn't known him before, had she?

Her paralegal-slash-friend's apparent relationship was new to Sunny but she was being foolish. A lot could happen in that time. Yet this unknown man alarmed her enough to make her arm hairs tingle. She needed to know about their connection, but how could she do it without exposing herself? She had to think.

Every morning before she drove to the city, Sunny read the city newspaper online, but there were never articles related to any investigation into Barley's death—no headlines, no arrest records, and nothing in the general news. Barley's death as news had disappeared a year ago into a black hole, out of sight and out of the city's collective memory. It very much preyed on Sunny's mind, much as she wanted to forget everything about those past ten—no, now almost eleven—years. That the murder was unsolved wasn't so much a matter of grief—if it ever really had been—but more the principle of the thing. Killers who took the lives of others, Sunny believed, should never escape the consequences of their crimes.

As weeks passed, Sunny saw that some people regularly lurked on the street outside René's office. She suspected they spied on René, too—not for the reason she did, but they could be a problem for her nonetheless. A DEA spy might interrupt her private investigation before she discovered something to pursue.

After yet another scorching day, Sunny drove home to Oak Alley, oblivious of the scenic, winding road she followed along the bayou levee. She was discouraged. This particular week had been an unproductive one watching Gaudet's home and office. Her sleek pair of washable white trousers and her sleeveless white cotton shirt weren't so sleek or neatly tucked in any longer. The grosgrain belt, striped red, white, and blue, to please New Orleans taste buds, was wilted from the heat. But her mood lifted when she turned into her long driveway, as it did every day. The yard looked beautiful. Jasmine ground cover perfumed the edges of the curving driveway with fragrant white blooms, and her rented house offered a lovely welcome.

Inside the cool house, Sunny dropped her keys, tortoiseshell sunglasses, and a crinkled bag of burgers and fries on a carved table at the front door. She sent her flat white shoes skidding across the floor, happy to be barefoot and out of the heat. She'd spent another fruitless day looking for...for...*anything*. The midsummer heat of New Orleans and her lack of success combined to leave her brain befuddled.

She padded into the kitchen and poured a glass of chilled sweetened green tea and lemon juice. She wiggled her toes on the cool tile floor, enjoying the feeling but thinking about her lack of progress.

It seemed she had few alternatives. One was to contact Tammy at the DEA to ask her for any new information, but she would have to convince Tammy not to report the conversation to her boss. That was a huge ask, and Sunny wasn't sure Tammy would do it.

Before she took that step, she decided she would visit Jan. It was risky, but Sunny knew her former paralegal kept her finger on the pulse of René's office. She would know if René had anything to do with Barley's death, and if so, why he'd done it. And she would know if he was doing anything else illegal.

Her loud doorbell rang into the silence, startling Sunny so that her tea sloshed over her fingers. She smiled, and still wearing the same sweaty, dusty clothes she'd had on since dawn, Sunny ran to the door. Her limp clothing would do, though she imagined her Aunt Hattie would have shaken her head in dismay.

She and David Kelley had fallen into an easy routine within days of his first trip to her door, especially once he made his visits a daily occurrence. Tonight, it was her turn to prepare supper for the two of them. Hence, the bag of burgers and fries she'd picked up on the way home, another thing that might have given her Aunt Hattie the vapors. She'd kept David in the dark about how she spent her days, having made a hooked-pinky promise with him never to quiz each other about work.

⁂

After eating her hamburger and nibbling a few French fries, Sunny unburdened herself to David, revealing her real name, and telling him about her husband's murder and the artificial life she'd led in witness protection. He seemed to take the cascade of information well, making all the right sympathetic sounds. At home in Sunny's kitchen, David took out the trash after their meal.

Up to that point Sunny thought everything had gone well. The problem came when she asked David for his help.

⁂

David Kelley had lots to think about when he reached home. His drive was brief, for which he was grateful. He had allowed himself half the bottle of wine because he optimistically thought that at last Sunny would invite him to stay the night. But by the time Sunny finished her story, he knew he had to leave her place, now that he'd heard what she had to say. The wine he'd drunk made him extra-cautious on the road, and his muddled thoughts rattled all over the place. He tried to concentrate, but he couldn't imagine how Sunny Valois was spending her days.

When he had first arrived, Sunny had opened the door and smiled. Her pretty face looked cute, smattered with freckles and devoid of makeup, an unnoticed smudge swooping like a mustache across half her upper lip. He was happy, a feeling of contentment coursing through his body.

What the hell? She doesn't give me any encouragement, but something keeps me coming back. At the door, he'd inhaled the dusty hints of her day mixed with a faint female, citrusy whiff of cologne. Her days must be spent mostly outdoors while she was in the city, but her clothes seemed more suitable for something like indoor desk work. He'd been trying to figure it out for weeks.

Tonight her hair had been tousled by the hot breezes, but her summery clothing appeared to be in good shape. That white streak in her hair fascinated him. He'd longed to touch it, but she'd never invited such an intimate gesture—at least, not yet. He had fallen deep into those dark amber eyes when she smiled so that it was hard to resurface and stutter a simple greeting. He knew he'd acted more like a schoolboy than a police chief. *I got hooked, all right.*

His warm, homey feelings had lasted while they munched their lukewarm burgers and slurped their melting milkshakes. They lasted even after he crumpled his burger wrapper and tossed it in the kitchen wastepaper basket, and even for a while after she'd begun to tell her story.

"David, let's try the wine I bought. When I finish this story, I have a question." Her story might turn out bizarre, but David was intrigued—and hopeful.

"I like wine. So, sure." He preferred beer, but why not. Things were getting interesting. Sunny retrieved the cabernet sauvignon and handed the unopened bottle and a cork gizmo to David, which he used while she pulled out two wineglasses. They carried everything into the cool, dim living room, and she settled in a comfortable armchair.

Sunny didn't cuddle beside him on the squashy dark velvet sofa, but she might end up there soon, David hoped. He later understood the chair had been a deliberate choice so she could watch his expressions and gauge his responses. When she was halfway through her story, and they were all the way through the bottle of wine, he belatedly realized he should have been guarding his emotions until he could check the facts of the tale she was spinning.

David cleared his throat. "What you're suggesting might work, Sunny, but tomorrow is out for me. How about we shoot for the day after." That would give him time to contact the DEA in New Orleans.

"Okay, I guess," she answered. "I hate to wait, but what's one more day? I've already been waiting for months. It's just that I need help, David. Maybe it's best to take a break tomorrow myself, and do some research here at home."

Me, too, David thought, moving to the door. He hugged her a quick good night and drove away. *Was she pulling him into some kind of con game?*

Chapter Four

Sunny did open her laptop, planning to spend the day in online research, but her instincts screamed there was no more time to waste. That forced her up and out of Oak Alley early the next morning despite a mild wine hangover. Squinting into the piercing early light of the eastern sky, she managed to marvel at the mass of colorful clouds, but their beauty was only a momentary distraction from her mission.

The city was quiet when she reached it, still early. Too early, Sunny knew, for her former paralegal to have left for work. The door of the quiet Victorian house on St. Charles Avenue, now a four plex, was unlocked. Sunny entered a faded hallway that smelled of mildew and dust.

Knocking on Jan Yokum's door, Sunny heard a cat inside meow a hungry sound. Sunny hoped Jan could answer some of her questions. If René was engaged in something illegal at her old law office, Jan would know about it. Without warning, she heard Jan's voice behind her in the hallway.

"Hello? You looking for someone?" Sunny's wine hangover dizzied her as she spun around, chastising herself for forgetting Jan would probably not be home.

"Jan?" Sunny had followed Jan long enough to know she spent her nights with the man whose movements seemed so familiar. Jan probably visited her apartment only for clean clothes and to feed and cuddle the cat she'd just heard.

Jan lurched back with a scream when she saw Sunny. Her keys flew from her fingers, clanging dully against the faded hallway. Shallow cans of cat food spilled from a bag, rolling across the worn tile floor. In the gloomy corridor, Jan's face appeared pale, and much older than the past year warranted.

"No! You're dead," she gasped. Sunny cocked her head, thinking Jan's reaction seemed somehow unlike her, over the top. The pallid, emaciated woman looked wild-eyed and frightened, instead of happy to see her. Jan sagged back against the corridor wall as though her legs wouldn't support her.

Sunny knew her own appearance had changed a great deal in the past year, for sure more than just her name. She'd lost a few pounds and wore countrified clothes, in an about-face from Cecile's sleek suits and stilettos. The biggest change was that her long hair was gone, replaced by a short haircut and the narrow swath of white that ran through it slightly off center.

Jan edged further away as Sunny approached. "I swear it was an accident. I didn't mean it, Cecile. Please don't hurt me."

Sunny cocked her head, frowning. *What? What's she saying?*

"I would never hurt a single hair on your head." Sunny reached out to Jan as she stood frozen as a trapped animal. Her friend's eyes darted about, looking for an escape.

"Come on, Jan. It's just me." Sunny's soothing voice settled the scared woman until she allowed Sunny to pet her arm. "Come on. Let's get out of the hall and go where we can talk."

It took coaxing, but Jan managed her timorous, shaky legs well enough to go into her apartment, where a tabby cat wound around their legs and meowed its hunger.

Jan's apartment showed evidence of her chaotic mindset. Through a pair of open pocket doors, Sunny saw papers scattered on every flat surface. Clean laundry sat on the tabletop waiting to be folded. Looking past that, Sunny saw the kitchen garbage can overfilled with trash. This was not at all like the Jan Sunny had left behind when she fled the city.

Still, vestiges of the old Jan remained. In the room where they stood, good, comfortable chairs sat near attractive lamps that revealed the old apartment's faded Victorian wallpaper. It showed Jan at her best, which was a far cry from where she was at the moment.

Once Jan recovered from her fright, the two women talked for the next hour. No longer boss and employee, their halting conversation was akin to that of new acquaintances. Jan acted jumpy but somehow accepting that Cecile had returned from the dead. Sunny, irritated with herself that she hadn't thought to record the conversation, tried to remember Jan's comments, because Jan was providing answers to some of her questions.

When Sunny described how she'd been told she was a widow within moments of regaining consciousness, Jan's eyelids fluttered rapidly, her neck becoming darkly mottled. Caught up in reliving the trauma, Sunny noticed Jan's reaction, but asked her nothing about it.

"After I was shot and Barley was murdered, the DEA wanted me as a witness in their investigation of René. I'm sorry to say they convinced me to play dead."

She looked at Jan. "How did I do? Did it look like the real thing?" Jan sat perfectly still, as though stunned. She looked devastated, then angry, like she was tasting an acid bile on her tongue.

"They—?" Jan probed.

"The DEA," repeated Sunny. "They changed my name and hid me, but they don't really care about me or who killed Barley. All they want is to prosecute René for drug trafficking. I'm the one who wants to find Barley's killer and close the case. And I need your help."

*

Jan remembered the days—nearly a year ago—when Cecile would arrive with a scarf wound high around her neck and wearing heavy makeup to cover her bruises. Her long sleeves stayed buttoned on the hottest summer days. The last straw for Jan had been the day Cecile tried to disguise a limp and sat in obvious pain. Cecile didn't complain, didn't say a word, but Jan found the injuries to her kind boss intolerable.

It was when Jan heard Mr. Gaudet and Cecile's husband, Barley, discuss "doing something about" Cecile that tipped her over the edge.

After everyone left the office that evening, she returned, unlocked the place, and placed a call to her new boyfriend from Mr. Gaudet's secretary's desk. The boyfriend had confided in her what kind of man he was, trusting her and not wanting secrets between them. Jan was in love with his warmth, his strength, and the gentlemanly way he treated her. She didn't care who he was or what he did. He was sexy. And, at that moment, he was useful.

Talking by phone that evening, she told him how Gaudet had instructed Barley to get the known hit man Mick Shaughnessy to "take care" of Cecile. She asked outright if someone could "do something" about Barley Forest. In her low contralto, she whispered, "I can't stand it. Cecile is more my sister than my boss. He hurts her so bad and so often. It's getting worse. He used to hurt her where I couldn't see the bruises. Now, he doesn't care how hard he hits her, or where. He doesn't deserve to live."

In his accented English, her boyfriend asked, "You sure it's Barley, Jan? Could it be sometin' else? A fall, maybe?" They talked about it for a minute, then the conversation switched to a more loving, personal plane before they finally said goodnight.

*

Jan's new boyfriend worked for Mr. Gaudet, too. Jimmy Costanza had been surprised by her brazen request concerning Barley, but it didn't bother him. Not at all. He had his own reasons for wanting Forest dead. Mr. Gaudet had replaced Jimmy with Barley. The firm's stuck-up new lawyer had got to be the boss's right-hand man. Mr. Gaudet thought Forest was more competent than Jimmy, and smarter, too, which Costanza knew was impossible. Mr. Gaudet had disrespected Costanza with the demotion, though he still got the old job's higher pay. He should've quit, but didn't, when Gaudet sent him to work in the garage. That made Costanza furious. His lowered prestige made him the butt of raucous jokes by the other employees. He laughed good-naturedly when they teased him, but it was like daggers in his back and as the weeks went by, the jokes got meaner.

Jimmy was appalled that Forest was abusing his defenseless wife, although he didn't know the woman very well. Where Costanza had been raised, men protected those who were more vulnerable, especially members of their families. Barley's despicable behavior gave Costanza one more reason to exact vengeance against a man he considered an enemy.

The night Jan called was the perfect night for him to take action. Jimmy wasn't in New Orleans, or even in the state of Louisiana. He would never be a suspect if Barley was murdered, since he was traveling on Mr. Gaudet's behalf. And the assassin Mick Shaughnessy was a friend of his.

Immediately after Jan kissed him good night through the phone, Jimmy called Mick. Shaughnessy would do anything if paid enough, including kill a man, and he was one of Jimmy's better drinking buddies. Jimmy and Mick agreed on the same fee to assassinate Barley Forest (making up for the lost fee for Cecile), provided he could get it done before Jimmy returned to New Orleans. He wanted to be sure there wasn't a single drop of blood on his callused hands.

He disconnected the call. How ironic, he thought, that he was paying someone else to murder, when he himself was a far better killer.

*

Mick Shaughnessy hustled off, leaving Shawn at their shared squalid apartment. This was a big payday and he wanted to be on time at the bar. He had killed the guy within an hour after Jimmy gave him the go-ahead second call. Shawn, Mick's accomplice, threw the gun away when they left Octavia Street and it disappeared without a trace into New Orleans rush hour traffic.

The men met for the payoff at Charlie's, their favorite New Orleans bar, located in a slowly disintegrating neighborhood close to downtown. It wasn't until Jimmy told him that Mick learned that Shawn's one bullet had taken two lives. He whistled, glad he wasn't Jimmy. His buddy's girlfriend wouldn't take that news very well.

"Two birds with one stone, huh?" Mick laughed at how weird that was, not caring. "I know for sure Barley's gonna stiff me now that he's a stiff himself."

Jimmy made two mistakes that night. He trusted Mick Shaughnessy. And worst of all, he put his trust in Jan Yokum.

Still jittery after having been surprised by Cecile waiting at her apartment door, Jan fed her cat, staying in her kitchen as long as she dared. She dripped a pot of coffee to share with her uninvited guest. Carrying a handsome tray, she walked back to the musty living room. This next part would be tough.

She'd known Cecile wasn't dead, but Cecile didn't know she knew, so she had to fake it. Jimmy had shared that shocking news when he returned from Puebla with his ribs bruised and suffering with a horrendous headache. Her boyfriend had been humiliated and terribly angry that he'd been ambushed and bashed over the head. He had raged that Jan's precious Cecile was not only *not* dead, she was bigger than life and much, much stronger than she looked.

Now Jan had to pretend she was ignorant of what had transpired. She would discuss Mr. Gaudet and his drug business with Cecile all day, if that would deflect her from talk about Barley and his murder.

Jan had long ago justified her role in Barley's assassination because she did it to protect Cecile, the boss who had given her a job she loved. That did *not* mean she would incriminate herself or the man she loved for murder.

"He still hasn't hired your replacement, Cecile," said Jan. She couldn't seem to stop her nonsensical jabbering. "I do most of the law work, at Mr. Gaudet's request. He reviews what I put in front of him, then imprints it with his notary seal.

"I never hear him talk about other activities, but he leaves all his paperwork lying around and product samples sitting on his desk. He doesn't try to hide anything anymore, and rough people come and go every day. Mostly men, but there are tough, scuzzy women, too."

Sunny leaned forward. "I hate that you live here all alone, Jan. Don't you have a boyfriend?" Jan jerked away, grabbed for her purse and jumped to her feet.

"Gosh, it's late. Sorry, Cecile, I have to go. We've been talking way too long." Hooking her hand under Sunny's arm, Jan helped Cecile stand.

"I'm so late. I really have to get to the office."

Drat. Well, that's that. Sunny hadn't handled that very well. She had hoped to ask whether Jan knew if René played a part in Barley's murder, but she said something that shut Jan down. Jan didn't know she'd been seen embracing a man, and Sunny wondered if he was Jan's boyfriend. *There must be something about the fellow she doesn't want to share.*

She let Jan draw her to her feet, but she resisted the attempt to move her toward the door.

"I won't leave until you promise not to mention to anyone that I'm alive and back in New Orleans."

Jan responded, "Who would I tell? Mr. Gaudet? I don't think so." She pulled Sunny through the door into the corridor and locked the apartment behind her. In the flurry of movement, Sunny didn't notice Jan hadn't promised anything.

Jan hugged her old boss, feeling honest affection. "I'm real happy you're alive, Cecile." She held Sunny at arm's length, wearing an intense expression. "You may think you need to know who killed your husband, but just let it go. You're better off without him."

Jan scooted off, leaving Sunny in the dim, musty corridor with her mouth hanging open. Sunny's expression was blank as she considered Jan's parting words. Something was a little off in Jan's behavior. Did Jan know something about Barley's murder? Dread settled around Sunny. Jan knew more about Barley's murder than she had said.

Sunny pushed through the humidity down the cracked sidewalk, protected from the sun by the Avenue's oak canopy, to the old truck. Shutting the door, she mopped her sweaty neck and analyzed Jan's conversation. Sunny had botched the visit with Jan so badly that David probably couldn't help her now. If she retrenched, made a list of what she knew, or *thought* she knew, something new might pop out and give her an idea of what to do next.

She could do nothing other than go home, cool off, and let things settle in her mind. The thought of a chilled glass of iced tea in this heat was an idea that was tough to beat.

David didn't know whether to be heartbroken or furious, or both. At a minimum, he knew Sunny's story had been truthful, as far as it went.

He hurried through his daily rounds of the village, then drove to the DEA office in New Orleans. He needed to know all about this...this Sunny Valois, especially after his phone conversation with the DEA. He left town more than an hour after Sunny had, still thinking she would be doing research at home.

Chapter Five

It had taken Chief David Kelley multiple tries and all his patience to get past the DEA/US Marshals receptionist when he'd called that morning. He imagined she'd relished denying him access the first time she disconnected. Not certain he reached the right place, David blurted two names Sunny had mentioned—Tammy and Gene—before she disconnected him again.

This time the open line hissed before he heard "Please hold." David again listened to the hiss, thinking, *What I won't go through to get the facts.*

A low-pitched, harried-sounding female voice came on the line. In an irrational moment, David wished the woman could see his uniform. That might add some *gravitas* to his call.

"Tammy Avenetti here. How can I help you?" Her flat accent was that of a Brooklyn native, unless she was from the Irish Channel in New Orleans. She was local, he decided, visualizing someone intelligent, with a woven lanyard dangling around her neck across a pearl necklace. She probably smelled like talcum powder.

"I hope so, ma'am. I'm Chief David Kelley from Oak Alley." He recited his official credentials. "I have questions about a new resident in our area. I have reason to believe she is under your purview."

"Purview, huh? That's a twenty-dollar word, if I ever heard one. Give me the name." The impatient voice said she didn't have time for this distraction. You have a DEA case number?"

"No number, but I have a story," David felt sheepish, unprepared, "that starts with a murder in New Orleans."

"Okay so far—whose murder?"

"Barley Forest." David heard something clunk, followed by other loud noises that sounded like she dropped the phone. He heard a curse, followed by a scrabbling sound and a sibilant hiss. When the flustered woman spoke again, she had transformed into an alert, fully engaged law enforcement official.

"I apologize, Chief Kelley. I had an unavoidable mishap, but all's well. Now, you referred to a Barley Forest? Who's the woman?" She paused, waiting for his response.

"She says she's Forest's widow and she's supposed to be dead. She doesn't use her real name and she's not dead."

"Just spit it out, chief. Tell me *both* of her names—real *and* fake." Over the phone, the clipped tone came through businesslike and irritated. David squirmed. He no longer saw the person he spoke to as a woman fondling her pearls.

"Either she's Cecile DuMond Forest or she's Sunny Valois, but I'm not sure which is real. She seems to prefer Sunny Valois."

To David's alarm, he could hear agitation ramping up in the woman's voice. "I'm familiar with both those names. I want to hear her physical description."

That was easy enough, thought David. His favorite pastime these days was looking at Sunny.

"She's in her thirties, I think. She's very smart. Has a great sense of humor. She's average height, slender, hits me at about the jawline." He closed his eyes, conjuring a 3-D image of the lovely Sunny. "Her smile sparkles. Freckles scatter across her nose. Short, shiny auburn hair except for an off-center white streak."

"You don't seem to have missed much, sir. Are the two of you in a relationship?"

"What? You mean romantic, something like that? We do see each other nearly every day—but, no." David cleared his throat, hearing the regret in his voice.

Tammy was astounded that Cecile was so near the city. "This Sunny, or Cecile, or whatever, lives right there in Oak Alley, that little town close to New Orleans? Is she alone?"

"I guess she's alone. Until yesterday I thought Sunny was exactly what she said she was. She says she works in New Orleans. Goes there every day, but who knows what she's really doing."

⁕

Tammy sprinted down the hall to Steve Morley's office, skidding through his doorway and crashing into his desk. Morley's pen left a stuttered trail across the page, causing him to grimace until he heard, "Boss, we know where Cecile is."

Tammy knew what Cecile was doing. How many times had she complained about the DEA's inability to find her cruddy husband's killer? Tammy didn't know whether Cecile was brave or stupid, but you had to give her points for taking things into her own hands.

Before she ended the call with Chief Kelley, she'd strongly suggested, ordered him really, to come right away to the DEA offices in downtown New Orleans. He had wasted little time getting there, then repeated everything Sunny had told him. Before Kelley left to return to Oak Alley, Mr. Morley allowed Tammy to tell him Cecile Forest's history as a professional courtesy.

After Chief Kelley left their office, Tammy settled at her desk and crossed herself like a good Catholic girl. She prayed the DEA crew could unearth—no! horrible word under the circumstances—could discover Cecile's current whereabouts in the sprawling city before she ended up just as cold and dead as that Barley idiot she'd married.

⁕

This was one time Gene was pleased with Mr. Morley's team meeting. The man's laser pointer vibrated in excited circles, looking like a superheated jumping bean on the whiteboard as Morley talked.

Gene turned sideways and leaned an elbow on the long conference table. Remaining perfectly still, he absorbed the news that Melba had been found in the village of Oak Alley. Their police chief had provided her newest name and address and Morley, in turn, thoughtfully shared the information with his team.

Gene interrupted, "Anybody here put eyes on her?"

"No," said Morley, "but Chief Kelley came to our office for debriefing. The man checks out, so we're pretty sure it's her. She's been in Oak Alley since early spring and that corresponds to when she disappeared from Puebla. Goes by Sunny Valois now."

Sunny, huh? Fits her. It pained Gene that he hadn't told Melba of his love for her. Privately, he acknowledged that his reluctance to declare himself wasn't because the agency had a rule against getting involved with a protectee. He would have lost his privacy and exposed his secrets. Growing up with just his mother, Gene had learned women punished boys for liking dirty magazines, and could always uncover a growing man's deepest, darkest secrets.

He sucked his teeth, finding it difficult to maintain the illusion of relaxation. Gene's thoughts roiled, caught between his obsessive feelings for the woman he called Melba and the crushing anger that had consumed him since she'd abandoned him and disappeared, leaving him stranded in Puebla. His DEA team made him the target of their derision and of his boss's insults. He looked like an incompetent fool. He wanted—had—to punish Melba for her behavior, and he had another, more private reason to find her.

He would take care of her punishment, and everything else, now that he knew where she was hiding.

Wasting no time after Morley's meeting, Gene slipped from the building unnoticed and hurried to his car. He knew the way to Oak Alley and was already planning his next steps. Only one lightly traveled road meandered through the tiny village, which had no more than three or four short streets. Melba's place would be easy to find. He didn't know her car, but he wouldn't have to track her down like a predator cat its prey. Chief Kelley had provided an address for Melba, or Sunny, or whatever the hell she called herself now. If his luck held, Gene brooded, he had time enough to inspect her place before she returned. Melba had a major surprise coming. The thought made him smile. She wouldn't know what hit her.

Ain't that a shame...

Chapter Six

During Sunny's drive home, scudding clouds released gushes of summer rain that obscured her view. Heavy drops hit the car's roof and fell to the hot road below, circulating as steam up into the clouds. A strong breeze buffeted the moving car.

I would love to drowse to the murmur of a breezy rainfall—if there weren't so much I have to do. Rain helps the grass and the soul, but it won't do a thing to wash away any of my anxious thoughts.

Sunny's problem was that she had no plan. All she had was information, and most of that was pure guesswork. Seven—no, make that almost eight—years of being a lawyer helped her recognize lies and dissembling when she saw them, but recognition didn't help decide what to do about them. Jan had been so erratic and confused during their conversation, her physical cues so odd, that Sunny intuitively believed Jan, and probably her boyfriend, had something to do with Barley's death.

She knew there'd been only one intended victim that night after the DEA told her they'd found only one deformed bullet at the scene. So, unless she'd been the target, and she saw no reason to suppose so, her injury that night must have been accidental. The expert's reconstruction concluded the gunshot passed through Barley first, then plowed a furrow in Sunny's scalp before embedding itself in a wall.

Sunny's challenge was to confirm her suspicion that Jan and her boyfriend had been involved in the murder, and prove it. Who *was* Jan's boyfriend? Sunny didn't recognize the man she had seen Jan kiss.

✻

Gene White explored Melba's big yard out to its perimeter before he breaking into the house using the battery-operated lock picks he kept in the trunk of his car. It was a matter of moments to get through Melba's front door, entering just as the rain began.

The place was nice enough, he thought, but it couldn't compete with the upscale safe house in Puebla. *She probably misses Rio Frio.*

He made a leisurely search of her place before he heard an approaching vehicle crackle down the gravel drive. Gene returned to the living room and peeked through the blinds, surprised to see an ancient truck pull clattering to a stop. *Is that Melba? Yes.*

Flattening himself against the wall behind the front door, his eidetic memory replayed the boss's presentation word for word. Gene's fanciful imagination made Melba's behavior an insult to him, again fanning his fury at the personal affront he'd suffered when she'd disappeared from Puebla.

He'd punish the damn woman, teach her not to try that again. And he'd found the perfect punishment in her own back yard. Something that fit into his plan.

David Kelley stared at the stormy weather past his wildly swishing windshield wipers, wondering what happened to the earlier bright blue and cloudless morning. He had expected this to be another in a line of mercilessly hot, late summer days.

It wasn't as though he hadn't been warned. The weather service had been accurate for a change, predicting heavy rain and strong winds because of a big storm further west. That was ludicrous, he'd thought, given the clear skies, so he disregarded the forecast and left his rain gear sitting useless in the trunk of his car.

To complicate matters, a wreck at the base of the bridge over the Mississippi brought him to a dead stop for an hour-long wait which bogged down his return to Oak Alley. He tried to reach Sunny by cell phone, but the call went to voicemail. Disgusted, he disconnected without leaving a message. He would tell her what happened and she would either understand why he'd checked up on her, or she wouldn't. She might tell him to take a hike and get out of her life.

Ashamed that he hadn't believed Sunny, David still thought the whole damn thing was bizarre. Agent Avenetti had given him her complete attention with no interruptions, having the receptionist hold her calls and take messages while he repeated Sunny's story. That meeting answered many questions, though there was so much information, it was difficult to stay on top of things—the Gaudet drug investigation, Barley Forest's role, the timing of his murder, the unproductive interviews with Gaudet's staff.

David had found the DEA office noisy. It was a disconcerting hive of activity, with some kind of task force ramping up, supervised by the chief agent. He wasn't told about any of that. It was none of his business, anyway.

Chapter Seven

On the way home, Sunny had tried to reach Tammy by phone, but she was in a meeting and wasn't available. She was told Tammy would return the call as soon as she was free. The receptionist took a message with Sunny's old name and her new phone number.

The bad weather worsened as Sunny approached Oak Alley and home. The wind was more like a tempest, closer to gale strength. Intermittent heavy rain threw itself in hard pellets against the thin metal skin of her car. She pulled to a stop in front of the house and peered through the windshield. Strands of moss tangled and swayed through the branches of the big oak outside her door. Dark clouds congealed in the sky, obscuring the setting sun. Sunny paid little attention to what she saw, past realizing she couldn't avoid getting wet. Her thoughts were still focused inward on how to deal with Jan.

Absorbed by her knotty problems, Sunny gathered the bags of groceries she'd bought on the way home and bumped the car door closed. She leaned into the stiffening breeze and hurried through the blowing rain. Shaking the drops from her short hair, she juggled the two heavy bags and trudged across the creaking boards of the porch to the front door. Setting down a bag, she inserted her house key only to discover the door unlocked. *Unlocked? I could've sworn I locked this door this morning. I'm losing it.*

Still, she hummed happily as she pushed inside, lugging the heavy bags across the threshold and anticipating David's visit. She liked David more and more, so funny, so smart. And cute. And sexy in a way that made her nerve ends tingle.

Unseen, rough hands snaked out, wrenching her arms away from the overfilled bags with bruising strength. Much later, she would find a bloody crescent had seeped through the fabric of her blouse from a fingernail that cut through the skin of her arm.

The grocery bags burst when they hit the floor, their contents exploding like Chinese fireworks all over the room. Shrieking with fright, Sunny struggled against the viselike strength of her unseen assailant that pinned her arms to her sides. Her neck muscles strained, and in a vain attempt to recall her self-defense lessons, she stomped her heels down hard, hoping to wrest herself away to safety.

"No, not again!" She screamed at top volume.

In the gloom of the room, her attacker clenched her from behind. *How did he find me? He'll kill me.* Her arms were pinioned to her sides. She couldn't move, so struggle was pointless and she stopped trying, motionless, frightened and quivering.

She swallowed, her throat painful and raw from screaming. Whoever this was, he was strong, more powerful than herself. When a much too familiar, unclean body odor hit her nose, she snorted. *What the...* She knew the voice that spoke in her ear, male, belligerent yet whiny.

"Melba, stop! I wanted to surprise you, that's all." Abruptly released, she staggered, catching herself with an outstretched hand.

Her assailant coughed out a malodorous laugh, unpleasantly like an outboard motor that failed to ignite. Sunny was dizzy with a flood of adrenaline. Blood still swooshed loudly in her ears. Working to stabilize and calm herself, she thought her thudding heart would crack her ribs. Air wheezed back into her lungs. She turned and looked at Gene, a man she had hoped never to see again, much less touch. *Where the hell did you come from? Did the man never bathe? Good gosh.*

"Yeah, right! How did you find me? And where's your car?" She began to pick up the fallen groceries, fury pushing her fear aside until she was thoroughly enraged.

Ignoring her questions, Gene lied, "You left the door unlocked. Not smart."

She distinctly remembered tugging on the door to be certain it was secure.

"No, you broke in!" She gauged Gene's behavior. He seemed a little off and a lot dangerous. His eyes bulged in a wild, frightening expression. She knew firsthand from her marriage to Barley, just how much hurt an irrational man could inflict, but in the last months she'd learned that bullies thrived when their victims showed fear.

She decided to attack. "You wanted to hurt me, Gene, admit it." Her voice rasped, hoarse from her screams.

Turning away, he squatted to pick up some scattered groceries, and offered an insincere apology with a smile that looked suspiciously proud of itself. Sunny would have none of it, gathering vegetables and cans with sharp, angry motions. Her lips squeezed tight in silent fury.

In an unspoken truce, Gene left the groceries on the kitchen counter and swaggered back to the living room, where he dropped onto the lumpy sofa, looking far too smug.

"Nice place, Melba."

Sunny walked to the front door, still shaky. Watching him the whole way, she pulled it open and made a show of looking at her watch.

"You haven't answered me, Gene, but I don't care. You have to leave. I have plans tonight and I want to get ready."

"What did you say?" Anger again transformed Gene's bland countenance. His jaw jutted with a menace that rounded Sunny's eyes and made her quail. He approached in a stalk, looming with utter craziness in his eyes.

Engaging him further was debatable wisdom, but Sunny wanted him gone, the sooner the better. "You don't get to tell me what to do, Gene. I want you to leave—right now." Reinforcing her words, she added, "As a matter of fact, leave and don't come back."

"I don't think so, missy," Gene snarled. "We have plans for you."

We? Sunny thought. Her alarm increased.

He seized Sunny's wrist in a blurring-fast move before she could move more than a step. She yelped when he banged the door wide open and jerked her through it, half-dragging her behind him. The gale winds out of the southeast carried stinging rain, blowing Sunny's hair into her eyes, plastering their wet clothes to their bodies, and pushing them further from the house.

"You're gonna learn I'm always prepared," he growled. "Wait 'til you see what's coming next. Do you even know what's in your back yard, Melba? Something really interesting."

Gene panted, his bulging muscles strained as he dragged Sunny through tall grasses flattened by the storm. He knew what he planned wasn't strictly necessary, but Melba deserved this punishment before he delivered her.

She stumbled, struggling to free herself from his fierce grip. He mumbled as he trudged, and she dreaded what might happen next. She spoke between gasps, her words halting and breathless.

"I don't *want* to go. Let me go. What have I ever done to you?" Why did awful men always find her? First Barley, then a killer, then a who-knows-what in Puebla, and now creepy Gene. Her thoughts caromed from thought to thought in a mental arcade game. Not all men she knew were awful. David Kelley was nice.

Where is *David? Why hasn't he come? He'll see us, and...oh, God! Both of them have guns.* Her fright escalated.

Gene pulled her past satsuma trees whose branches were laden with their ripening globes of edible sunlight. They blew like a *corps de ballet* in the wind, releasing a tantalizing citrus smell. Sunny worried irrationally that the fruit wouldn't survive the storm. Helpless, a honeybee tumbled past her nose. Where had this wind come from?

She tripped over a muddy hillock and lost a shoe. She bent to retrieve it, but Gene jerked her wrist painfully. Sodden and dripping,

Sunny could only stagger behind him, leaving her shoe behind and trying not to fall.

She wheezed out a question, in an attempt to slow his pace. "I didn't see your car. Where'd you park?"

"None of your damn business, that's where."

Gene's long strides steered them toward the far property line, a long way, two hundred feet, from the house. The wind grew stronger, buffeting them from side to side, grasses and small objects hurtling past or striking them painfully.

His behavior confused Sunny. She had thought their relationship was a decent one for two people who met only because her husband was killed. She'd been courteous, making small talk with him. She'd fed him on his visits to Puebla. His horrid anger was unwarranted, and now he was hauling her God knows where in the middle of a wild storm.

Every time Sunny's one bare foot touched the ground, she shuddered, afraid of what might happen. All manner of critters lived in country yards like this. Snakes hidden in the weeds would strike if caught by surprise. Sunny's foot itched with vulnerability.

Where are we going? South America? She smothered a manic giggle, though the situation wasn't close to amusing. They scrambled across a depression that extended the width of the property. A large grass-covered mound loomed at the far end of the low area.

"What *is* this?" Sunny asked, momentarily distracted.

She limped now, dodging the fire ant hills and nettles studding her path, though Gene seemed oblivious to them. The more drenched she became, the more difficult it was to keep her footing. Fiery pain radiated into her armpit from her wrenched shoulder, the tendons and muscles threatening to separate from the bones.

Gene didn't answer, but tugged her to a dripping standstill at the back side of the tall, rounded mound. A heavy, weather-beaten wooden door stood ajar, its frame set deep in the grassy mound.

"See this?" He gave Sunny's wrist a painful yank with each word. "This's a bomb shelter, probably built during the 1960s when the Russians were putting missiles in Cuba."

Sunny, hauled around by this crazy man, pelted by driving rain, and buffeted by the howling wind, couldn't care less. She thought only of the relief she'd feel when her arm was her own again. She squinted into the gloom of the shelter. It was apparently dry inside and she imagined what kind of critters might've taken refuge there.

"Why are we here? I didn't know about this...this *thing*."

"Melba?" Gene's voice vibrated with a dangerous new tone. He was drenched, rain dripping off his nose. His wet clothes clung to his concave chest. His shoes were heavy with mud.

"What?" She yanked, trying to free herself, and earned a casual backhand blow to the jaw that forced her to whimper. If she just had enough courage to break her own wrist like a trapped animal, she might gain freedom. She doubted she could survive the pain.

Gene's eyes were wild, glassy. "I loved you. Until you betrayed me."

"What? What are you talking about?" Breath scraped from Sunny's lungs. She gaped, hovering somewhere outside herself, staring in panic. His words were so incomprehensible, she stopped resisting.

"You have to know that, Melba," he said, not believing her surprise. "And you put *me* in an impossible situation when you ran away."

"And *you* love *me*. We could have a perfect life together. We still can—right here in Oak Alley—for the rest of our lives, if this is where we want to be."

What could she say? *Why didn't I see this*? Sunny felt unexpected compassion for this strange man. *In the months I've known him—and during all the meals we shared—not once, not once, did he ask a single personal question. Not once! He doesn't know me, who I am. I could never love someone so self-involved.* But this wasn't the time to reject him.

If she said anything now, he might hurt her out of anger, but his screwy notion that she loved him was absurd.

"You love...me?" she said. "A stupid girl like me won't make you happy." A stutter betrayed her discomfort. The man was in his own world. He made no sense and his firm grasp kept her imprisoned. It was obvious he believed she would try to run.

She peered back at the house through the rain, daring to hope David was coming their way, but the early twilight created by low, black swirling clouds made it difficult to see.

"I know everything about you. I've read your confidential file," he answered, "and the minute I saw you lying unconscious in your house, I wanted you. But it's too late for that. Now I have a new mission."

His expression was one she'd seen many times on Barley, one of lascivious possession. Gene, much bulkier than Sunny, had her trapped in the shelter doorway.

She took a chance and pushed away, trying to get past, but he pulled her back as easily as a rag doll, then released her and gave Sunny a thrust that sent her sprawling into the shelter.

"You're not going anywhere until Gaudet says so," he ground out through his clenched teeth. On hands and knees on the dry dirt inside the earthen shelter, Sunny thought, *Gaudet?,* then watched Gene slam the heavy angled door shut, leaving her in complete darkness.

"This is 'just in case,'" Gene yelled through the door. "I think you need a little quiet time before I take you to see Gaudet."

"You're insane!" Sunny choked, her sore throat scraped raw. She was unable to budge the door. "Open the door, Gene! It's dark in here. What are you doing? Gene?" She yearned for her cell phone, useless back at the house.

"Help!" She banged the door with both fists, struggling against the unreasonable fright that threatened in the dank blackness surrounding her. No light could penetrate the door.

Sunny heard Gene yell, "I locked the door. You won't get out, so don't bother trying. I'm leaving for a while. Maybe we can talk about our future when I get back, but if you have plans for tonight...so sorry."

She heard nothing further. The sounds of blowing wind and pelting rain became muted, like a volume control turned down from high to low. Sunny shivered, cold and soaked to the skin. *How long,* she wondered, *will Gene keep me here? No one knows where I am.* The dark shelter smelled of mildew. At least it was dry.

Chapter Eight

David debated whether to swing by his apartment and freshen up or go straight to Sunny's place. He'd repeatedly dialed her cell phone, but his calls had gone right to voicemail. Did it matter whether he looked his best? Either way, she wouldn't be happy after he told her about checking out her story, and then his visit to the joint US Marshals and DEA office in New Orleans.

No, she wouldn't be pleased, but it was a good thing he had made the call. His eyes had been opened until they were bug-eyed, about all the events swirling around this poor, pretty girl.

That marshal who acted as Sunny's minder had to have forged her exit paperwork to cover up her disappearance. The Marshals' office informed David that Sunny was no longer under their protection and of no official interest to them. They *were* curious, however, about where she was and why she'd left Puebla without saying a word.

David had asserted himself and hadn't let himself be pushed aside once he penetrated the DEA offices in New Orleans. He was determined not to leave without having his questions answered. He'd glared at the deceptively fresh-faced young woman standing in front of him. It was all he could do not to wag a finger in her face.

"There's something screwy here, Agent Avenetti. You say Sunny left you in the lurch, but that woman would never break her word to anyone. Okay, I concede she seems to be hiding from something, but she's just a sweet librarian. All I want to do is to find out what she's afraid of, and why."

Tammy could see that Chief Kelley's interest was more personal than professional. She could also tell he didn't have a clue who

"Sunny" was, but she could do something about that part. His good looks as much as his credentials persuaded Tammy to tell him Cecile's story. Goodness knows, Cecile needed someone like David Kelley to take a personal interest, so Tammy escorted him to a quiet corner.

"Sit down, Chief Kelley," she said, brushing back her hair. Tammy gestured to the small table there in the reception area alcove. He plopped into the nearest chair, which he discovered was extraordinarily hard and uncomfortable.

"Okay, first off, we're surprised a gifted lawyer like the woman we call Cecile and you call Sunny, was reluctant to cooperate with us as a federal authority, as though she suspected we had plans that weren't always in her best interest. And I'm not saying she was right or wrong about that."

"Lawyer? Sunny's a lawyer?" David interjected, dumbfounded. That rocked the foundation of his belief in Sunny. "She told me she was a librarian." He wondered about the many layers of Sunny's life. How much would he have to peel away before he uncovered the real Sunny?

"Technically, that's true. In her defense, David, Sunny *is* a degreed librarian, but yes, she's a successful lawyer, too. She had a thriving practice here in New Orleans before we, the DEA, got involved. Because you're law enforcement, I'll tell you her story. It's confidential, so keep it to yourself.

"I'll start from the beginning and tell you what we know about Cecile DuMond Forest—also now known as Sunny Valois."

The story took some time, and Tammy concluded with her personal disappointment at Cecile's recent behavior.

"Initially, we thought she'd hooked up with her minder, Marshal Gene White of the US Marshals Service. Everyone here knew he was obsessed with her. But then, he's here with no idea where she's gone.

"The worst blow to me personally—when I thought she was involved with Gene—was that she still had such poor taste in men."

"Still?" asked David.

"Yes. I'm talking about her murdered husband, Barley Forest." Tammy held up her hand, when she thought David was about to interrupt again.

"We'll talk about him another time. Agents and their protectees occasionally get involved; that's nothing new. But none of us could wrap our heads around the idea that a class act like Cecile Forest would run away without saying thank you or goodbye. We knew she had better manners than that, me especially. It was completely out of character, but it *might* have been something Gene White would do."

"Until he brought us her exit documents, that is." Tammy sighed. "She apparently left for reasons that had nothing to do with Marshal White. The Service can't always control a protectee. Cecile Forest—or Sunny Valois, or whatever she calls herself today—is an American taxpayer, and we—the US Marshals Service and the DEA—work for the taxpayers. We took her bad behavior on the chin and got back to work on our main job, which is to find enough evidence to convict René Gaudet of drug trafficking.

"And concerning Marshal White?" She shrugged. "The jury's still out, but we were watching him. And about an hour ago, *he* slipped away from us. We can't find him. He was at Mr. Morley's briefing, but now he's gone. *My* money says he's on his way to Cecile because, in the briefing, Mr. Morley repeated exactly what you told us about where she is now.

"Marshal Gene White knows where to find your Sunny."

The blue lights of David's cruiser flashed the entire way home. Once over the Mississippi, his foot was heavy on the accelerator, exceeding the speed limit and blowing through every blinking yellow light in the small towns along the way. He expelled a prolonged breath as he sped home, overwhelmed by the information he'd heard in New Orleans. It hurt that Sunny had only selectively shared her story with him, leaving out the worst parts, but he worried about her.

Pulling to a stop in front of his cramped headquarters, he dodged through the rain to get indoors where he paced his small office, unable to organize his thoughts or to stay still. Trees blown by the wind scrabbled their branches like skeletal fingers across the building's tin roof. He dragged back the shade and did a double take to see the tall grasses blown flat by the strong winds. Raindrops pelted like birdshot against the windowpanes, making him recoil, but David didn't give a damn about the storm.

On the way back to Oak Alley in his cruiser, he had heard the weather station mention strong thunderstorms brewing to the west, spinoffs of the hurricane hitting the Houston area. He didn't care about that, either. At that moment, weather was immaterial.

David's main concern was Sunny and her safety, but how much he cared about her was the real bombshell. He had more emotional investment in Sunny after fewer than four months than he'd ever had in another woman. She had never indicated she felt the same way, but first things first. Right now he needed to digest what Tammy told him, then tell Sunny he knew who she really was. Later, he would figure out a way to coax her feelings out of her.

A crew of DEA and US Marshals would join him in Oak Alley early tomorrow. In the meantime, he worried about the missing Gene White and his obsession with Sunny. Would the man actually show up? David knew she would open the door to him. He was a man Sunny would assume she could trust.

David thought about the serious conversation he would have with Sunny over dinner tonight. He'd take two bottles of wine to soften what he had to say, ending with the news that the DEA and the Marshals would be at her door tomorrow morning, probably by the crack of dawn.

Chapter Nine

David shuffled past Sunny's car, preoccupied by his thoughts, barely giving the vehicle a glance. He didn't wonder why Sunny took so long to open the door to his knock, because he was concentrating on what he planned to say. Instead he stood on the porch in the rain, his ankles getting wet, before he decided to call her cell again. No answer, but he thought he heard a faint ringing inside. She had to be home. Her car sat just a few feet away at the foot of the steps.

Hitting redial, his call went directly to voice mail—again. David glared at the illuminated face of his phone as though it deliberately blocked the connection. Using his fist, he hammered the glossy maroon of the solid wooden door, wincing at the pain to his knuckles. Wind gusts skirted the porch overhang, snaking around his umbrella and dousing him until his elbows dripped.

What was taking so long? *About right. What is it that makes the good ones run and hide? Is Sunny the type to ignore a visitor? I feel like limburger cheese—one whiff of me and she runs away. We have a date, and she* knew *I would be here.* His knuckles hurt worse as he pounded and began to worry. Was she okay?

Anxious now, David jiggled the doorknob, expecting it to be locked. The door silently swung open.

Hunh! Grim, David knew he could enter without permission as a wellness check. In this less populated area, he answered only to himself as the sole police presence. Water dripping from his clothes, his shoes squelching, David edged into the stifling house, calling for Sunny.

A bright green object that lay just inside the door caught his eye and gave him pause. That was no place for a celery stalk. And there was a can of chicken broth that had rolled to a stop against the baseboard at the arched opening to the kitchen. Beyond the arch, a purse lay on its side on the pale granite counter, its contents spilled helter-skelter. Cans and jars sat nearby. Sunny's small key ring sprawled next to her purse.

A storm alert came from within the purse, surprising him. It was the sole noise in the house except for his footsteps and the fabric of his shirt scraping the wall. The house exuded a staleness, a gloomy emptiness. He strained, but heard nothing unusual, no click of a gun's safety or a shuffling shoe. The wind whistling outside and the rustling leaves and branches were loud enough for him to question the silence of the house. David made a large target, so he shielded himself, crouching below cabinets and behind walls as he moved.

If Sunny was in the building, he wanted to find her quickly but the dilemma of whether someone else was there slowed him down. Caution was important. An intruder might be armed and well-trained in combat and weaponry. David had to be ready to attack first. He would have one chance to get the upper hand. This was dangerous and tricky, but Sunny and her safety were important.

If the marshal was holding Sunny captive, they could be anywhere. David prayed he wouldn't trip—especially over a body. The mere thought made his heart slam in his chest. *What happened here?* He grimaced, then took a chance and yelled "Sunny?" loud enough to be heard throughout the small house.

He had a bad taste in the back of his throat. Why had he left his gun in the cruiser? He'd not thought it necessary at the time, and now he was unwilling to leave the house to get it. Sweat oozed down the back of his neck and he swiped it away, jerking at a deafening peal of rolling thunder. *This is a horrible storm and the humidity is from hell.*

Intuition told him a search was pointless, but this weird feeling Sunny was calling his name kept David moving from room to room. *Where could she be?*

Police training forced him to be thorough, to look under every bed and into every closet. He gulped back a groan at evidence of Sunny's tidy attention to detail. Nothing overdone, but not spartan, either. Just right. He paused in her fragrant bedroom to inhale her scent. The chaste bed was neatly made, her sensual femininity apparent, not in ruffles and bows, but in sophisticated contrasts between textures and in the muted shades of aubergine and aqua.

A deep yearning spread into his heart to hold the owner of this room. The feeling was new to David. He badly wanted to tell Sunny how much she meant to him, but he had no idea where she could be. *Where was she?*

He grabbed his phone, retrieving Tammy Avenetti's personal number.

"Yeah?"

"Tammy? She's gone. Looks like she was surprised."

"Chief Kelley, is that you?"

"Yes. Listen up. Sunny...er, Cecile. Her car is here, but she's gone. Her house was unlocked and the kitchen has groceries dropped on the floor. It's isolated here and storming outside. She didn't just walk away. Your people need to help me." Desperation crept into his voice, making it husky.

"*You* listen, David. We won't come until after the storm has passed. You're in the middle of a hurricane. You do know that, don't you?"

"Hurricane?" He bit the inside of his cheek. "Not here. There's one over Houston."

"Not there, David. Here. The storm swung east and intensified while you were meeting with us. That's what I'm saying. It's all over the news. It hit land a couple hundred miles west of New Orleans, so Oak Alley is right on the eastern edge of the hurricane's path.

"We still plan to be there early, so hang in there." She disconnected.

David, disheartened, hoped morning wouldn't be too late for Sunny. He retraced his steps to her front door. He'd search tonight on his own.

⁕

The DEA after-hours service patched Tammy's call to AIC Steve Morley having a quiet dinner at home with his family. As he listened, he occasionally cursed, startling his wife and making his children giggle.

There were parts of that damn Gaudet case that seemed a torment he might have to deal with for the rest of his frigging life.

"Tonight? Dispatch agents?" Morley's jaw tensed. He struggled to sound reasonable. "Early morning's the plan, Tammy. You know that."

"But she's disappeared. Sunny's gone." The practical Tammy, always down to earth, now sounded hysterical.

"Tammy? You don't wanna hear this, Tammy, but forget about this for now. Get some rest." He listened some more, then capitulated.

"Okay, let's compromise. You call the crew. Tell them to mobilize an hour earlier than planned. The storm will have moved out by then."

Disgusted, he disconnected the call. Tammy had reported Chief Kelley's closing words. *What the hell? I am not an asshole.* He pushed away his half-eaten dinner

⁕

Howling hurricane force winds knocked Sunny's front door into David's chest, leaving a painful bruise, when he tried to begin his search. Using all his strength, he grappled with the door, pushing it closed, then he locked it and engaged the deadbolt.

He stared out a living room window as the locked door vibrated under the power of the wind. Needles of rain pinned sodden leaves against the window glass. *I hope my cruiser makes it through the night out in the open. Not likely.*

He realized a search tonight was impossible, and his shoulders sagged. Almost as bad, by morning the storm would have erased any tracks Sunny and her kidnapper had made. About now, David could've used a little company to complain to, but the only person he had to talk to was himself.

"Where did that messed up piece of garbage take her—if it's the marshal and not somebody else? Nah, it's him."

At the very moment David spoke those words, Gene White, the messed up piece of human garbage, was holding on to a swaying tree in the lee of the storm a hundred feet from Melba's new place. He was having second thoughts about the deal he'd made with René Gaudet. True, he would earn a half million dollars when he delivered Melba, but he hadn't counted on a hurricane.

He was lucky the DEA had included him in their investigation of Gaudet after he was assigned to Melba's case. Otherwise, he would never have been able to find her this afternoon.

Wearing official dark US Marshals rain gear and using binoculars, White caught occasional glimpses of David and fumed. Gene had driven up Melba's drive, had come to release her from the makeshift confinement, but he'd seen a police cruiser parked in front of her house. Throwing his car into reverse, he'd accelerated back to the road and parked on the shoulder a quarter mile away. He hiked to Melba's place through the woods, avoiding most of the shrubs and vines violently whipping in the gale. He dropped the binoculars to his side, secured by a cord around his wrist, and struggled to stay on his feet in the blustery wind.

Having a cop, or anyone, in Melba's house threw a monkey wrench into Gene's plans. He wanted to be her hero when he rescued her from the bomb shelter, but it was supposed to be private. Anything else would ruin the effect. He settled in to outwait whoever was in there. He'd save Melba after they drove away. *Why would anyone be checking on her in a hurricane*?

He laughed quietly, knowing Melba wouldn't be found, and wiped drops of storm water from his face. From his years of experience as a US Marshal, he knew the local police didn't know what they were doing. He shrank back under the whipping, overhanging branches, into the protection of the tree trunk, trying to make himself smaller.

A dog began to bark, getting louder and becoming more insistent. Gene had to leave, unwilling to answer questions if someone saw him. He forced his way back to his car in the storm. He found a cheap motel down the road and waited for the storm to pass.

Melba was destined for a longer stay in the shelter than he had anticipated, but she was safely hidden. He fretted her punishment was a little worse than he'd planned, but he had no other choice. It wasn't his fault.

Chapter Ten

Which is it? Is black the absence of color, or is it all colors combined? I can never remember.

All Sunny really knew was that a starless midnight couldn't be any blacker than where she sat right now. She couldn't tell whether her eyes were open or closed. She'd been trapped long enough to be unbearably thirsty, her mouth and throat cottony dry. Mealtime had come and gone. She fantasized mouthwatering thoughts about the sizzling steak she had planned to serve for dinner.

That sicko Gene! Sunny swore only mentally, never out loud, a habit ingrained in her by the nuns at school, but her internal curses were about to become bitter.

She gingerly closed her fingers into fists. She couldn't see her nails, but she could tell most of them were snagged and broken—probably bleeding—though that was a guess. Her fingertips burned like fire, raw and sore after many futile attempts to dig her way out. After she kicked off her second shoe, she'd felt her way barefoot along the walls, stubbing her toe painfully one time against a large, empty, open container with a handle—a bucket. A moldy chair provoked a scream when she tripped and it sent her sprawling in the dust, but she was happy to find it and eventually sat down.

Head bent, Sunny analyzed the path that had led to her current predicament. As much love as her great-aunt Hattie provided her after Sunny was orphaned, with the able help of her friend Uncle Karl, she had never felt secure enough to make many independent decisions. Even after Aunt Hattie died while Sunny was in college, it was Barley who forced the decision for them to marry. And look how that worked out.

That took Sunny to thoughts of her "best friend," Mary Ann. In retrospect, Sunny understood that Mary Ann had been an amoral opportunist from a very early age. It wasn't surprising, in that context, that she and Barley had combined forces to keep Sunny off balance and subdued until they could steal her future and her fortune. It was Barley's death and Sunny's injury that gave Sunny an opportunity to explore the internet, and the interest and time to do a deep dive into the psychological causes of her lack of assertiveness and tentativeness, along with suggestions on how best to overcome that behavior.

Sunny had worked on her mental strength for months, and now her personal confidence matched the professional confidence she'd always had in her legal practice.

If she could just get out of there...

A sob erupted from her throat, sounding loud in the inky dark. Sunny thought of the *tête-à-tête* she had planned to have during dinner. David probably thought he'd been stood up. How could he know what happened? She hardly believed it herself, but here she was.

Sunny's thoughts settled on the tiny brown mole she had seen on his left earlobe. She missed David's sweet little mole, and his company, too. Too bad he didn't know how she loved being with him.

No, it occurred to her, her blind eyes wide, *I crave being in his presence. I want to touch his warm skin and feel that warm baritone vibrate with my ear against his chest.*

And now she might never see him again.

Ten—no—eleven years ago, she'd allowed herself to be talked into marriage by an unscrupulous, lying bastard. She hadn't known better—one harbor, she'd thought, was as safe as any other. Once Barley was killed, Sunny believed she was better off with no man, but David and his considerate behavior was forcing her to rethink that.

Without her phone, it was impossible to track how much time had passed in the darkness, but the heavy humidity was keeping Sunny's hair and clothes damp. She shivered, not from chill, but from shock or perhaps trauma. Probably both. With her ear pressed to the door, she could hear howling winds and the pounding rain of a raging storm, but inside the shelter was dry—so far.

Raindrops sprayed against the padlocked door, sparking a new fear that critters would somehow squeeze under the door for shelter. Sunny's skin crawled. Was it night or day? It seemed she'd been in there forever. She swallowed, craving water. Thirst would soon become her worst problem. Sunny despaired, staring into the absolute darkness.

Gene is delusional, locking me away to force me to love him—that Stockholm syndrome stuff. No, he's going to leave me here. My dead body will rot in this horrible place, but at least I'll join the rest of my family.

Contorted pretzel-like in the musty chair that had earlier sent her sprawling, Sunny drifted off to sleep. She dreamed fitful dreams of laughing with Ginny, Joyce, and ReJoyce in the library as a menacing lizard lay in wait. A nightmare of Barley's hands squeezing her throat followed that.

She struggled awake to an eerie silence and utter darkness. Her muscles ached and her empty stomach spasmed with hunger. Her fingers felt swollen and sensitive with darts of shooting pain. Wavering to her feet, Sunny felt her way to the heavy door and tried again to claw at the hard dirt walls, but her damaged fingers couldn't handle the pain.

A pinpoint of light that had pushed through an infinitesimal chink at the top of the door caught her eye, releasing an overwhelming joy in her that she had made it to a new day.

Through the door, Sunny heard an unmistakable gurgle of moving water. She didn't recall having seen a stream, though she might've missed it under the circumstances.

If she could have just one sip of that tantalizing liquid. Just one sip. Her tongue stuck to the roof of her mouth, without enough saliva to help her swallow. She had no urge to use the bucket today, though she had used it twice the previous day. *That's a bad sign.* Feeling this awful, so soon, meant things would quickly become much worse.

Feeling her way back to the uncomfortable chair, Sunny sank into the only thing in the ghastly place which provided anything close to relief. She stared at the pinpoint of light, her bleeding fingers curled against her chest. She was thinking that the bomb shelter had been built to protect people, as she drifted back to sleep, not to imprison them. What awful fear forced someone to build a bunker?

Chapter Ten

Groggy from his restless night on the couch, at dawn David Kelley cracked open Sunny's living room blinds. David had stayed at Sunny's house through the night—most of it jackknifed on a loveseat that passed for a couch—in the remote hope she would return. He couldn't bring himself to commandeer her bed, certainly not without her lying beside him, and without her permission.

The DEA folks had awakened him with a text saying they would reach Oak Alley in an hour or two. Everyone knew the storm had destroyed clues to Sunny's whereabouts, but they were well-trained, tenacious investigators. David, chafing at the passing minutes, scared and wishing he could hurry their arrival, thought of himself much the same way.

His eyes were red-rimmed and gritty with exhaustion. The remaining traces of the attractive laugh lines near David's eyes had wilted overnight into deep grooves. The evening before, he'd scavenged paper and pen to list places where he could search for Sunny, and in the morning he woke bleary-eyed, still half-sitting, the pen still in his fingers.

David trudged to ransack Sunny's cabinets for coffee, pausing to peer out the window over the kitchen sink. Gone were the howling winds and pounding rain, replaced by birdsong and water steadily plopping from leaves. The day was shiny and new, with broken branches and torn leaves scattered on wet earth, under a cloudless sky of bright sunshine. Other than leaves and debris tossed pell-mell in the soggy green grass, the blown-out storm had left few traces.

When he found ground coffee beans stored in Sunny's refrigerator, David whispered his gratitude in a drawn-out, sibilant "yesss." Sunny had the soul of an aficionado when it came to coffee, which he confirmed in minutes, inhaling the welcome robust aroma and taking his first delicious sip.

After he'd chugged two extra-sweet cups of strong coffee, the cobwebs of exhaustion dissipated. Clad in yesterday's rumpled, creased clothes and sporting a day-old beard, he wasn't at his best, but so what? David dumped out the used coffee grounds and brewed a fresh batch to have on hand for the DEA folks.

He thumbed through a thin, well-thumbed phone book he discovered sitting on a small protruding kitchen shelf. Running a finger down the names beginning with 'H', he hoped to find Octave Hebert's telephone number. Known as Mr. Octave, he was the owner of Sunny's Airbnb rental. He'd been around too long not to be listed even in an old phone book. Like the many other senior citizens in town, he was an early riser. Within days of David taking the job as police chief in Oak Alley, he learned most of the old-timers got up with the sun to congregate at the town's small diner. Their group made up the historical consciousness of the pretty little village, and they possessed an enormous breadth of knowledge. They had graciously invited David to join them, which he often did.

Mr. Octave didn't answer David's call, and no machine demanded he leave a message. David disconnected, intending to try the call again in an hour or so. The old man had either gone to Mass to nourish his soul, or, like his contemporaries, to the diner to nourish his body. David voted for the diner. The oldsters tended to traipse to the diner after a big storm to check damage reports and offer what help they could.

When he could finally reach Mr. Octave, David hoped the old man would have noticed any strange vehicles in the village. At the very least, he would know all the best hiding places.

Chapter Eleven

Louisiana has endured many hurricanes, and the glancing gale winds of the previous night were considered minor. The eye of the storm dissipated within hours of making landfall a hundred miles west of Oak Alley. However, the sheer amount of torrential rain was calamitous, beating the sugar cane crops down to the ground and melting the rich, dark soil into gelatinous, oozing mud.

Throughout the night, sheets of rain had sluiced down. The heaviest rainfall in a hurricane occurs to the east of its eye, as the waters of the Gulf are drawn up into a counterclockwise vortex. This natural phenomenon had inundated Oak Alley with an unmanageable quantity of water in a perilously short span of time. Once a storm saturates the ground, the remaining water drains back into the Gulf. The storm cycle isn't instantaneous, but it does move quickly.

It starts with rivulets that merge into ditches, which then overflow into coulees, streams, and non-navigable tributaries. Leaves and debris push into bayous whose boisterous waters overrun their banks in their rush to the sea. Such flooding is temporary and nothing new to the residents of Oak Alley. It inconveniences hardly anyone, but this particular instance was different.

The flooding had an extreme effect on Sunny Valois.

*

David was experiencing a caffeine buzz, his third cup of coffee half empty, when the DEA knocked at Sunny's door. Though sleep deprived, a surprisingly chipper Steve Morley stood waiting outside, badge in hand. Tammy stood behind him, disheveled but not about to miss anything to do with Cecile, who she already thought of as Sunny. Behind her, four other agents hefted assorted equipment.

Morley raised his credentials when David cracked open the door and, speaking in a rapid monotone, made a formal announcement.

"Sheriff Kelley, the United States Drug Enforcement Administration is taking control of this crime scene. The disappearance of Mrs. Cecile Forest may be connected to the René Gaudet investigation through the possible involvement of his minions. We request your approval of our participation, but must advise you we shall proceed with or without it."

The DEA parade began to file into Sunny's house before David answered.

"No call for formality, Morley," said David, annoyed, but using a mild voice. Too much caffeine had him wired to explode, but good sense kept his irritation in check. He needed these people more than they needed him.

Reminding himself they were the good guys—*just not guys with good manners*—who had come a long way to help, he added, "I'm good with that. We need to find Sunny, the sooner the better. I made a fresh pot of coffee. Follow me."

Three SUVs had pulled up near his cruiser. The place had begun to look like some kind of staging area—one David hoped would end in a celebration and not in a more sober conclusion. He had something to show Morley and the agents.

David carefully removed the three protective garbage bags he had thrown over footprints he had discovered in the mud at the foot of the kitchen steps. They were in poor shape, but seemed to point to the rear of the property.

A DEA tech built a frame around them for a plaster cast. The best print was of a man's worn shoe sole with the inside of the heel eroded. The second print, smudged as though dragged, was smaller, likely a woman's shoe. He would make its cast, too, but it would probably be of little use.

Other techs fumed doorknobs, door frames, and the cans of food on the kitchen counter for fingerprints. On-site equipment scanned the prints in real time and seamlessly connected to national databases. David's prints were instantly identified, not that he cared, since he was in the national fingerprint registry through his police career and his former military service.

Morley pulled David aside. "We found Cecile's prints..."

"Sunny's prints," David interrupted. The skin around Morley's pinched nose and mouth paled to a bloodless white, but his tone remained disconcertingly affable. He grimaced a smile.

"Yes. Sunny's prints were identified as Cecile Forest's, since her law license required that she be fingerprinted. Also, when Barley Forest was murdered, we took her exclusion prints.

"There are unknown prints which probably belong to a grocery checker. They can be chased down, if necessary, but we found the kicker.

"We found prints we didn't quite expect—those of Marshal Gene White. He touched many items—doorknobs, cans of food, counter tops, other things.

"Considering that none of us knew Sunny's location until yesterday morning when you called, we believe Gene either alerted Sunny to escape, or, worse, he captured Sunny for an unknown reason. After our briefing yesterday, we looked for him, but he must've left immediately after we reported her location in Oak Alley."

David felt a lump clog his throat. This... this situation was his doing. The reason Sunny vanished, voluntarily or involuntarily, was because he'd called New Orleans. But why leave through the kitchen door, where there was no walkway? Were they trying to mislead him or the DEA?

Sunny's truck still sat outside the house, awaiting its owner, steaming in the hot early morning sun of a cloudless day. If it could speak, what questions could it answer? The tall Johnson grass beside its wheels reached for the sky. The pastureland of Sunny's backyard lay somnolent and still.

David fretted as he watched agents move systematically across the soggy yard in a grid pattern, searching for evidence. He redialed Octave Hebert's house phone. The call might be meaningless, but it was another pebble he could skip across the pond of the investigation. It helped him feel useful.

Morley left the house to check the surveillance cameras in the village which might have captured video of Gene's car. The man obviously loved the hunt, and his cheerfulness was somewhat disconcerting. As he left, he took the creaking steps an awkward two at a time, talking jerkily as he hustled past David.

"Looks like Oak Alley has three cameras—one at either end of the bayou bridge, and one at the only gas station in the village. We might see a license number and what kind of car White's driving. Cross your fingers."

David mentally smacked himself for not thinking of that. He gave Morley a thumbs up before the DEA man jumped in an SUV, executed a perfect J-turn, and roared away, leaving David to contemplate his inadequacy.

*

Mr. Hebert answered David's call on the third ring.

"Mais, hallo?" Octave Hebert, with the diminished hearing of an octogenarian, didn't understand the chief. David spent valuable minutes reassuring the agitated oldster that Sunny didn't want her money refunded. The elderly man became more affable once he understood David's request and agreed to a quick meeting at his mother's former home, now Sunny's residence.

David waited for Mr. Octave outdoors, counting the myriad small dents and scratches left on the cruiser by the storm. The clean air that followed the storm helped restore his energy, though the day was becoming progressively hotter. Hardy insects droned in the long grasses, a soothing symphony for his frayed nerves. The humidity was dense, like standing inside a transparent cloud. Birds chirped and tweeted in the branches of a spreading oak, ignoring the human activity below. Nature returned to its interrupted work unmindful of mankind, and if Mother Nature knew Sunny's location, she kept it to herself.

Mr. Octave's old truck squealed to a stop beside Sunny's even more ancient truck. The old man shook his head as David approached. David looked a question at him.

"First time for ever'thing," he said. "Weren't never this many cars at Mama's, even at her wake."

"These cars are from New Orleans, Mr. Octave. They're looking for Sunny."

The frail oldster harrumphed and slowly climbed the steps to the porch of his childhood home. He turned his hearing aids up to full volume and listened intently as David spoke, lip-reading, too, as the police chief talked. He occasionally asked an intelligent question for clarification, then answered by nodding, sometimes no, sometimes yes.

Mr. Octave abruptly sat ramrod straight and, touching David's arm, asked, "Did you search the bomb shelter?" His gnarled forefinger pointed toward the rear of the property. "*Maman* and Papa built that thing a long time ago to protect us from Russia. I almost forgot about it."

David leaned forward. "Where exactly, Mr. Octave?" At the answer, David jumped up, his chair rocking wildly, and ran straight through the house, hollering for the agents.

"There's an old underground bomb shelter out back. Hurry!" Tammy, caught in the draft of David's wake, followed, taking three steps to every two of his. He flew down the kitchen steps, calling Sunny with every stride, his heart pounding.

Chapter Twelve

Deeply concerned for the safety of their friend, David Kelley and Tammy Avenetti frowned at the storm waters flooding through the deep ditch behind Sunny's house. Tammy pointed at the protruding mound which divided the rapidly moving stream.

"Is that something?" She shucked her weapon and holster, throwing them to the ground.

David's heart lurched, his eyes wide. Was Sunny in there? He waded into the churning waters, struggling to maintain his footing in the strong current. Tammy followed, heedless of her laced boots and heavy denim jeans. The water came up to her ribcage.

"Sunny?" There was only silence, but they pressed on. "Sunny!"

Inside the bunker, Sunny was dreaming. She sputtered, floating in a cold, dark ocean. She choked on an inhalation, thinking she heard a voice. Water plugged her ears. *Am I awake or asleep*? *Awake! Wet!* Cramped in the uncomfortable chair, rising water was up to Sunny's waist.

Fully conscious now, she yelled, "Help!" in a hoarse voice. The mound was leaking like a sieve. Jumping to her feet, Sunny turned and climbed onto the soggy chair seat, then straddled the armrests, stabilizing herself by placing her hands on the low ceiling. She hoped that would be enough. The water continued to rise. She shivered, her teeth chattering. Even in the dark, Sunny knew there was little space remaining between the water's surface and the dome of the shelter.

Terrified, Sunny prayed she wouldn't die here alone, where she might never be found. "Help!" Her hoarse voice muted her shouts. She thought, *Do I hear someone? That Tammy?* The voice faded away. *No! My imagination. Not Tammy, no one...*

Sunny vibrated with a shocky chill, but that was hardly the problem. It was already too late for that. Water lapped at her chin as she strained upward on her toes. The earthen roof was firm, solid against her skull. She would drown before she could be found.

Again she heard the voice. "Sunny?"

It *was* Tammy. *She's here.* Water eddied unseen around Sunny and slowly inched up, lapping at her chin.

"Help!" She stretched her neck and lifted her chin into the life-giving air. A second voice gladdened her heart.

"Hold on, Sunny." In response, she sputtered a scream.

"It was Gene. Watch out for Gene. Water's at my mouth. Hurry, David! Help!"

"Gene can go to hell. Let's get you out."

The water continued its incremental rise while David struggled to wrest the door open. The peg securing the shelter door's hasp had swollen as it absorbed water and now refused to budge. His inner feelings scrolled through his brain as he fought the door. Sunny, in great danger herself, had thought to warn him about Gene.

"Back away, David." David looked up and gasped. Tammy stood on top of the dome, pointing her gun at him. She had retrieved the weapon she left back on drier land, then waded back, holding it over her head until she reached the bomb shelter and clambered on top.

"What the hell?"

"Stand back." Tammy made a shooing motion. "I'll shoot off the hasp."

David surged away from the door, grasping Tammy's intent.

She braced her squelching shoes, held her weapon with both hands, aimed straight down and snapped off a shot. Muddy water exploded in every direction, dirtying their faces and obscuring the hasp.

She needed a second shot, taking it as soon as the sediment dissipated enough for her to see. David lunged for the handle, straining against the current that trapped the door shut. There was silence within.

"Get here, Tammy. Hurry."

Tammy dropped her weapon onto the mound and jumped into the water. With their combined strength, they managed to lay the door back against the shelter's exterior wall. The flow of water held it fast. Submerging, David and Tammy barely saw Sunny standing on her tiptoes on the arms of a chair.

Sunny's head grazed the ceiling. Water lapped at her nose. She snorted, fighting to stay above water and trying not to move. Tammy crawled back on the mound outside, yelling to Sunny that David was coming in for her.

David held his breath and swam into the flooded, claustrophobic shelter, barely seeing Sunny in the deep shadows. Grabbing her leg, he pulled Sunny down. Half-remembered military training helped him hold her as she tried to escape his grasp. He secured his arm tightly across her chest, one hand in the softness of her armpit. She struggled frantically while he kicked his strong legs and swam her to safety, his lungs clamoring for air.

Tammy was soaked through and through. She kneeled atop the mound and peered into the dirty water, nibbling her filthy nails and mumbling, "This is taking too long. What should I be doing?"

At that moment, Sunny's head popped out of the flowing current, followed by David's, both of them coughing and sputtering. Sunny squinted in the unaccustomed sunlight to see Tammy grinning down at them. She clung to David, who clung right back and brushed her head with a surreptitious kiss.

She choked again and spat, whispering, "Your smile, Tammy. It's wonderful."

David shook her gently. "Hey, what about me? I risked my life for you."

Sunny beamed and squeezed him. "Yes. I love you, David. I love your smile, I love you. Now get me out of this damn water." Her voice trembled, her body shaking.

"Let's get to the house. Can you walk?" When she tried to rise, her legs gave way.

"I'm a little shaky."

Tammy scooped up her weapon, held it high over her head, and jumped into the current next to Sunny.

"Hold on to us, baby girl," she said. "We'll get you home. I'll update the boss."

Mr. Morley needed to know about this. When they'd waded out of the water, Tammy retrieved the water-resistant phone she'd thrown down with her gun on a damp hummock of grass. The exhausted trio squelched slowly across the soggy field back to Sunny's house.

Chapter Thirteen

Steve Morley had good reason to be distracted when Tammy called him.

"You found Cecile? Where? Good grief!"

Morley debated whether to tell Tammy what he'd found, but he didn't want to step on her good news. "Great news. I'll be there before you're dry."

He'd been reviewing footage from the village cameras during the search for Sunny, and had discovered digital photos of a car crossing the bayou bridge. The image was pixilated, but the driver could be Gene White. He had emailed the digitized information to the DEA tech wizards for possible enhancement. That done, Morley went to the third location on his list, the only service station in Oak Alley.

The station owner turned out to be a tech geek whose equipment had crystal clear video showing Gene's face. A second portion of the video captured Gene's license plate.

The owner began shaking Morley's arm while Morley was still staring at the screen.

"What the...?" Morley yanked his arm away and reached for his weapon before he realized the man was peering through his big plate glass window and pointing.

"Look yonder, son. There goes your man right there. Ain't that who you're looking for?" Morley gaped as Gene drove by. Yelling his thanks, he ran to his car, his tires throwing gravel as he pulled out in pursuit.

*

Sunny had been punished long enough, Gene thought, certainly far longer than he had planned. He looked about him at the beautiful day, the freshly washed moss hanging in great swaths from the giant oaks that flanked the street. He would deliver Sunny, regardless of how much he loved her. He had made a deal.

He drove sedately to Sunny's house. In his rearview mirror Gene saw an SUV approach, which he dismissed as normal traffic. SUVs were everywhere these days. Out of courtesy to the driver behind him, who was using his phone while he drove, Gene activated his blinker as he turned past the sheltering oaks onto Sunny's street. His car traveling only a few yards, Gene's mouth dropped open on a quick intake of breath. Several familiar-looking cars were parked helter-skelter in Sunny's yard, their windshields reflecting the burning sun. He punched his brake to the floor and skidded to a halt just long enough to throw the car in reverse.

Trying to leave before he was detected, Gene gunned the motor, but was violently thrown backward then forward before he could turn to look over his shoulder, his forehead impacting the rearview mirror so hard he was temporarily blinded.

The grind of metal screeching against metal deafened him and he tasted blood when he bit through his lower lip. Stunned, Gene didn't register the armed men running in his direction.

In the vehicle Gene rammed when he reversed, Steve Morley cursed, trying to draw his weapon as he fought his deployed airbag. His dignity fared worse. The white powder airbag contents coated him from the top of his head halfway down his DEA shirt. His crew pulled their weapons before they realized it was their boss who was behind the wheel of the steaming vehicle.

Stunned and bleeding, US Marshal Gene White stumbled from his car. At the menacing sight of Steve Morley, he blanched and shrank back.

Morley clenched his fists, wanting to slug White. "Somebody find me a damn towel," he growled, letting his fists drop. He grabbed someone's handkerchief, scrubbing his face and dusting off his clothes. He started to order two agents to secure White's wrists and ankles with zip ties for transport to New Orleans, but then hesitated.

"Wait—I need Cecile Forest to identify White as her kidnapper. Then you can leave." The agents escorted the limping, bleeding man through the front door just as David and Tammy supporting Sunny came into the kitchen from the back yard.

Gene heard Sunny's hoarse scream before he saw her. Barefoot and dripping, she shrank from the man who'd imprisoned her, hugging the far wall. She stood rooted to the floor behind David and Tammy, until David turned and folded the soaked, trembling woman against his drenched shirt.

"He can't hurt you, Sunny," David laughed. "Look at the man. He's bleeding. His wrists are zip-tied and he's a mess."

The disheveled Steve Morley, also a mess, pushed past the agents who held White as their prisoner, and pointed at him.

"Is this the man who kidnapped and imprisoned you, Mrs. Forest?"

"Yes," she nodded. "Yes, it is, but something's wrong with him. Until this happened, he was always so kind to me."

"I'm gonna let someone else decide whether he's sick or not. Now that you've identified him, we'll get him out of your sight and locked up." He flicked a glance at Tammy. "Help Sunny get cleaned up and dry. And tell her what's been going on."

Chapter Fourteen

Tammy helped Sunny to her bedroom and closed the door, turning to her friend. "Let's get you cleaned up, but you have to be hungry. I'll grab you some food, and then I'll explain."

"Thanks, Tammy, water first, please. And I smell coffee. I need lots of coffee."

"You got it, girlfriend." She returned to the kitchen while Sunny's dirty, wet clothes dropped to the floor in the en suite bathroom.

Returning with two bottles of water and a plate piled high with buttered toast, sausage, and broiled peaches, Tammy joined Sunny in the bathroom. She shucked her wet things, too, kicking them in a corner, and wrapped her body and hair in thirsty white towels, waiting her turn in the shower.

"Jump out and stay in here to eat, Sunny. I'll catch you up on everything while I shower.

"That Gene's crazy. To be honest, we already knew that *before* he kidnapped you. Gene never learned the complete story from the beginning about who hurt you, because he left before we fit the pieces together.

"You were right about the one thing we were wrong about from the very beginning. Don't get me wrong. René Gaudet *is* a bad guy, but he wasn't part of what happened to you and Barley. I have permission to tell you what we know about your case, Sunny, if you want to know."

Sunny vigorously toweled her wet hair between refreshing nibbles of juicy watermelon chunks and swallows of coffee. Wiping her mouth on a dry washcloth, she gave an affirmative nod.

"Are you kidding? I want to know everything. Don't hold anything back."

Chapter Fifteen

Bright afternoon sun streamed through Sunny's bedroom window. Random leaves still stuck to the glass, blown there by yesterday's hurricane. The light brightened the pleasant feminine room and the two freshly dressed friends.

Tammy continued with her story as Sunny ate. "Okay, so we finally, finally, got the POTS/VOIP report."

Sunny raised her hand, speaking through a mouthful of food. "The what? Sounds like government nonsense."

"You could say that, I guess. Means Plain Old Telephone Service and Voice Over Internet Protocol. Lots of folks think VOIP is untrackable, but they're wrong. It just takes a long time. We traced all the calls made at Gaudet's office. His paranoia made it easy for us because he kept a record of almost everything." Tammy paused.

"Wait. Let's back up. We checked his automated office log first. All Gaudet's employees swipe cards when they enter or leave the building. The day your husband died, the log shows your assistant, Jan, left later than most other employees. What caught our eye was that she checked in again, after everyone else was long gone."

Sunny stopped eating and her lips trembled as her suspicion grew.

"The report we received yesterday showed one 23-minute call to a cell phone, just minutes after she reentered. The call wasn't made from Jan's desk—it came from Gaudet's secretary's desk. Alyssa certainly hadn't made the call. She and her husband were at her mother's bedside in an ICU at least an hour's drive from New Orleans.

"The automated internal list recorded that the call connected with a company cell phone checked out to Jimmy Costanza. In Jan Yokum's interview, she told us Costanza is her boyfriend."

Sunny touched her fingers to her mouth. "I suspected she was in a relationship. What happened next?"

"Jimmy stupidly used his company cell phone to call a known contract killer, who then killed Barley within a few hours. Then we had to work it out, but Jimmy finally told us he went to his favorite bar when he returned to town.

"Our agent hung out there for about a week and called the number from Costanza's phone whenever anyone new walked in the door. When a man standing at the bar answered, we arrested him on the spot. He pointed the finger at Jimmy almost immediately in return for a reduced sentence."

Sunny was overwhelmed, holding her friend and quietly crying. "Thank you, Tammy. And, thank you to the DEA for catching that murderer. I hope he spends the rest of his life in prison."

"You're welcome," said Tammy, "though we thought it might undermine our efforts to snag Gaudet, since he wasn't involved in the murder after all—except for one thing we discovered as we looked through his subpoenaed documents.

We—really, it was me—noticed another anomaly in the daily check-ins and -outs for Gaudet's office. I summoned Jan Yokum back to the DEA office yesterday afternoon to ask why she and her boyfriend skipped work the day after you were attacked in Puebla. She told me Jimmy was sick as a dog and she took him to a particular outpatient clinic to see about it.

"It took a couple of tries to reach the doctor, who turned out to be a veterinarian. He remembered his human patient. The man wasn't sick; he was beat all to hell, had a concussion, two cracked ribs, and two black eyes. There's no patient confidentiality for an animal doctor, so we have the x-rays and notes. Jimmy used an alias for himself, but Jan Yokum signed him out of the vet's using her real name.

"Yesterday evening, a DEA squad dropped in on Jimmy and put him under arrest for murder, attempted murder, assault, and attempted kidnapping. No one was surprised to discover Jan there, instead of at her place, and it saved them a trip. She was immediately arrested for her role in Barley's murder. Both Jimmy and Jan are locked up, awaiting arraignment. Jan asked me to check on her poor cat. Jan admits the sweet little thing hardly ever saw her after she fell in love with Jimmy Costanza.

⁕

"Incidentally," said Tammy, "if you hadn't decided to call Karl Schmitzer in the first place, we might never have gotten access to Gaudet's office records. After he confronted Schmitzer and threatened him, Gaudet told him he knew you were alive and where you were. Schmitzer called us—the DEA—and reported the incident.

Gaudet could only have known you were alive by illegally hacking into your bank records. Based on that, a judge issued a warrant to search Gaudet's office and that's when we hit the mother lode. Besides retrieving the VOIP information, we found computer files with details of drug inventory and buy-sell transactions that will put René Gaudet behind bars for many years.

Epilogue

Sunny breathed in cool twilight air and looked skyward as the soft, gentle breezes shook a few yellowing leaves from the trees her great-aunt had planted so many years ago. This was home, her home, her favorite place. She had missed being here, and loved being back among friends. She smiled at David Kelley standing close beside her, and looked at the casual group who chattered on her patio.

An elderly couple sat on her metal glider, their shoulders touching. Karl Schmitzer and Odette Freyou, Sunny's friends, had both been very close friends of Sunny's deceased great-aunt Hattie. It was easy to see they were in love, a romance sparked when the DEA asked them to jointly maintain Sunny's home and yard in her absence.

The group was discussing a *Times-Picayune* newspaper report about the dismantling of a wide-ranging drug distribution ring that had been operating across the South. Sunny's friends knew the backstory that the unraveling all started with Barley Forest's abuse of his wife. An abuse that Sunny's assistant, Jan Yokum, wanted to stop—permanently.

The goal of the DEA's New Orleans chief, Steve Morley, from the beginning had been to put René Gaudet in prison, preferably for the rest of his life. Morley had a grand time promising reduced sentences to Gaudet's lackeys in exchange for verifiable information, which culminated in multiple guilty verdicts against his main target.

Jan Yokum admitted she'd asked Jimmy Costanza to have Mick Shaughnessy kill Barley instead of Cecile, who had been the original target. Jan pleaded guilty to her role in Barley's death, but in light of extenuating circumstances (her action had prevented Cecile's likely murder) received a two-year sentence, plus two years of probation.

After serving her sentence, she returned to West Virginia and dropped out of sight.

Morley offered the tips of the spears, Mick Shaughnessy and Shawn Leary—the two who killed Barley and wounded Sunny, formerly known as Cecile, with a single deflected bullet—a reduction to second degree murder, which they agreed to in exchange for testimony against the man who hired them, Jimmy Costanza.

Jimmy Costanza pleaded guilty, while insisting he had his own reasons for killing Barley Forest. He received a reduced sentence by giving verifiable information about René Gaudet's illegal activities. Having twice operated as Gaudet's second-in-command, Costanza knew all his boss's secrets.

All this provided Steve Morley's division of the DEA with a bonanza of names and locations that they used to dismantle a drug ring operating in five southern states.

Tammy Avenetti was enjoying this day with her happy group of new friends. As a US Marshal, she'd been loaned to the DEA when Morley decided to hide Sunny. It had been her job to liaise with Sunny, nothing more, but as time passed, she assumed a larger role. Morley recognized her initiative and enticed her with a bigger paycheck to work for the DEA. Sunny becoming her friend was a welcome bonus.

It had been Tammy's idea to put Barley's belongings in his Jaguar and park it on St. Charles Avenue in front of the home of Mary Ann Fitch's parents, where she was living with her baby son, Barley Fitch. Tammy then transferred the title and mailed it with the keys, but without comment, to Barley's lover.

Neither Tammy nor Sunny forgot the Puebla library sisters, Ginny, Joyce, and ReJoyce. Tremell Senegal stayed on their radar, too.

Sunny Valois and David Kelley drove to Puebla so she could introduce him to her wonderful Texas friends. The librarians hugged David and danced with him around the library. They showed off the two new bathrooms that had been financed with an anonymous donation. They would never learn that Sunny, whom they knew as Melba, was the donor. Nor would they learn it had been Sunny's philanthropic call to Karl Schmitzer that had led to the unraveling of a drug empire.

The librarians and Tremell *did* learn most of Sunny's story, going back to the day she was shot, and that she had re-established her law practice, working from an office established in her Uptown New Orleans home.

Driving home from Puebla to New Orleans seated next to David, Sunny had counted her blessings and squeezed David's hand. She now knew how it felt to be in love. She had fallen in love with this smart, handsome, available man. A man who loved her in return.

Just the month before, Karl, Odette, and David had helped her celebrate her 33rd birthday at her Octavia Street bungalow.

Karl Schmitzer, dapper as always, and part of her life as far back as she could remember, was now in his nineties, his hair snow white and his skin thin, his hands densely freckled.

He had pulled Sunny aside, holding out an envelope that contained a one-page spreadsheet that listed the total value of two trusts he had set up with Sunny's great-aunt Hattie, the greatest love of his life. The monthly disbursements from her maintenance trust had been accumulating all the while Sunny was in the Witness Protection Program. The sum was substantial, even after funding the Puebla library's restrooms. And the mind-boggling assets of the main trust that Karl had secretly been managing would also be transferred in their entirety into Sunny's name in two years on her 35th birthday. She would be a tremendously wealthy woman, the sole recipient of the cumulative riches of generations, and she'd have plenty of time to consider how she could best use the money.

Those were things Sunny could think about some other day. For now, she sat on her patio, her fingers twined with David's, and closed her eyes. The low murmurs of her friends' quiet conversations and the sawing sounds of cicadas swirled about her through the cooling air.

Soft breezes rustled the crisp autumnal leaves as dusk descended. Sparrows twittered and doves cooed as the birds settled, roosting in Sunny's trees.

Disclaimer

This is a work of fiction. Any resemblance to actual events or persons, living or dead, is entirely coincidental. Streets and geography may have been altered to improve the story. For those sensitive to the issue, there are occasional mentions of domestic abuse.

This is the First Edition. Edited by Tom Welch. Cover designed by 100 Covers. Author's website: https://bellamygayle.com/ . Printed in the USA.

Bellamy Gayle began her writing career as a sports stringer for a local newspaper in Cajun country, followed by a monthly column in a regional woman's magazine. Her other activities afforded a wide variety of writing experiences, from politics to a development director for a nonprofit organization, with stops in real estate and owning travel agencies back in the day. While serving as president of the local Writers' Guild, Bellamy learned the basics of novel writing, meeting many gifted writers.

Gayle's dusty stacks of short stories grew until NaNoWriMo (National Novel Writing Month) nudged her to write KEEP ME SAFE, a full-length murder mystery which is the first novel in the Sazerac Series. The second book of the series, AN ORDINARY WOMAN, scheduled for publication in 2023, is in the editing phase and will be followed by a third novel, tentatively titled ODETTE: RUN FOR YOUR LIFE, currently in the blocking phase.

Gayle and her husband live in south Louisiana's Lafayette Parish, happily listening to the summer sounds of the cicadas and visiting with the neighborhood cats named Baby, Bob, and Blackie, who regularly drop by. The couple has a passel of grown children, with a swarm of precious grandchildren scattered across the nation.

Don't miss out!

Visit the website below and you can sign up to receive emails whenever Bellamy Gayle publishes a new book. There's no charge and no obligation.

https://books2read.com/r/B-A-PIDN-LBHZB

BOOKS 2 READ

Connecting independent readers to independent writers.

About the Author

Bellamy Gayle began her writing career as a sports stringer for a local newspaper in Cajun country. A monthly column in a regional woman's magazine followed. Other work afforded a wide variety of writing experiences, from politics to a development director for a nonprofit organization, with stops in real estate and owning travel agencies back in the day. A member of the local Writers' Guild, Bellamy studied the basics of novel writing and met many gifted writers.

Bellamy's stacks of short stories grew until NaNoWriMo (National Novel Writing Month) nudged her to write a murder mystery which became the first novel of the Sazerac Series. The second book, AN ORDINARY WOMAN, is in the editing phase. A third novel, tentatively titled ODETTE: RUN FOR YOUR LIFE shall follow.

Gayle and her husband live in south Louisiana's Lafayette parish, happily listening to the summer sounds of the cicadas and visiting with the neighborhood cats Baby, Bob, and Blackie, who regularly drop by. The couple has a passel of grown children and a swarm of precious grandchildren scattered across the nation.

Read more at https://bellamygayle.com/.

About the Publisher

www.ingramcontent.com/pod-product-compliance
Lightning Source LLC
LaVergne TN
LVHW091028080826
845145LV00002B/405

* 9 7 8 1 7 3 6 5 2 8 2 1 1 *